M000159076

ALICE

THE WANDERLAND CHRONICLES

J.M. SULLIVAN

Bleeding Ink
Publishing

Alice

Copyright © 2018 by J.M. Sullivan

Sale of the paperback edition of this book without the cover is unauthorized.

Bleeding Ink Publishing

For information contact:

Bleeding Ink Publishing

253 Bee Caves Cove

Cibolo, TX 78108

www.bleedinginkpublishing.com

info@bleedinginkpublishing.com

Cover design by Author Branding Essentials

Editing by Jessica Reino

Book design by Bleeding Ink Publishing

ISBN: 978-1-948583-03-9

First Edition: August 2018

❀ Created with Vellum

For my wonderful husband, Steven. Thank you for following me down the rabbit hole.

"Twas brillig, and the slithy toves
Did gyre and gimble in the wabe:
All mimsy were the borogoves,
And the *momerath* outgrabe."

Lewis Carroll, *Alice's Adventures in Wonderland*

DOWN THE RABBIT HOLE

H is head exploded. I'd never seen someone's head explode. I never thought I would. Maybe in the movies, but not in real life.

It's amazing what a 12-gauge can do at close range. The gun wasn't even ours, just a rusty old rifle we found on the side of the road. It only had one shell left. I don't even know why I picked it up. It was just supposed to be used as a safeguard, but it gave Dinah and me enough time to put some distance between ourselves and the monsters. I guess it did its job.

No one ever stops to think how one day life can be mind-numbingly ordinary and then the next, completely go to shit. Not that it matters whether you think about it or not. What matters is how you deal with it. Like Dinah says, "We can only play the cards we've been dealt. It doesn't do any good to wish about things you can't change."

Alice wiped her tired eyes and peered at the journal on her desk. She scrunched her nose as she looked at the crude sketch she had drawn next to her entry. While it was no artistic rendering, her pencil had captured the raggedy, emaciated figure with its unhealthy soot-gray skin and vacant dead eyes quite accurately. Her brow furrowed as she remembered how it looked after the gun bucked--face half gone with its thick blood forming a gruesome shower. It took hours to wash the black stains from her silvery hair.

She studied the haunted creature glaring at her from the page. A shiver shot through her, ending in a violent twist of her stomach. The ghost of a scream echoed in her ears and she was ten years old again, hiding in a ransacked gas station with her mother. Her hands trembled as she remembered pleading in hushed tones for her mother to stay behind the cashier's desk with her while the creatures outside howled in rage.

We have to get out of here before they come inside. If not, we'll both be trapped. Her mother's forest green eyes filled with a sadness Alice had never seen in them before. It was wrong; her mother was never sad. She was joy—*life.*

Alice's lower lip quivered. She hated what came next. Begging. Tears. *I love you, Alice.* Running. Yelling. Terror. All followed by a flash of ripping, bloody claws.

Death.

A teardrop fell on the monster in the paper, blurring the graphite lines. Alice brushed it away quickly, smearing the picture further. She ran her hand back over it angrily, wishing she could wipe out the memory the same way. When she pulled her hand away, only a gray blob remained, ruining the page.

That's appropriate.

Alice thought about the way the monsters had shown up and ruined everything. Her stomach turned as she remembered the first time she saw them. She had just crawled out of bed and walked into the living room where her mother was watching her favorite news station. Rounding the corner, she heard confused shouting and terrible screams above the reporter's voice.

"...*I can't tell you exactly what happened in Washington*

District this morning, Trey, but it seems a mob of citizens turned violent and began attacking other pedestrians on the streets outside Borogove Industries..."

Her voice died out and Alice stared at the screen in stunned silence. It was a nightmare. The cameraman panned the shot to a large pack of men and women in business suits rampaging the streets. At least, they looked like men—except they were mauling people.

Suddenly, the screen blacked out.

"That's enough of *that*." Alice's mother set the clicker on the coffee table and compulsively started tidying the room the way she always did when she was upset. She went to the kitchen and brought back a dust cloth and some varnish. "Here. Help me with this." She handed the cleaning supplies to Alice. "I think it would be best if you stayed home today."

Alice never made it back to school. By the time the evening news aired, all major channels were reporting unnatural attacks surging out of the Phoenix area. Momerath, CNN called them, a mixture of "moment" and "wrath," since a person could turn into a raging killing machine with less than a moment's notice. She supposed it stemmed from the media's obsession with conjoined nicknames like "Bennifer" and "Brangelina." She didn't get it, but the name stuck.

That was six years ago. Now, at sixteen, she should be a junior in high school, but instead of her mother teaching her to drive, Dinah was teaching her how to keep rampaging monsters from tearing her to pieces.

Alice sighed and flipped lazily through her journal. Bits and pieces of the world after the Plague jumped out at her as she skimmed the pages.

... Momerath reported in all fifty states. . . military fighting back, but it's not enough...people say it's gone international. Flip.

3

...They can be killed! . . . have to destroy the nervous system. . . ask Dinah what the heck that means... Flip.

...There's more than momerath. . . there are Carriers too. . . people who have the virus, but don't show it until it's too late...

Alice paused to look at another rough sketch she had drawn inline with her entry. It was a box that she had split into two sections. The first showed a little stick girl lying in bed, coughing. The next box was the girl standing on the bed with her arms raised and long claws reaching out from them. The word "momerath" had been written above in scratchy red pen.

Alice remembered that entry. She drew it after she had snuck downstairs to watch the news with Dinah and her mother one night after she had been sent to bed. They sat on the couch together, her mother's pale hands clutched Dinah's as they watched the report in stunned silence.

Terrifying images flitted across the television screen, and she had to strain her ears to hear the hushed volume to make sense of what she was seeing. A man was on the screen, pale and shaky as he spoke with the reporter.

...we just thought she was sick—the doctor said it was pneumonia...

He trailed off, his voice broken. The background switched to gruesome pictures of a mother and two boys lying on the floor, their bodies disjointed and mangled. Another picture flashed to a different angle, revealing the mother's eyes, wide with fear. The rest of her face was missing. The final photograph showed a decapitated momerath, dressed in a frilly pink nightdress with golden plaits twisted around the stump of its bloody neck. Alice had to clap her hand over her mouth to keep from crying out so she didn't get caught. She had nightmares for months after that.

She took in a deep breath and looked once more at the picture. Now that she was older, the image didn't torment her any longer, but it still made her stomach squirm. She flipped the page again, burying the memory.

...CDC says the Plague is a virus. It lives in the blood, makes it bad somehow...momerath kill because they need clean blood... Dinah won't tell me what it means. Mom won't let her. I wish Dad was here. He could explain it to me...

This time, a blaze of anger surged through her chest. How much time had she spent wishing he would come back? *Too much,* she thought bitterly. What a waste of her time. Angry Flip.

Alice sighed and shut the cover of her journal. "That's enough depressing thoughts for today," she grumbled, tapping her pencil against the desk. "Maybe tomorrow, you can relive the day Mr. Carroll left. That's *just* what you need." She snorted. "Yes. Then afterward, you can seek professional help for talking to yourself."

"It would probably be a good idea," a musical voice agreed, startling Alice from her monologue. "It's getting kind of creepy." Dinah stood in the doorway, brown eyes crinkling as she flashed a teasing grin.

Alice rolled her eyes but smiled at her older sister. Technically, her *adopted* older sister. Both girls had been taken in by the Carrolls when they were babies. First Dinah, then Alice a few years later. Standing beside each other, it was obvious they weren't related. Though both girls had pretty faces and petite frames made slender by strict food rationing, all similarities ended there. Barely older than twenty-two, Dinah was gorgeous, with beautiful dark skin and rich mahogany eyes. She kept her curly ebony hair cut short and out of her face, which only emphasized her natural beauty.

Alice was the complete opposite. Her smooth, porcelain skin was so fair Dinah often joked that she could glow in the dark, and she was probably right. Her hair was the same: pale blonde that looked silver when the sun hit it right. It was one of her favorite features, which is why, even though it drove her crazy half the time, she never cut it. Paired with her high cheekbones and heart-shaped lips, it accentuated her dusky blue eyes and gave her a striking appearance. She wasn't a captivating beauty like Dinah, but she wasn't plain either.

Alice scoffed, used to her sister's teasing. "Whatever. I only talk to myself because I don't have anyone else to talk to. It's a coping mechanism."

Dinah slapped her hand across an imaginary wound on her chest. "You can talk to *me*. I'm always here for you, little sister," she said, wrapping her arm around Alice's shoulders to hug her tight. "Because. I. Love You." She squeezed her close with each word for emphasis, then finished by planting a sloppy kiss on her cheek. Alice shrieked and hurried to wipe her face on her shoulder. Dinah laughed and let her go.

Alice huffed and tried to glare at her sister, but only succeeded in letting out an unattractive snort. Like their appearances, the two girls had completely different personalities. Though Alice whined about not having anyone to talk to, it wasn't a valid complaint. Even if people were around, her preference was to stay at home, reading or writing in her journal. If she did have to go out, she would rather watch the people in the Sector than have to interact with them. It was probably where her habit of talking to herself came from. Dinah always teased her about it. But then, Dinah didn't have problems talking to anyone. One would think the apocalypse could put a damper on anybody's spirit, but not Dinah's. She had an easy smile and quick quip to offer to anyone in the Sector, especially Alice.

"You about ready to head out?" Dinah stretched lazily against the doorjamb. "We need to make sure we get back before dark."

Alice groaned. Scavenging through abandoned homes and old belongings was depressing and made her feel guilty. It set her nerves on edge.

"Don't give me the pout." Dinah grimaced at Alice's sulky expression. "We have to eat."

"I know," Alice whined, "it's just so *creepy*." She shuddered for emphasis.

"That may be true, but it doesn't make it any less necessary."

Alice wrinkled her nose. Dinah was right—as always—but low stock in the pantry didn't make traipsing into momerath territory any more appealing. "Can we at least stop at the library on the way back?" She needed new reading material. She had gone through all her other books at least twice already. Her favorites were on their fourth or fifth read-through each.

"Sure," Dinah promised. "But that means we need to get going. We don't want to run out of daylight, and I have to stop at the Peterson's before we leave the Sector. Mrs. Peterson says the baby has a fever and wants me to check her out."

"Alright. Let me get my books and I'll meet you out front." Alice picked up her backpack and searched the room for the borrowed books scattered around her room.

"I don't know why you bother returning them." Dinah shook her head "It's not like anyone is going to notice they're gone."

Alice shrugged. One of the things she hated most about scouting was taking things from people's homes. It didn't matter if the owners were long gone or dead, it still felt like stealing. Returning library books might have been completely irrelevant, but it gave her guilty conscience a reprieve.

She scanned her room, making sure not to forget anything. Her eyes landed on a picture of her family prior to the world falling apart. It was taken a few months before the Plague began, on a weekend trip to Huntington Beach. Alice could almost smell the salty sea air and feel the sand between her toes. She and Dinah leaned together with their mother holding melty ice cream cones on the pier next to Ruby's Diner. Mr. Carroll had been long gone, but it didn't stop them from having a blast. They spent the day playing sand volleyball, swimming, and hunting for seashells before ending with dinner and dessert on the pier. They asked a stranger to snap their picture and before he could, Mom smashed her cone in Dinah's face, covering her nose in vanilla ice cream. Alice smiled, remembering how she shrieked when Dinah snorted, spraying ice cream everywhere.

Curious how a memory can make you happy and sad all at the same time, she thought, looking wistfully at the picture.

"Maybe those are the best memories of all," she said, then realized she was talking to herself again. Sighing, she swung her backpack over her shoulder and hurried downstairs to meet her sister.

2

Alice followed Dinah down the Sector's Main Street. The Petersons didn't live far. Considering the commune's small size, everyone lived relatively close to each other. Main Street wasn't even really a street. It was a common area where Sector residents spent their days. Ratty kids ran up and down the pavement playing tag with each other, weaving in and out of makeshift stalls where vendors would hawk their wares. Loud voices clambered over each other as men haggled over payment. Paper money was a thing of the past. No one had use for it anymore—now people bartered goods or services for things they needed. Alice was willing to bet that was why Dinah was going to the Petersons' today. Before the Plague hit, Dinah attended school to be a nurse. Though she never graduated, she had almost completed her course. It was more qualification than most people had, so now she worked as the community's resident caretaker.

"It shouldn't take long, I just need to stop in and see the baby," Dinah said. "It sounds like she's got a bit of a cold. Seems to be going around right now." She sneezed, as if to emphasize her point. "See what I mean?"

Alice didn't answer. She was busy wondering what she was going to do when it was time for her to start contributing to the house. For now, she helped Dinah with scouting and shadowed the occasional house call. But she wasn't skilled like Dinah. To be fair, Dinah had a head start. She had wanted to be a nurse since she was little and had seen Mr. Carroll come home in his scrubs. She said any job that let her work in her pajamas had to be a good one.

Alice couldn't remember much about Mr. Carroll. Most of what she knew came from the stories Dinah would tell.

"Dad used to be different from the way he was before he left," Dinah would begin. *"He was happy and fun. His work was important to him, but he always made time for us too. And the time I got so sick, he was the one who took care of me. He had to take weeks off work, but he did, staying with me to make sure I was alright. It's too bad you didn't get to see the best of him."* Here, Dinah's smile would always fall to a frown. *"Then something changed. He and Mom started fighting a lot and he wouldn't come home until really late at night. When he was home, he would lock himself in his office and stay there for hours. I'm sure he still loved us, but his work consumed him."*

Dinah's stories didn't help Alice understand why she would want to pursue a career in the medical field. It sounded terrible. But Dinah must have seen something good in it. Then again, Dinah always saw the good in things. She also had an extra eight years with Mr. Carroll. Alice tried not to dwell on it, but sometimes when she thought about all she had missed out on, bitter resentment would gnaw at the pit of her stomach.

A sharp pain on the top of Alice's head jerked her from her thoughts as Dinah rapped knuckles against her forehead. "Hello! Earth to Alice! Anyone home?"

"Ow! Hey!" Alice massaged the spot her sister whacked.

"You zoned out again." Dinah shook her head in disbelief.

"Did you hear anything I said? I swear, it's a miracle anyone tries to keep you company."

Alice scrunched her nose and stuck out her tongue at her sister. "I'm *wonderful* company," she said.

"Obviously." Dinah rolled her eyes. "You definitely keep yourself entertained, that's for sure." She huffed. "Anyway, *I was saying* Mrs. Peterson is concerned about a fever and cough the baby has. I guess she's been like this for a few days, so the worst is probably over. I'm just going to pop in for a minute and I'll be right down. Wait here, okay?"

"Yeah, sure." Alice didn't want to go upstairs anyway. The Petersons were nice people, but Alice didn't think they realized they were living in an apocalypse. They had six kids and Mrs. Peterson was pregnant *again*. Their house was always loud and busy and messy. No thanks. She would stay down here with the street vendors and their noise. It was less obnoxious than the kids. She sat on the stoop of the apartment building and gazed out at Main Street. Several stalls had sprung up and four of the Petersons were playing outside, chasing a striped tabby cat with a couple of other boys from the Sector. A few women cackled loudly, exchanging commune gossip while neatly folding stacks of laundry to take home.

Over the busyness, a familiar voice rang out across the pavement. "News from the outside! Updates from outside the Sector!" Alice turned towards a gangly boy about her age walking through the streets, yelling at people he passed to make an exchange for information. He was skinny with mousy brown hair that grew just past his oversized ears. They suited him, considering he was the self-appointed Sector messenger. As such, it was his job to find and share any news coming into the commune, and he was good at it. How he always seemed to be the first to get the scoop, Alice had no idea.

"Oi! Alice!" His face lit up as he waved and hurried to cross the street.

"More news, Lewis?" She punched him softly on the shoulder. "Don't you ever do anything besides make up stories?"

"No stories, only God's honest truth!" Lewis's voice rose as he countered her jibe. "Heard it from a group we met travelin' out of the city and headin' to the country—Buckeye, I think. Had family out there or somethin'. They said there might be a way to fix everything! Said they heard about some doctor who was working on a cure. Made it sound he was kind of crazy though. Guess he'd have to be to not have given up yet. But think! What if it worked? What if he found a cure?" Lewis's features sparked in excitement as he spilled his news, too enthused to attempt to work out a trade.

Alice shook her head as she listened. "What if rivers flowed in the desert?" she sighed. Lewis exasperated her, always talking about life before the Plague and how it would be if everything was different. He was a dreamer. "It would be nice, but it's not gonna happen, Lewis. You shouldn't spout off talk like that, giving false hope to people. It'd be better if they focused on surviving. It's more important than some silly dream."

"But Alice, dreams are how people get by in a place like this," Lewis countered. His freckles faded with his smile. "We gotta find somethin' to hold onto, else we'll all go mad."

"You'd be better off holding on to your head," Alice quipped. Lewis couldn't read past a fourth-grade level—he had no business trying to get philosophical on her. She glanced at him and her expression softened when his shoulders slumped in defeat. Lewis couldn't help but dream; it was who he was. She let out a guilty groan before forcing a small smile to her lips. "Look, Lewis, I gotta go." She nudged his shoulder apologetically. Dinah and I are going on a supply run," she said. "Try not to make up too many more stories while I'm gone."

Lewis brightened, all hurt forgotten. "Ain't stories, Alice. You'll see. One day, sure enough, you'll see." In a flash, he was off, yelling again to catch the attention of someone willing to trade for information.

"Sure thing." Alice waved as she walked back to the Petersons' building to meet Dinah, who had walked out of the complex and was sliding the wooden barricade back into place. "You ready?" she asked, hurrying to her sister.

"Always." Dinah coughed at the dust the barricade kicked up. "Let's get out of here. The baby is sicker than I thought. I'm not sure what it is, but she's going to need stronger medicine than I have. We'll have to see if we can find a pharmacy while we're out. We'd better get moving."

Alice matched Dinah's brisk pace away from Main Street. They walked back the way they came, towards their apartment building, but instead of going in, they kept south, not stopping until they reached the abandoned outer edge of the Sector. No one wanted to live in the buildings closest to momerath territory. Alice didn't blame them. She still remembered how hordes of the monsters used to scrape along the sides of the fence searching for points of entry before eventually giving up and shuffling off through the desert.

After the momerath departed, people eased up a bit, but no one was keen on setting up camp on the edge of the Sector. This worked in the girls' favor, since what they were about to do was technically not allowed. People weren't supposed to leave the safety of the Sector, and it wasn't easy. To keep momerath out, two heavy chain-link walls had been set up with barbed wire bordering the tops. The inner fence served as a backup in case the first one fell. Between the fences was an added layer of protection: a five-foot gap filled with more coiled barbed wire. The ground was littered with shattered glass and sections of two-by-four with huge nails sticking up at every angle, intended to slow down anything that risked walking through it. Lewis had told her there were even supposed to be land mines scattered in as well.

So far, the safeguards had held and no breaches had been reported. But that was only because the girls had never been caught. They had been sneaking out together for almost four years, after Dinah decided Alice could be trusted enough to help.

Alice followed Dinah to a large group of withered pricker bushes. Behind them, Dinah had cut a small hole into the inner chain fence and cleared out an incognito path they could cross safely. With careful steps, they followed it out, just like every other trip they made. When they reached the outer layer, they used a small mesquite tree to hoist themselves up and over. Outside, scattered Joshua trees provided cover for the girls to bob and weave through until they were out of sight.

They had left so often over the past few years, it only took a few minutes for them to break out. Once they were through, the rest of the trip was pretty uneventful. Tolleson was part of the web of smaller towns that made up one huge suburb. They all merged into the sprawling metropolis of Phoenix, which meant Alice and Dinah didn't ever have to go far to reach a new area to scout. Thankfully, since Dinah needed stronger medication for the baby, they wouldn't scour homes today. Instead, they found an old shopping center with a pharmacy inside. They crept through the aisles, careful not to make any noise. There hadn't been any signs of momerath, but it was better safe than sorry. Sorry meant you were dead.

At the pharmacy, Dinah snuck behind the counter to search through the few remaining medications for antibiotics she could use. On the other side of the counter, Alice checked the shelves for basic health care supplies and filled the small bag Dinah had given her, then peeked back to the pharmacist's desk to check for her sister.

Where is she?

It shouldn't have taken long for Dinah to get what she needed. Her bag wasn't that big. The store had also been picked pretty clean, so there wasn't much to choose from. Alice wouldn't have been surprised if someone had helped themselves to the controlled medicines in the back as well. After the Plague, most people became opportunists.

Granted, she thought, *we're doing the same thing—but it's different.* She argued with herself, attempting to ease her conscience. *We're only taking what we need. And I'm not happy about it. That counts for something, right?* A small pang twinged the pit of her stomach. She pushed it away. She didn't have time for post-apocalyptic guilt trips. Survival was more important. She glanced nervously around the store, watching for movement.

Where is Dinah?

Silently, Alice slunk back to the counter. She strained her ears, listening for the sound of her sister rifling through shelves, but couldn't hear anything. The building was eerily quiet. Her heart pounded erratically. She stretched on her tiptoes to peek over the tall counter, searching for Dinah. Nothing. She was about to whisper for her when something lunged over the counter.

"Hey!" Dinah growled and grabbed Alice's forearm. Alice nearly peed herself. Panicked, she gasped in a huge breath of air and choked on it. She burst into a fit of coughing. By the time she could finally breathe, Dinah was doubled over in hysterics. She stood next to Alice, her hand on her shoulder.

"Oh...my...God." She dissolved into a fit of giggles. "I'm... sorry." She paused, succumbing to more laughter. "I couldn't..." Alice rolled her eyes as Dinah let out a loud snort. "...help it. You should have seen your face." Tears streamed down her cheeks as she fought to compose herself.

"Ha. *Ha.*" Alice bristled; her heart still beat violently against her chest. She scowled at her sister, but couldn't stay angry for long. Dinah was a mess. Clutching her side and leaning against the counter for support, she was practically falling over. Finally, the lack of oxygen caught up to her, and she broke into a fit of heaving coughs before slowly standing.

"Serves you right," Alice hissed. "I could have died of heart failure."

"Oh, you're fine." Dinah wiped the tears from her cheeks. "You need to lighten up. Come on, let's get the rest of our groceries. Then we can go to the library." Just like that, she crept to the grocery aisles as if she hadn't nearly scared Alice out of her skin. Like there wasn't anything to be worried about. Alice shook her head, resigned.

That was Dinah.

Dinah behaved the rest of the time they were at the store. They filled their bags with anything imperishable they could carry. When they were finished, they zipped their bags and left for the old library.

Though the library was technically part of Tolleson, it remained outside the area that turned into the Sector. It was a little under a quarter mile beyond the fence at the end of the commune, so even though Alice could see it from the safety of the Sector, she was only able to go when they went scouting. It was infuriating. Dinah knew how much Alice loved books, though, so she took Alice whenever she could.

The library was exactly as Alice remembered it. Even through the apocalypse, it remained the same, a small haven in the middle of the end of the world. The smell of books lingered in the air, and the silence that was so awkward everywhere else was perfectly acceptable and welcome here.

"Go find your books. I'll wait for you." Dinah picked up an old tabloid and plopped into one of the oversized armchairs in the front sitting area. A cloud of dust puffed out of the faded

burgundy fabric and flew in her face. She coughed and waved the dirt away. "Ugh!" She spluttered, turning to face the window. She looked warily at the dimming skyline. "You'd better hurry up though," she said. "We need to get home before dark."

"I'll be quick," Alice promised, walking to the checkout desk. First, she needed to return her old books. "Here you go," she said softly to the imaginary librarian as she set them on the counter. "Right on time, so there won't be any late fees."

Smiling at her own joke, she ventured to search for the perfect books. *Fantasy, this time,* she decided. She settled on three titles—*Peter Pan, The Phantom Tollbooth,* and *A Wrinkle in Time.* She collected them together and knelt to tuck them safely into her backpack. She was in the middle of squeezing *Peter* between a pack of cookies and a case of noodles when she heard a small crash followed by what sounded like the dulled thudding of books toppling to the carpet. She sighed and rolled her eyes. Probably Dinah trying to scare her again.

"Very funny, Dinah," Alice singsonged, walking to the end of the aisle. "You're not going to get me twice," She leaned around the shelves to see where her sister was hiding.

"What are you talking about?" Dinah called from behind. A nervous thrill shot through Alice's chest. She whirled around, dismayed to find her sister.

"Wait." She pointed dumbly. "If you're here, what was..." Her voice trailed off as she turned to where the crash came from. A shadowy figure lunged at her, letting out a guttural howl. Alice lurched back into Dinah. For one awful instant, she took in its patchy hair, milky eyes, and missing fingers. Alice froze, paralyzed until another gurgling cry from the momerath snapped her into action.

"Go, Dinah! Go!" Alice pushed against her sister. Dinah didn't have to be told twice. She clamped her hand around Alice's wrist and yanked, dragging her towards the library exit. Behind her, Alice heard the ragged, wheezing breaths of the momerath furiously chasing after them. They moved quickly through the rows of books, hustling to the main entrance. She scanned the dusty library, looking for anything to use as a weapon. An ancient book cart had been left in the middle of one of the aisles, overloaded with untended literature. Alice shoved it backwards as hard as she could, hurtling it into the momerath pursuing her. The rusty wheels moved for the first time in years, causing the heavy cart to groan in protest until it stopped abruptly, followed by a loud crash. Alice had the satisfaction of hearing the momerath cry in rage as the obstacle smashed into its decaying body.

"Don't look back, *don't look back*," Alice coached herself. She urged her legs forward. She knew checking behind would only slow her down, but curiosity overpowered her will. The momerath was on her heels, less than six steps away. Dried blood caked the sides of its wounds and coated its fingers, the only evidence it had torn its own flesh to shreds. It limped after them on a horribly shattered ankle, forcing its weight on the side of its foot instead of the sole. Still, it was fast. It prowled after them in a fresh burst of speed, a stark contrast to the raspy gasps coming from its chest.

"Now is really not the time to be talking to yourself, Alice!" Dinah wheeled around the corner of the self-help section towards the main entrance. "Pay attention!"

"I'm doing fine, thanks!" Alice snapped back. "But if you don't pick up the pace, we're going to be dead meat!" *Pun intended*, she thought.

They escaped the corridors of books and Alice pushed to catch up to Dinah. She could make out the shaky rattle coming from the momerath's chest—it was still too close.

"We're almost there! I can see the door!" Dinah's cry pulled Alice's attention forward. The front entry waited for them as peacefully as it had when they first came inside. Looks really could be deceiving.

Only thirty feet...twenty feet to go. Alice's sides burned as she pushed her body to its limit. *Keep going,* she instructed herself. *Ten feet...* They were going to make it.

Suddenly, Dinah was no longer beside her. Alice turned and saw her tuck and roll off the dusty carpet. Her heart lurched as the momerath lunged, rage flashing in its dead eyes. Luckily, Dinah fell well and kept moving, almost seamlessly. She scrambled up, commanding Alice to keep running.

"Are you okay?" Alice screamed, acutely aware of how shrill she sounded over the lump of her heart in her throat. At least it was beating a little more regularly now that Dinah was up and running again.

"I'm fine," Dinah said. "I just tripped. I might have twisted my knee, but I'll be alright. Just...keep...going." Alice could hear how winded her sister was. She glanced over and saw beads of sweat sprouting from Dinah's forehead, her face flushed with exertion. Worried, she turned to see how far they were from the door and almost cried with joy when she saw they had made it. She pushed all her energy into slamming the front door open, bursting through with Dinah on her heels.

The extra energy used was worth the effort. Right after Dinah passed through the frame, the momentum from the swing slammed it shut. The heavy glass door barreled into the momerath, shattering the door's paneling and sending the monster sprawling flat on its back.

They didn't stick around to see what happened next. Alice clutched Dinah's hand, sure the momerath was mere seconds from getting up and following them home. They sprinted the rest of the way to the commune, weaving around lonely Joshua trees before finally flinging themselves up the branches of their mesquite tree and dropping into the fencing median of the

Sector. They didn't stop until they slid themselves through the rabbit hole in the fence and climbed out from behind the pricker bush. Alice didn't even care about the twigs caught in her hair and clothes. They made it. She couldn't believe they had made it.

Finally safe, she scooted out from under the bush and lay flat on the desert floor, exhausted. She greedily gulped air, relishing the way it felt whooshing in and out of her lungs. Turning to her sister, Alice felt the gritty earth on the side of her cheek. Unlike her, Dinah stood hunched, gasping. Suddenly, her ragged breaths turned into a large bout of coughs, and she fell to her knees, her arms the only thing keeping her from collapsing to the ground.

Alice was up in a flash. "Dinah, are you okay? You weren't bit, were you?" Panic flooded her chest, freezing her in place.

"No, I don't think so. It didn't even come close to me," Dinah said. "I was pretty awesome, if I do say so myself." She pretended to pat herself on the back, but Alice didn't miss the way she warily eyed her arms.

"We'd better check you out anyway." Alice extended her hand to hoist Dinah up. "Let's get you home and cleaned off."

It was dark by the time they made it home. Dinah went straight upstairs to clean herself up while Alice shuffled to the kitchen to prepare a makeshift dinner. Beanie Weenies with canned peaches and a glass of cola were on the evening menu. She set the plates on the table, looking at their sad presentation. *What the hell*, she thought, dropping four cookies on each plate, *we earned it.*

"All clear." Dinah toweled her hair as she walked into the kitchen. "Got a pretty good carpet burn on my back from when I hit the floor, but otherwise I'm clean." She lifted the hem of her shirt to show Alice the evidence.

"Good," Alice said, although *good* didn't begin to cover it. If Dinah had been bitten, or the momerath had gotten her... She wasn't going to think about it. Dinah was fine. There was nothing to worry about.

"Good," Dinah agreed, a huge yawn escaping from her mouth.

"Tired?"

"Yeah." Dinah stretched out her arms. "Actually, if you don't mind, I'm going to take my food to my room and head to bed. I'm pretty beat." She reached for her plate.

"That's fine. I'm gonna head up and read for a bit before I go to bed too," Alice said. Truth be told, she was going to suggest Dinah go to bed anyway. She looked awful. Dark, heavy bags had started to form under her eyes and she couldn't stop yawning. It had been a traumatic day though, and Alice was tired too. Hitting the sack early wouldn't hurt either of them.

"Thanks, Alice. You did great today, by the way." Dinah flashed her a small smile. She turned and padded up the stairs to her room. The door shut softly, and the house was quiet.

"Yeah, way to not get eaten, Alice," she told herself. She picked up her plate and dropped it in the sink, not bothering to rinse it. She would clean it in the morning. Right now, she was exhausted and ready for bed. "Maybe next time you can actually kill the thing instead of just knocking it out." She grimaced, fully aware it was only dumb luck that had saved them. She walked upstairs to her room, wondering what she would do the next time she ran into a momerath— if there was a next time. All she knew was if it did happen, she didn't ever want to be that helpless and scared again.

The next day, Dinah didn't get out of bed. At first, Alice wasn't worried. It wasn't uncommon for her sister to sleep late the morning after a scouting day. Usually she would plod down the stairs to make breakfast before noon. Alice busied herself by cleaning the house and starting her new books. By the time the sun crossed midday, Alice figured it was time to check on her. She pulled herself from *Peter* and returned her pile of books to the top of her desk. The stack hit with a loud thud, and the impact jostled her journal from its spot on her table. It flopped to the floor, hitting spine first and landing open faced on the floor.

Frustrated, Alice leaned forward to retrieve the book, but froze when she saw where it landed. The book opened to a page stained with tears. The paper was wrinkled, distorted by the salty drops scattered across it. The top of the page only had three words written in broken cursive at the top.

Mom is dead.

Alice rubbed her face as memories stormed her mind. She wondered what life would have been like if the momerath never showed up. Different scenes danced through her thoughts until, angrily, she pushed them away. Imagining happy endings wouldn't make them true. The momerath *had* come. And they were here to stay

Alice's gut twisted. She still couldn't think about her mother without tearing up. But before she could get lost in grief, a sound ripped through the house that made her heart drop. A hoarse, grinding cough resounded from her sister's room down the hall. It sounded like a cough from someone who had smoked for eight years or who had pneumonia or... Alice paused as another horrendous cough shuddered through the house. There was an abnormal harshness to it, like something was hidden in the depths of Dinah's chest. Like—

Alice's world crumbled.

Desperately, she replayed the scene from yesterday's chase. *We were ambushed at the library. Dinah was behind me, out of the momerath's reach. I dodged him and we ran away. She fell, but showed me she was clean when we got home. No scratches, no marks, nothing. Nothing happened.* But the sound coming from Dinah's room didn't fit, unless...

Dinah was a Carrier.

And if Dinah was a Carrier, that meant—No. *No.* Dinah just had a cold or something. After all, it was November, the middle of flu season. She probably caught something from the bratty little Peterson twins when she was checking on the baby. That was it. *Nothing to worry about.*

Another gut-wrenching cough ripped from behind Dinah's door. She was sick. Very sick. Alice couldn't breathe. Her chest squeezed tight against her heart and it felt like someone slapped her in the face. She had to talk to her sister.

"Dinah, are you awake?" Alice fought to keep calm.

More coughing. Dinah's voice came out barely above a whisper. "H-hey, Alice. Come in."

Alice cracked the door and peeked in. Dinah didn't *look* like she was carrying a deadly rage-inducing Plague. Just exhausted. But when Alice crossed the room, she could see something wasn't right. Huge bruise-like bags formed under her sister's eyes and her beautiful dark skin had turned pale and ashy. And with the door no longer acting as a barrier, she could hear the slight wheeze interlaced in every breath Dinah took.

"Are you okay?" She sat carefully next to Dinah's feet at the edge of the bed. She seemed so fragile, Alice didn't want to crush her.

Dinah couldn't answer right away. Another huge series of coughs racked her chest, taking over her whole body. After the fit subsided, Dinah wearily fell into her pillow. "I'm fine. Just not feeling great. I must have caught something at the Petersons'. The baby was sick, you know." Dinah rubbed absently at her collarbone. Each word sounded raw and painful. "This stupid cough is starting to make my chest hurt though."

"I'll bet," Alice agreed as she gently brushed her hand across her sister's hairline the same way Dinah always did for her. "Let me feel your head. Are you warm?"

Alice swallowed as she checked her sister's temperature. Everyone knew high fever was one of the early symptoms of the Plague.

Dinah was on fire.

Don't panic, she thought with forced reassurance. *These symptoms could all easily be explained by the flu.*

"No, actually, I'm freezing. Could you bring me another blanket?" Dinah shivered and pulled her comforter around her chin. Blue rings surrounded the bases of her fingernails, covering her skin in a purplish tinge. This was no flu. That kind of skin discoloration was exclusive to the Plague. There was no denying it. Dinah was infected.

A burning sensation seared Alice's nose and she scrunched it to chase it away. This always happened when she was about to cry. She hated it. It was a nuisance, and sometimes it downright hurt, especially when there was going to be a lot of tears. This was one of those times.

But it couldn't be.

Don't let her see you cry. She can't know anything is wrong, Alice scolded herself. She walked to Dinah's closet and reached to the shelf above her clothes. There was a raggedy purple blanket stuffed between some cardboard boxes. "Here you go." She tossed it to her sister and laughed when it landed on her head.

"Thanks," Dinah deadpanned. "You're awesome." Any other sarcastic remarks were lost as another violent set of coughs escaped her throat.

"Hey, relax." Alice tenderly brushed her hand against Dinah's sweat-drenched hair. She put on a brave face, but inside, her head was spinning. "I'm going to go downstairs and read for a while. I'll check on you in a little bit. You sleep."

"Okay," Dinah rasped. "Sounds good. Thanks, Alice." She rested against her pillow and let out a huge yawn. "Sorry I'm being such a bum."

"Don't even worry about it. I got this." Alice winked, then tucked the blanket under Dinah's chin. "You worry about getting better. Love you." She hurried to leave before the tears she felt burning her eyes could pour out.

"I love you too," Dinah said through another yawn. She rolled over onto her side. Even through the blanket, Alice could see her ragged breathing. A slight wheeze sounded through the room. Alice quickly closed the door and fell against it, letting her head thud lightly against the wood.

The minute the door clicked shut, the tears she had reined in came flooding out. She bit her lip to stifle a cry. The house seemed to close in around her. She was suffocating. She had to get out—now. Without thinking about where she was going or what she was doing, Alice fled down the street, not bothering to look back.

She ran as far as she could without leaving the Sector. She had never gone outside without Dinah before, and she had no intention of starting today. She ran to the outskirts of the community, far enough to see the makeshift fence surrounding the Sector. It encompassed the whole area, beginning—or ending, whichever way you considered it—just before what used to be the exit to the I-10. Inside, there was an advertising billboard with a happy family hugging each other underneath the words, *Welcome to Tolleson!* The ad was dingy and torn, no longer inviting. Five feet from the base of the billboard, a set of ladder stairs led to the top of the structure.

Alice often came here to think. Being so close to the edge of the momerath territory made it a quiet space where she could be alone with her thoughts. It was fitting her autopilot brought her here now. Like every time, she approached the base at a brisk run and used her momentum to spring off the metal to grab the bottom rung. Once she had hold of the ladder, she hoisted herself up the rest of the steps.

Hard part over, Alice hurried up the rungs to the billboard. It was a climb, but the view at the end was worth it. From the top of the board, she could see over the crumbling concrete freeway and follow the road as it snaked to the heart of Phoenix.

After her trek up, Alice was too tired to cry anymore, so she simply sat on the ledge and stared at the city. She wasn't sure how long she stayed there. It didn't matter. It stayed the same as always. Dead.

It isn't fair, she thought. Everything in Phoenix—no, everything in the whole damn world was dead. She gazed at the old freeway, a tangled maze of abandoned vehicles. Cars, trucks, and the occasional semi sat empty on the road. Some were completely totaled, slammed into by other panicked drivers trying to escape the city. Some had been ransacked for parts useful for other fleeing vehicles. Most just sat there waiting, as if they were merely idling, stopped for a moment until their owners came to reclaim them.

A sudden movement between a red Prius and a blue sedan caught her attention. Shambling aimlessly between the vehicles, a lone momerath made its way down the freeway. It shuffled listlessly, animated without a purpose. Its clothes hung off its body, barely staying on its emaciated form. The Plague had not been kind to its physique.

"Must be rough catching your own food these days," Alice muttered bitterly to the starved figure. Everything about it screamed death and decay. Its skin was sallow, and its head twisted at an unnatural angle. Definitely broken. Still, it kept on, walking around as if nothing was wrong. Like it shouldn't be dead.

Dark thoughts churned in Alice's mind as she considered the death of her world. Like some external symptom of the virus had killed off the whole planet. These creatures that couldn't die themselves just killed everything—and everyone else—instead. And Dinah was next.

No, she wasn't.

Not Dinah. Dinah was so alive. Even through the end of the world. Dinah, who had always taken care of her even though they weren't even really related. It didn't matter to her, though. Dinah had immediately accepted Alice into the family. And when Mr. Carroll left, Dinah never blamed Alice, although Alice secretly blamed herself. Even after Mom died, Dinah stayed with her. She didn't hesitate, though it meant she was stuck forever playing mommy to some girl her parents brought home when she was younger than Alice was now.

Alice's nose tickled, warning of the tears threatening to come.

She sniffed and roughly wiped it with the back of her hand before brushing her cheeks clean of the few drops that escaped. "Enough, Alice." Now was not the time for tears. Now was her chance to make up for all her sister did for her. It was her turn to take care of Dinah. "Time for you to fix this."

Alice stood and beat the dust off her clothes. She turned to take one last view of her home. To the west were the White Tank Mountains, calm and unmoving. To the east, the ghosts of lonely buildings downtown stretched from the valley in the horizon. Phoenix.

Phoenix! A thrill ran through Alice as she dared to hope. Could it have been only yesterday Lewis told her about the doctor working on a cure? Alice had laughed then, but now it seemed the only thing that could help her.

Her mind spun so fast, she didn't pay attention as her legs pulled her through the streets back to her house. *Find the doctor. Get the cure.* Of course, it wasn't that simple. She was pretty sure the doctor—whoever he was—didn't just stand in the middle of the street advertising his work. Not to mention the fact he may not even have a cure, or... *Stop. One step at a time,* she instructed herself. First, she needed to make sure Dinah would be taken care of while she was gone.

Lewis.

She found him wandering around Main Street still trying to peddle his information. The way his shoulders slumped told her it wasn't going well.

"Hey, Lewis! Don't forget to come pick up your payment for our trade," she yelled loud enough to hold the attention of the nosy Sector-dwellers. "Dinah has it waiting at home." She was pleased to see a few nearby vendors perk their ears in interest. Maybe she could drum up some business for her friend.

She hurried to where he stood, then peeked over her shoulders to make sure her audience had lost interest. A few still looked on, but from where they stood, they wouldn't be able to hear anything Alice didn't want them to.

"We got a bunch of supplies on our last scouting trip," she said softly. Lewis was the only person who knew about their excursions, and she intended to keep it that way. "Next time you come over, you can take your pick of what you like."

"Aw, Alice, you don't have to do that," he said sheepishly, the tips of his ears pink.

"Sure I do. You gave me some really great information. You deserve to get paid for it." She clapped him on the shoulder. "And..." She paused. Her face scrunched into a half wince. Lewis was *not* going to like what she was about to ask.

He groaned and covered his face with his hands. "I know that look," he moaned. "What do you want?"

Alice pulled back her lips in an exaggerated smile. It was lost on Lewis, who didn't look up from his hands. "I need a favor—a *big* favor."

"What do you need?" He sighed and pulled his hands so they only covered the lower part of his face.

Alice glanced nervously over her shoulder once more to make sure nobody was listening. The other Sector residents had long lost interest in her conversation with Lewis and had gone back to yelling at each other across Main Street. Still, she lowered her voice to be safe.

"Dinah is sick," she breathed in a rush. "*Really* sick. We don't have the right antibiotics to give her, so I've gotta bring some back." Alice couldn't bring herself to physically say Dinah was a Carrier. Mom always used to say speaking words made them true, and that was something she couldn't have on her conscience.

Something in her face must have given her away, because Lewis gave her a shrewd look and asked, "How sick is she?"

She bit her lip. "I could be gone a few days," she evaded the answer. "I need you to keep an eye on her—check in on her every now and then. Make sure she doesn't leave the house..." Her nose pricked and tears flooded her eyes.

Lewis's hand fell from his face. His eyes were wide. They darted around her nervously before he leaned in to hiss, "You don't mean..."

She sniffed. "Help yourself to whatever you want at the house. I'll be back as soon as I can."

"Alice, you can't be serious!" The low voice Lewis had worked so hard to maintain flew out the window. "What am I supposed to do—"

Alice clapped her hand over his mouth and pushed him back against the wall. She whipped her head over her shoulder to make sure they were still alone. A few vendors glanced over at the disturbance, but none left their wares. "For starters, you can keep your voice down!"

Lewis's eyes blazed as he pushed her hand away from his mouth, but his voice dropped to a hiss. "This is crazy. You know that, right?"

Alice opened her mouth in retort, but sighed it closed with a slump of her shoulders. "I know," she said in a weak voice. "But I have to try."

Tight-lipped, he searched her face. His brows furrowed and she gave him one last pleading look through tear-filled eyes. He sucked in a slow breath and let it out in a heavy sigh.

"Alright," he groaned, "I can't believe I'm saying this, but I'll do it." He scrubbed his face with his hands again.

Alice's eyes widened and she had to fight back a squeak of surprise. She threw her arms around his neck and hugged him tight. "Thank you."

"Yeah, well, you owe me," he said as he disentangled himself from her grip.

"Anything I hear on the outside is yours exclusively," she promised. Her cheeks flushed with excitement. "I have to go.

Watch out for Dinah," she reminded him. "Thank you, Lewis. You don't know what this means to me." She flashed him a grateful smile, then she was off. She shot through the streets, making a mental list of what she needed.

It took her less than ten minutes to pull everything together to leave. She didn't pack much; no need to be weighed down by nonessentials. In the end, a toothbrush, some toothpaste, her gray hoodie, and a full change of clothes was all she packed. No shoes. They were too bulky and her black combat boots were better for travel. The rest of her space was dedicated to supplies, and those were rationed to carry as much water as possible. Even in the fall, the desert got warm. After momerath, dehydration was her biggest threat.

Before she left, Alice stopped outside Dinah's room. She pressed her ear to the door and listened carefully for her sister. She snored quietly as she slept, but every now and then, her breathing turned raspy and irregular. She was getting worse.

"I love you, Dinah," she whispered softly. "I'm going to make sure you get better. Just hang on." The warning tickle shot down her nose and Alice turned and walked away before she started crying again. It wouldn't fix anything. She took a deep breath and headed to the front door.

"I can do this," she told herself. And with that, she was off to find the doctor.

4

The distance from the Sector to Phoenix was less than fourteen miles. Alice figured walking at a brisk pace, she could cover a mile every fifteen minutes. Factoring in a rest break or two, she estimated her trip taking around four hours, which was good considering she was leaving later in the day than she should. The sun had already passed high noon when she left the house. She was cutting it close. Really close. She was going to have to run. She didn't want to be out in the open when night fell. Daylight didn't hurt the momerath, but they preferred the dark. If she didn't find somewhere to lay low for the night, the odds would not be ever in her favor. Her best bet would be to get into town at least half an hour before the sun set so she could stake out a place to sleep. She doubted there would be a Super 8 she could check into.

"Worry about it later, Alice. First, you need to get there." Her nerves were starting to get the better of her. She tightened her grip on her backpack and moved quicker. She trekked the side streets of the I-10, avoiding the main freeway where she had seen the rogue momerath earlier. She was on the outskirts of the inner city when the sun darkened to a burnt orange—sunset was coming. She was making good time, but she still needed to find a place to settle in for the night.

Phoenix was massive. Buildings towered over her, cold and empty. Everything felt different here than back home. Scarier, somehow. In small towns, it didn't seem strange when there wasn't a whole lot going on; the quiet made sense. In the city, where things were supposed to be noisy and moving, the stillness was almost suffocating. Her chest tightened as she walked through the abandoned buildings, working to stay hidden in ghosted streets.

"Alright, you've made it this far, now you need to find somewhere to sleep," she murmured under her breath. It was a funny situation to be in, wanting to break the terrible silence but needing to be quiet to not draw attention to herself.

Alice wondered exactly what she had gotten herself into. She was alone in a huge, unfamiliar place, searching for some doctor she didn't know anything about except he *might* be working on a cure to the Plague—potentially in the city she was currently in. "Great plan, genius," she muttered under her breath. "Maybe you should have painted a big old target on your back for good measure."

"Why would you do something like that?" A mocking voice from behind sent Alice jumping out of her skin. She screamed and whirled around, fists raised and ready to attack. They quickly fell to her sides when she realized she was facing a boy not much older than herself. Though her heart still raged against her chest, her surprise quickly turned to anger when she saw he was laughing at her.

"Did you just let out a battle cry?" he asked, his rough voice tinged with mirth. "What are you going to do, yell me to death?"

Alice wasn't sure how to respond. Though it was a completely valid question, she was furious he had the nerve to laugh in her face. Her cheeks warmed with embarrassment, and instinctively, her hands balled back into fists.

"Who—"

"Quiet." He clapped his hand over her mouth and pulled her towards him as he pressed his back flat against the wall of the alleyway.

Alice's anger morphed into a wave of panic. She struggled against the boy's arms, but he tightened his grip. He leaned in and whispered in her ear, his breath warm on her cheek. "If you don't quiet down," he said, his voice pitched deliberately low, "we're both going to die."

Alice stopped fighting as the words sunk in. *Both...*

The moment she realized what he meant, she heard the clang of metal followed by a guttural howl. Her heart caught as she strained to hear where the momerath was coming from. She wanted to run, but the boy's arms circled around her like iron shackles. She vaguely wondered if he could feel how violently her heart was beating.

"There's a reinforced minivan parked on Washington Street not far from here. On my count, I'm going to let go and we're going to run for it." Though there was urgency in his words, he spoke in a calm, steady tone. Paired with the deep tenor of his voice, it was almost soothing. "If you don't keep up, I will leave you behind."

Well, it *had* been soothing. *So much for chivalry,* Alice thought, but nodded to show she understood.

"One...two...*three!*" The boy twisted his body and pushed her into the alleyway. He ran with a grace Alice had never seen before, dodging the rubble of the alley like nothing was there. He moved so gracefully, a brief image of a predatory cat flashed through her thoughts. She did her best to keep up, trying to match her awkward steps to his nimble ones. Her legs were shorter than his, though, and she missed a step, kicking an abandoned glass Coke bottle and sending it clattering loudly across the sidewalk. Another howl shot into the night, closer now than it had been before.

The boy cursed and scowled at her. His golden eyes narrowed in annoyance before he spun forward and pushed on, moving faster. Alice kept pace, listening to the wild cries behind, waiting for the sound of rasping breaths to catch them. Her chest tightened with every step, and her breathing came out in uneven gasps. Desperately, she pushed on, and soon they reached an old minivan parked on the side of the road, as promised.

"In here." He flung the door wide open before practically throwing Alice in. "The frame has been reinforced with steel. They won't be able to get in. But just in case, there's a gun under the front seat. Use it if you need to." He didn't bother to explain how. Apparently, in the city, they had training in that sort of thing. Alice's head spun as she tried to process all the information. She felt dizzy, but the boy wasn't done giving orders.

"Don't come out 'til morning," he growled, piercing her with his golden gaze. Another animalistic screech sounded through the streets. The momerath were close. The boy glanced over his shoulder anxiously and grabbed the door handle. He tensed his arm to swing it shut.

"Wait!" Alice cried, realizing her voice sounded more than a little frantic. A million thoughts ran through her mind—*Whose car is this? Why did you bring me here? Where are you going? Why are you leaving me here?* These questions and more clashed into each other, demanding an answer. The winning query spilled out before she could stop it. "Who are you?"

The boy flashed her a sly grin and tightened his grip on the door. "I'm Chess," he said. "Welcome to Wanderland."

5

It was a long night. After the strange boy—Chess—shut the door and ran, Alice curled up in the corner of the van into the smallest ball she could manage and held her breath. She was afraid to make any sound or movement the momerath could detect. Raspy cries surrounded the vehicle, and for an unbearable few moments, Alice was certain she was going to die. Silent tears streamed down her cheeks as the van jostled under siege. She bit her lip to keep from crying out before the momerath eventually gave up and shuffled away.

After what seemed like an eternity, the city fell quiet. Still. She stayed tucked in her protective huddle for another ten minutes after she heard the last momerath cry. Once she was sure there were no more nearby, she slowly untangled herself and looked nervously around the minivan.

Crouching low to the floor, Alice prayed what Chess told her was true. To his credit, the van seemed secure enough. The windows were tinted and painted over, making it completely impossible for anyone to see in—or for her to see out. The inside of the vehicle was, as Chess claimed, reinforced. Every surface was steel-plated, with the exception of the windows, which had metal bars strategically placed over them. Alice also found the gun hidden under the carpet beneath the driver's seat: a black pistol with *Luger 9mm* etched in the side. Tucked next to it was a sleek machete sharp enough to split a hair and a pocket can of INFERNO pepper spray. Alice had no training on how to hold a gun, let alone shoot one, so she left the Luger in its place and pocketed the INFERNO. Then she carefully set aside the machete and continued rifling under the chair to see what else she could find. Resting underneath the gas pedal, she found a discarded glass vial with the words *Drink Me* printed on the label. She made a mental note to ask Chess about it if she ever saw him again.

It was clear the minivan was not designed for comfort. The only seat in the whole vehicle was the driver's, and Alice guessed it was just there because it was required to operate the machine. Everything else was completely gutted. It looked like the vehicle may have been used as some sort of weapons base; the walls had mounts installed to house a variety of tools. If the two pieces she found under the driver's seat were any indication, they were all pretty hardcore. One of the mounts even held a handcrafted sheath for the machete Alice found. When she tried to tuck the blade in, it fit like a glove.

Bits of trash and broken glass littered the floor, and she wondered if the van's owners had to make a hasty exit. It made her wary of Chess and how he knew about it. The only clue she had to any of her questions was a tattered old Nine of Hearts tucked in the mirror of the driver's sun visor. It didn't help.

Alice flopped back against the van's hatch. Finally sitting and semi-safe, her exhaustion caught up to her. A huge yawn escaped her mouth, and her eyelids fluttered closed. Outside, the night was filled with the distant shouts of the monsters who had claimed the city. Shrill, broken screeches pierced the quiet, sending shivers down her spine. She tightened her hold around the blade beside her. Sighing, she closed her eyes and slowly counted to ten to clear her mind. Fatigue gripped every part of her body, from her stiff leg muscles to her aching back, but she was afraid to fall asleep. She was thankful Chess had provided her shelter, but she didn't trust it. Her eyes burned, heavy with the strain of keeping them open. She nodded off a few times, only to be woken by the unholy sounds of the momerath. Eventually, her will was overpowered and her overtired body drifted to sleep with the terrifying soundtrack of the city playing in her dreams.

Alice woke a few hours later, startled at first by her foreign surroundings. Heart pounding, she snatched the machete next to her and jumped into a defensive stance. She scanned the area for threats. Satisfied nothing had breached the security of the van, her nerves slowly calmed. Remembering where she was, she surveyed the inside of the van again. It was still dark, but the paint on the windows had lightened, hinting that the sun had risen and morning had come.

Alice sat and took out a water bottle and one of the granola bars she had packed. She nibbled on the pastry absentmindedly, preoccupied with sorting her thoughts. She had a couple of options. She could sit in the van and wait for Chess to come back and ask him if he could help her—*if* he ever came back. Or, she could leave and attempt to find the doctor on her own. She didn't know much about Phoenix, or have a clue where to start, but if she waited, she would lose time. Dinah couldn't afford that.

Decision made, Alice gathered her belongings and slung her bag over her shoulder, wearing it like a messenger's bag. She strapped the machete to her back, resting it securely along her spine. Once it was in place, she pulled her hair into a messy bun to keep it out of her way in case she needed to reach the blade. Her bangs, too short to be held captive by the tie, fell in front of her eyes until she swept them away with a flip of her head. With only a moment's hesitation, she gripped the door handle and clicked the lever to unlatch the door, exposing her to the city once again.

Sunlight flooded the van, burning bright against her eyes. Using her hand as a shield, she gazed at the city, peaceful in the early morning. There was no sign the streets swarmed with monsters the night before. It was desolate. The asphalt and concrete of the buildings absorbed the heat from the sun and made it warmer than the Sector, almost stifling. It was brighter, too—glass windows covering the downtown skyscrapers gleamed as the light reflected off their surface and bounced off to bake the streets below.

Alice let the heat sink into her skin. The sun was amazing, warming her through her bones. She let out a contented sigh, prepared to leave, when she heard rustling coming from down the street. Quickly, she ducked back into the minivan and quietly slid the door closed, leaving it cracked a sliver so she could peer outside. The small space didn't give her room to see much, but she heard the crash of a metal garbage can followed by hurried footsteps. Her breath caught, and she felt to make sure the machete was within her grasp. More footsteps approached, this time followed by a man's voice, muttering unintelligibly. Alice pressed her ear to the door, straining to make out what he was saying.

"I'm late...I'm late," the man said as he passed the minivan. He was older, sixty or so if his hair color was any indication. Most of it was still intact, a shock of white against his tanned skin. His facial features hinted he could have been younger, but stress had taken its toll on him. Worry lines etched his forehead and he fretfully craned his head back and forth, nervously eyeing his surroundings.

"Late. So, so late." He brought his wrist up to check his gold watch. "She's going to be so upset with me. Why am I always late?!" He ran his fists through his hair, forcing the snow-white strands straight from their roots. Alice's forehead creased in concern for the man's sanity. She wondered if that was how she sounded when she talked to herself and made a mental note to stop immediately. She peered intently at the man to learn as much as she could about him without actually engaging him. Aside from the erratic behavior, he seemed well put together.

He approached the van, providing Alice a better view. He wore a solid gold watch that could have passed for a Rolex, and dark square-shaped glasses sat on the bridge of his squat nose, drawing attention to his electric blue eyes. He had an average build, not tall but not short, and she could easily tell he wasn't overweight. He wore a neatly-fitted collared shirt and dark khakis with a pair of scuffed brown leather shoes. Over his clothes, he wore a crisp doctor's coat with a plastic name badge with large print identifying him as Dr. Waite R. Abbott.

Oh no. This couldn't be the doctor she came to Phoenix for. Not this potentially crazy, pathologically late old man. He couldn't possibly have the cure for the Plague. Her heart sank as she thought of Dinah and how much she needed one.

"Can't be late. I have to get the antidote and take it to the Queen," Abbott muttered, haphazardly smoothing down the hair he had just pulled up.

So, it was him.

Well, it makes sense the only doctor still working on trying to find a cure would be a bit... unstable. But fitting didn't make it any more comforting. Alice watched him hurry down the street to whoever was waiting on him. At a loss for how to convince him to help her—and more than a little unsure whether he would even be able to—she watched the curious man hustle down the street, mumbling to himself about the time. He seemed harmless enough, so naturally, Alice did the only thing she could: she followed him.

6

"Maybe I'm the crazy one," Alice whispered as she hurried after the doctor. "After all, I'm chasing down a random doctor who's potentially insane. That can't be normal."

But what's normal anymore? her mind argued back as she huffed along. *There are people who tear apart and eat other people.* She shuddered. *And I'm pretty sure I read somewhere that crazy people don't question their sanity. That counts for something, right?*

Her personal debate was cut short by a sudden change en route. She had been following Abbott from a distance when he quickly started zigzagging across streets and ducking into alleyways and she had to concentrate so she didn't lose him.

She tracked him until he turned the corner of Roosevelt Street. She wasn't far behind, but when she rounded the corner, the street was empty. Abbott was nowhere to be found, but she couldn't see anywhere he could have gone. There were no roads for him to take, and she wasn't far enough for him to have run any farther without her seeing him.

Where is he? Panic flared in the pit of her stomach. *You lost him.* She glanced nervously around the street. She had no idea where she was. Abbott's winding path had completely turned her sense of direction upside down. *You should have talked to him when he passed by earlier instead of trying go all James Bond and tail him through the city. He probably thought you were trying to kill him or something.*

Her mental tirade ended abruptly when a large hand clamped over her shoulder like a vice. Her heart kicked into over-drive, shooting adrenaline through her body. She clutched the blade on her back and whipped it in front of her as she turned to face—the doctor?

"Who are you? Why are you following me?" he demanded, unfazed by the machete she was holding between them. His blue eyes pierced hers, previous agitation gone. His demeanor was so different from the man she had seen in front of the van that she wondered if maybe she *did* lose him in a different alley. But this was him. He had the same white hair, the same striped shirt, the same name tag.

"Doc-doctor Abbott?"

"Who's asking?" His eyebrows knotted together as he raked his gaze across her face.

"I—I am." She stumbled over her words, still trying to figure out what had changed so much in the man. "I need to find an antidote for my sister. She's sick. I think it's the Plague—"

"She's dead then," Abbott gruffed. "MR-V doesn't have a cure. Your sister's as good as gone." His voice was harsh, but Alice saw pain filling his pool-blue eyes.

"But, you said—" She faltered, but began again, strength-ening her resolve. "By the van, you said you needed to bring the antidote to the Queen." She didn't bother to mention she had no idea who that was. She hoped her bluff would be enough.

"So that's when you started following me," he said, more to himself than Alice. "Well, I'm sorry to have misled you, but what

I said was true. There is no cure." He glanced at his watch. "Even if I wanted to, I have nothing I could give to you. Or the Queen." He rubbed his hand over the deep creasing wrinkles in his forehead, as if trying to smooth them. "I've been working for so long, and have found nothing. So much time—"

Suddenly, the doctor's body went rigid. His eyes darted frantically around the alley, terrified, like he had lost himself.

"Time...*time*. Late. I'm late—" he whispered through pale lips. His posture tensed like a tightly wound coil and his hands began to tremble. He raised his watch and Alice noticed its crystal face was broken. The glass was cracked and the two tiny hands were frozen in place, never moving from 3:30. This didn't matter to the doctor, who ran his hands through his hair as he wildly swerved his head side to side, chasing away some unseen demon. Without warning, he shot down the street crying at the top of his lungs, "Can't be late! I have an important date!"

"Wait! Mr. Abbott!" Alice chased after him. "Where are you going?" The doctor ignored her and kept running, compulsively checking his watch as he tore a twisted path through the empty streets.

"Dr. Abbott, can you hear me?"

If Abbott did, he didn't show it. He was as distracted as the first time Alice had seen him. *What makes him act like that?* The doctor had been fine until he brought up the time, then his whole demeanor changed. *Curious,* she thought. *Very curious.*

Another quick turn, and Abbott was hurtling through a run-down alley littered with trash surrounding the oversized Dumpsters that lined the walls. Against the bins, someone had assembled a collection of cardboard boxes and pieces of discarded furniture to use as a makeshift shelter. The doctor, unaware of his surroundings, rushed past the hovel, loudly lamenting his tardiness.

Startled by the sound, something rustled violently inside the lean-to and a female momerath sprang out like a hellish jack-in-the-box. It let out a menacing snarl as it scanned the side street to find what disturbed it. Trailing behind Abbott had left Alice in its direct line of sight and exposed. The momerath flung its head back to release an earsplitting roar, deafening Alice with its shrill pitch. The doctor didn't even stop to see what was going on.

"Dr. Abbott!" Alice cried, terrified to be caught with the monster alone. But the doctor was gone, turned down another side street in the city's grid.

The momerath hissed, drawing Alice's attention to its inhuman form. Its pixie hair was matted with dirt and blood, and its skin was streaked with filth. It wore the remains of an old dress, the color indistinguishable from the grime caked onto it. It stood disoriented until primal instinct kicked in and it propelled itself directly at Alice, eager to tear her apart.

Alice was a stone. Nothing moved except her heart, which beat erratically against her ribcage in a desperate attempt at escape. The panic in her chest built until a surge of adrenaline coursed through her veins, filling her body and stilling her nerves. She knew what to do.

She fell into a defensive stance and raised her machete in front of her, arms outstretched. It was heavy in her arms, but she held position, even as the momerath drew nearer. Her ears buzzed with the excess energy flooding her body, but she held fast. She would not run. She didn't have time.

Less than five feet away, the momerath let out one last raspy screech and launched at Alice, arms swinging as it tried to rip into whatever part of Alice it could reach. Faster than she ever moved before, Alice sidestepped the momerath and swung her blade. She made contact and sliced a huge gash in the creature's arm. The momerath let out an angry hiss then whirled around to face her again. It lunged for Alice, its milky gaze locked on her throat. Unpracticed with the machete, Alice jerked it back over her shoulders like a baseball bat. She squeezed her eyes shut and swung, another war cry escaping her lips as she lashed out at the momerath.

Crude as it was, the attack worked. The machete made contact with the momerath's neck as it dove for Alice. The combined momentum was enough for the blade to slice clean through the sinew of the creature's neck. Alice peeked her eyes open when she felt the resistance against her weapon disappear. She froze in horror when she saw the momerath's headless body lying on the asphalt, arms still reaching for her, twitching as if they hadn't received the signal to stop moving yet. Her stomach flipped and she ran to the wall and retched, losing what little breakfast she ate that morning. When she was done, she stood and wiped her mouth clean with the back of her hand. Curiosity getting the better of her, Alice dared one last peek at the momerath. It still lay there, but mercifully, its limbs had finally stopped moving. She took in a steadying breath and exhaled loudly.

"Well, what do you know?" a familiar mocking voice chirped behind her. "You aren't completely useless after all."

7

"You!" Alice whirled around, fatigue forgotten. Her blazing temper returned the color to her cheeks as she fixed a fierce glare at Chess. He was laughing at her *again*. "What are you doing here?" she demanded. Her arms shook, and she was unsure if it was rage or exhaustion.

"I came to check on you," he said as though it was the most obvious thing in the world. "At first I couldn't find you, but then I followed the noise." He studied her. "You do know sound attracts momerath, right? Even during the day."

"Of course I know that!" Alice raged. What did he think she was, an idiot?

Chess's only response was an amused grin tilted sideways by the quirk of his neck. He scrutinized her like a puzzle to solve. He had a lean build, but even under his dingy gray leather jacket, it was easy to see he had good muscle tone. The fade of his jacket almost exactly matched his ash-colored hair. He wore it short, trimmed on the sides and only slightly longer on top. It was a stark contrast to his olive skin and amber eyes. Standing in the sun, they gleamed a startling shade of gold until he moved and the light hit him at another angle, making flecks of green scattered throughout dance in the sun.

"So, what's your game?" His eyes crinkled behind his cheeks. "Are you trying to call out all the 'rath in this place, Blondie? It could be fun, I guess." He tapped his chin, making a show of his consideration. "Personally, if I was playing, I'd hope for Fighters, not Flighters." He smiled like he knew a secret she wasn't privy to.

"Flighters?" she asked automatically, then shook her head, frustrated he had distracted her again. She held up her hand to keep him from interrupting. "My name is Alice." She brushed her bangs from her eyes to give him the full effects of her glare. "Not Blondie."

"Nice to meet you, Alice," he said as he circled her. He flipped the end of her ponytail as he passed behind her. "But you've gotta admit, Blondie has a nice ring to it."

Alice planted her hands firmly on her hips. "Not really." She'd never been called "Blondie" in her life, and she wasn't about to let it start now. The last person who even called her by a nickname was Mr. Carroll—*and we all know how that turned out,* she thought bitterly.

"You know, your eyes get darker when you're mad. Like a storm on the ocean. Not that I've ever seen one." Chess treated the whole conversation like a game. He had switched the direction of his jaunt and was now tracing lazy circles the opposite way around her. It was making her dizzy. "It's kinda cute."

To Alice's dismay, her cheeks flushed at the compliment. Her face needed to get with the program. She schooled her look and rolled her eyes, forcing them into submission as she let out an unattractive snort. "Don't tell me this is how you talk to all the girls."

"Nope. Just you." With a graceful twist of his body, Chess hoisted himself on top of the rusty green Dumpster. He smiled from his perch and leaned forward to ask her, "So. What's a pretty girl like you doing in a nasty place like this?"

"I—" His question caught Alice off guard. So far, Chess seemed to prefer teasing her; she wasn't expecting any sort of serious conversation to come from him. She also wasn't sure she wanted to answer. She didn't know anything about him, except apparently, he called himself Chess. But he had sheltered her and provided her with a weapon. *And,* she reminded herself, *you still have the INFERNO if he gets too fresh.*

"I'm looking for the doctor who's working on the cure for the Plague." His amber eyes bored into hers, unwavering. "At least, I was. I found him, I think, but then I lost him again."

Chess's eyes sparked, all seriousness gone. "Lost him. *Again.*" He snickered.

"Yes. Well, it was that or be lunch," Alice snapped. "So I think I made the better choice." She crossed her arms, daring him to contradict her.

"Absolutely!" Chess raised his hands in a placating gesture. He tried to wipe the grin from his face, but even with his lips turned down, his other features betrayed him. "I was just wondering: what's your plan now, Princess?"

Alice grimaced. Princess was worse than Blondie. Not wanting to give him the satisfaction of seeing her riled, she spoke as matter-of-factly as she could. "Find him, obviously." It was her turn to play know-it-all.

"How are you gonna do that?" He leaned forward to rest his elbow on his leg. He dropped his chin in his hand and watched her with an amused expression.

Crap. He called her bluff. "I'm going to follow him," she said haughtily, hoping she sounded convincing.

"You know where he went?" There was that smug smirk again. *It's a good thing he's sitting on top of the bin, otherwise I'd smack that stupid smile off his face,* Alice thought. She wasn't sure she had ever met anyone as intentionally irritating. But as much as it pained her to admit, he had a point.

"Well, no. Not exactly." She was fully aware her confident façade was fading fast. She huffed and straightened her shoulders. "But I saw which way he went. And if I wasn't stuck here talking to you, I'd probably have caught up to him by now."

"So it's my fault?" Chess's grin widened.

"Pretty much." She turned to follow the direction she saw the doctor leave. "Now if you'll excuse me."

Before she could pass, Chess dropped from the Dumpster to cut her off. Alice sighed dramatically and flashed him a bored look. He didn't notice.

"Since it's my fault you lost him, I feel I should make it up to you." He placed his hand over his heart in mock apology.

"You could help me lose *you,*" Alice suggested innocently as she tried to move around him.

"Ouch." Chess sidestepped in front of her again. Man, he was tall. Standing close, she had to crane her neck to see his face. "You wound me, Sweet Pea."

"Not. My. Name."

"Right. What I was *going* to suggest, before you so inconsiderately stomped on my heart—" He clutched his chest and spluttered theatrically. *Too bad Hollywood isn't around anymore,* Alice mused. *He could have had a lucrative career.* He definitely had a flair for the dramatic.

Chess continued, ignoring her nonplussed stare. "—was that I could take you."

"But then I would have to put up with you longer." She wrinkled her nose in distaste.

Again, Chess ignored her. It was starting to become a habit of his. "Double win for you. You find what you want, *and* get my company." He beamed, obviously pleased with his argument. "What do you say, Buttercup?"

"Alice. My name is *Alice.*"

Part of her wanted to say no simply on principle. Then she wouldn't have to put up with him—or those stupid nicknames— any longer. But another part of her knew she had no idea where to go, and principle or not, her pride was not worth Dinah's life. She let out a small groan. "If I let you come, no more nicknames."

Chess's smile widened. "You got a deal, Sw—Alice." He caught his slip and coughed awkwardly in an attempt to play it off. "You know, you got spunk. I like you." He slung his arm around her shoulder and led her down the alleyway.

"Lucky me." Alice's voice was flat as she shook her head in defeat. *This is going to be interesting,* she told herself.

"You have no idea," Chess said.

"What?" Alice asked.

"Hmmm?" Chess glanced at her innocently. "Oh, I was just saying you have no idea how lucky you are you met me. Considering how awesome I am and all."

"And so humble," Alice added with a pointed look. Surely it wasn't possible for someone to *actually* be that cocky.

"Humble. Hey, I like that. Yeah. Humble, that's me." Chess poked his chest with his thumbs. "With a capital H."

Alice's jaw actually dropped. Apparently, she was wrong about the cocky thing. She shook her head, but couldn't keep a smile from quirking the corners of her lips. "Let's just find the doctor," she said, a traitorous laugh escaping at the end of her sentence.

"Your wish is my command, m'lady." Chess beamed. He dropped into a low, flourishing bow before he strode in front of her, ready to guide her through the city.

THE POOL OF TEARS

8

Turned out Chess was an expert on the inner workings of the city because he lived there his whole life. Before the Plague broke out, he lived in a small two-bedroom home in the Coronado Historical District not five miles from downtown. He told her his old house was still intact, and he even used it as a shelter from time to time. Alice wondered why he didn't stay there, but when she asked about it, Chess pretended not to hear. Instead, he chattered on about Bank One Ball Park—only idiots called it Chase Field, he said— and how it was basically a momerath free-for-all.

"Needless to say, we won't be catching any games this season." He swung an invisible bat as he walked. Alice noted he was a southpaw. His imaginary bat connected with its target and Chess covered his eyes, pretending to follow it out of the park. Alice watched in amusement. She had never seen someone with such a carefree attitude. It almost made her jealous.

"If no one is here, why did you stay in Phoenix?" she prodded.

"Where?" Chess's brows knit in confusion then shot up

when understanding dawned on him. "Oh, Phoenix. Right. I forgot people still called it that," he said, winding up for another pitch.

Alice was confused. "What else would they call it?"

"Everyone around here calls it Wanderland." He swung and missed. *Strike*.

"Wanderland?"

"Yeah. After the Plague started, most people took off or turned. Not many stuck around, so the only action anyone saw was the 'rath wandering the streets." Another miss. *Strike Two*. "Seemed fitting."

Alice nodded, imagining Wanderland the first months after the Plague. With so many people, it had to be a nightmare. She shuddered. Chess wasn't bothered and prattled off on random tangents. After striking out, he had given up his baseball bat and now dribbled an imaginary basketball. Alice wondered when the last time he had a real conversation with another person was. He was content to casually remark on anything, but any time the discussion delved deeper than surface level, he quickly switched gears. She didn't think he had many real friends, if any. But in his defense, it was hard to make friends these days. If it wasn't for Dinah, her own social life would have been nonexistent. It wasn't like social media survived after the technology crash. Even if it had, she highly doubted Apple would have been able to success-fully market an iMomerath product line.

"You there, Spunky Brewster?" Chess interrupted. He waved his hand in front of Alice's nose to get her attention. "You do that a lot, don't you?" His head quirked to the side in his trademark pose. Alice called it "Curious."

Pay attention, she scolded. That was the third time he caught her lost in thought. Flippant as his attitude was, he was very observant.

"You promised no nicknames," she reminded, hoping to show

she wasn't completely oblivious. "But, in reference to your question, yes, I'm here. With you. *Still.*" They had been creeping through the city for the past hour, and although Chess swore they were going the right way, she was beginning to wonder. "Are you sure you know where you're going?" she asked for what was probably the twentieth time.

"How little you trust." He shook his head in mock dismay. It was amazing how he could *tsk* and keep his smirk firmly in place.

Alice rolled her eyes. She had been doing that a lot since Chess joined her. "Alright, Mr. Navigator." She assigned the nickname hoping for a reaction. He didn't care. "Do you have any idea when we'll get...*wherever* it is we're going?"

"Yep." Chess was undeterred by her attitude. "Right about... now." He stopped and held out his arms in a grand gesture. "We're here."

"Here..." Alice trailed off, warily eyeing the building in front of her. It was a huge skyscraper with *Borogove Industries* printed in bold at the top. The majority of the building was sleek, tinted windows. The only exceptions were the base and top of the building, which were dark gray stucco. Outside was plain, with only a matching gray stucco plaque surrounded by two cypress trees proudly displaying the company name for decoration.

Borogove Industries. Unremarkable, yet, she was struck by a gnawing familiarity she couldn't place. It wasn't fear or anger, something about it just felt—*off.*

"You okay?" Chess bumped into her shoulder.

She shook her head to chase the sensation away. "Yeah." She paused. "Yeah, I'm fine," she quickly repeated, as much for herself as for Chess. She took a few cautious steps toward the building, then stopped at the small staircase leading to the front door. Staring at the front of Borogove, a vision washed over her and suddenly she was somewhere else—*A cold, dark room that stank of formaldehyde and felt cold as ice. She was young, only two or three years old, and she wasn't alone. Two other children shared the room with her, a boy and a girl who stared at the ceiling with blank expressions. They huddled under their blankets, but it was still freezing. Their beds lined the wall of the room, each one separated by a strange railing with a curtain attached, strange for a bedroom. Her bed was placed at the end of the long room with the boy's beside her, too far to make out his features. She strained to see, but, footsteps approached outside the room and a deep voice called for her—*

"Hey, Space Cadet, it's your turn." Chess clapped his hand on her shoulder, startling her from her reverie. Embarrassed, Alice flipped her ponytail and let out a quick breath.

"So this is it?" She forced a bright tone, but she was unable to hide the tremor beneath it.

Chess studied her a minute more, then shrugged. "Yep. Borogove Industries. If you need a doctor, this is where you'll find him." He spoke with authority, but Alice was doubtful.

"How do you know?" She surveyed Borogove once more. It wasn't different from any other building they passed. She wondered what made it so special.

"Easy," Chess said airily. "I'm the master of the city." His eyes sparkled as he teased her. He paused, clearing his throat and scratching his head innocently when Alice impatiently placed her hands on her hips. "Or it could be this is the only building in the entire city with its security system active." He pointed to a black video camera hooked to the building.

Alice was dubious. Just because cameras were installed didn't mean they were functional. If they were, she wanted to know how the company kept the system running. And why they were still working. If she had a full-time job before the apocalypse, she would have taken the end of the world as a sign for an extended vacation.

She crept toward the door. When she stepped onto the

bottom stair, the camera on the corner swiveled its face to where she stood. It stopped, focusing its lens with a mechanical buzz. A tiny orange light began to blink, indicating it was recording. Alice's nerves fluttered under the scrutiny.

"Have you ever tried to get in bef—" Alice stopped midsentence. Chess was no longer with her. She turned to find where he went, but the pavilion was empty. He had vanished. She was standing in front of Borogove completely alone. Chess had ditched her *again*.

9

"Seriously?" She couldn't believe Chess had ditched her twice in less than twenty-four hours.

Talk about commitment issues. She didn't understand why he kept leaving. *You were the one who kept whining that he wouldn't go away,* she reminded herself. But it still didn't explain why he kept showing up to begin with. He was definitely an odd one. Alice didn't think she'd ever figure him out. Then again, she hadn't completely decided if she wanted to.

"Get over it, Alice. There's no time to worry about the potential psychological issues of some stranger." *Especially if you're not going to address your own psychological issues first.* Alice ignored it.

She looked at Borogove. The only marked entry was the large sliding glass door with the company logo plastered across the center of it. *It can't be that easy,* she thought as she approached the entrance.

It wasn't. Up close, she could see the inner barricades the dark glass had masked before. Large metal panels pressed against the glass, running flush with the doorframe. She couldn't see how they secured to the wall, but it didn't matter. No matter what she tried, the doors didn't budge. The barricades were doing their job.

She let out an exasperated sigh. "Perfect," she whined to no one in particular. "Foiled by a door." She peeked over her shoulder, half-hoping Chess's habit of randomly appearing might bring him back. It didn't.

Figures.

A flash of white drew her eye to the side of the building. Alice turned and saw Dr. Abbott nervously crouched outside before a large gray door swung open and he hurried in.

"Hey! Wait!" Alice ran after the doctor, hoping to catch him. Before she could, the steel door slammed shut, clicking loudly as the lock latched in place. She pressed against the door with all of her might, but it didn't budge. She jumped into it, throwing all her weight against the metal, but it only made her shoulder hurt.

"Now what?" She rubbed her throbbing arm. She wondered if she could pry the door open or undo its hinges. But that wouldn't work. The door was solid steel and completely seamless. It didn't even have a handle. Clearly, it opened from within.

That's not going to help. She slid her hand down the smooth metal. On the side of the door, a ten-digit electronic keypad with a built-in fingerprint scanner flashed green.

"Guess I know how Dr. Abbott got in." She bit her lip. "Now, how do I?" On a whim, she pressed her pointer finger to the scanner, covering the little screen in the center. She held it there, unsure what to expect, until it beeped.

"*Unknown personnel,*" a soothing female voice crooned over the intercom. "*Please verify identity.*" A tiny square window beneath the keypad opened and a small metal tray extended from it. It held a small glass vial filled with bright blue liquid. Curious, Alice picked up the glass to examine it closer. Its only marking was a plain white label that read *Drink Me.*

Alice shook the bottle, then uncorked the top and lightly sniffed its contents. It didn't smell like anything. She pulled the vial back and eyed it warily. Clearly, she was meant to drink whatever was inside, but she didn't trust it. Hesitating, she peered at the entrance in front of her. The doctor was in there.

She placed her hand on the door, the only barrier between her and the doctor. Resigned, she balled her fist and pounded it against the door, her body's small protest against her mind's instructions.

"Here goes nothing." She steeled her nerves and drew the vial to her lips. She hesitated only a second, letting the cool glass rest against her lower lip. Before she could talk herself out of it, she threw her head back and poured the contents down her throat.

Bottle empty, she dropped her arm with the small vial clutched in her hand. She hunched in on herself, her eyes squeezed shut, prepared for the worst. Nothing happened. She waited a moment longer then slowly opened one eye, daring to peek around, wondering if anything had changed.

"Vision—unimpaired," she confirmed as she performed her own physical assessment. "Touch—" She dug her nails into her fingertips, feeling them bite into her skin. "Normal. Skin—" She brought her hand in front of her face and rotated her wrist. "Clear." She patted down the rest of her body, only slightly disappointed when she discovered no new extremities.

"Talk about anticlimactic," Alice muttered, and pocketed the empty bottle in her bag. She checked the door, hoping something had changed. It hadn't. She rocked on her heels, debating what to do next. She was about to start pounding on the door when the smooth voice came on the speaker.

"*Identity verified. Non-Carrier. Enter keycode to proceed.*" Alice's fist dropped in shock. It worked! She was in! Well, almost. She gazed at the keypad, at a loss. She didn't even know how long the correct combination was. Ten digits. Endless possibilities. Millions of wrong answers and only one that could open the door.

Alice growled. *Why does this have to be so difficult?* She wiped her hands over her eyes, feeling a throbbing pain in her head. Her mind spun as numbers and memories jumbled together in a tangle of nonsense. She massaged her temples to ease the pressure building in her skull. As she did, a series of numbers flashed through her brain.

3...5...1...6...6...4...8. The numbers appeared slowly, dancing across her vision like a pulse before they began to move quicker, merging together until they formed a single unit. 3.5.1.6.6.4.8. ... 3516648.

The numbers meant nothing to Alice, but she couldn't shake the feeling they were important. The edges of her mind gripped the frayed ends of a memory, but couldn't seem to hold onto anything. All her thoughts slipped through her mind like smoke wisps leaving only 3516648.

Raising a trembling hand, she punched the code. She stepped back, watching the door with bated breath. She bit anxiously at the inside of her cheek until the bitter taste of blood hit her tongue. The monotone box spoke again, distracting her from the pain.

"*Invalid code. Access Denied. Vacate the premises immediately.*" Its demure tone contradicted the warning. It confused Alice until a shrill whistle rang out, wrenching from Borogove into the rest of the city. It was so high-pitched, it hurt her ears—her teeth vibrated as it buzzed through her eardrums. She cringed and pressed her head against her shoulder to dull the sound.

Alice wasn't surprised when the momerath shot out the nearby alleyway, startled by the alarm. She was sure everything in a five-mile radius could hear the noise emanating from the building and figured it was only a matter of time until unwelcome guests appeared. What did surprise her was when, instead of attacking, it tore down the street in fright. She didn't have long to dwell on it though. As the momerath fled, its shrieks called the attention of others. These behaved the way she expected. They shambled into the clearing, abandoning their decrepit hiding places following the commotion, ready to attack.

She needed to move.

Fast.

She tightened the straps of her bag, securing it firmly against her body so she could run unencumbered and took off. Behind her, an unnatural howl ripped through the air. The low, guttural tones clashed with the high-pitched scream of the alarm. This time, Alice hardly noticed the pain in her ears. More animalistic shouts joined the first, each one closer than the last. Her chest tightened and she had to fight to breathe. It was too late. The momerath were coming.

10

The momerath rushed closer and sudden clarity burst through Alice's hazy thoughts, startling her to action. She whipped her blade from its sheath, gripping it tight in her hand. The rhythm of her heart accelerated into high gear, beating erratically against her chest. Her ears throbbed as blood rushed to fill her veins, and her tangled thoughts morphed into an organized plan. First, she needed a defensive position. Standing exposed on the side of Borogove left her open to attack from too many angles. She needed to get higher up, out of the momerath's reach. That way, she could at least get the drop on them.

She scanned the area and saw a small fire escape hatch on the Firm-Tech Corporation building next door. She took off at a run, hoping she could reach the base of the steps. The access point was almost identical to her billboard in the Sector, except the bottom was a good eight feet off the ground. Her shoulders bunched as she flexed, praying she jumped high enough. A raspy yowl in the distance spurred her on until she was sprinting as fast as she could. The wind whipped past her face, stinging dust against her cheeks, but she didn't slow. The second before she hit the side of the wall, she threw herself into the air, desperately clutching at the bottom stair. She kicked her feet, using her momentum to bound off the wall and onto the ladder.

She landed higher than anticipated, firmly gripping the fourth stair from the bottom. From there, she easily brought her feet onto the landing steps. She crawled onto the flat, cramped space as an angry, gut-wrenching cry sounded beneath her.

The largest momerath she had ever seen stood under the landing, glaring up at her. Scratches ran across its face at every angle, making it look like it had been in a horrific knife fight. Its skin was darker than most other momerath she had seen, and her stomach sank when she realized that was how Dinah would look if she failed. It was flanked on its sides by three more 'rath, one each to its left, right, and behind. They all glowered at her, but waited on the 'rath in the middle to make a move. If Alice hadn't known better, she would have thought the monster in the middle was their leader.

But that was impossible. *Right?* In all the years since the Plague began, she had never heard of anything like that. She would definitely have news for Lewis when she got home. Another set of furious snarls pulled Alice back to the present. Her insides twisted with nervous energy, but her head remained clear. She had the vantage point. Now she just needed to defend her position. She raised her machete in a show of power and glared down the leader, who sneered in rage before letting out another shriek.

Alice waited for the pack to make the first move. She lowered into a crouch, ready to propel herself into action. Once the 'rath finished its cry, it let out a quick, coughing bark to the others.

The two 'rath on its sides surged forward. They jumped the fire escape, clearing the eight feet as if it was nothing. Alice gripped her blade, feeling the ridges of the handle dig into the flesh of her palms. Though her heart pounded faster, her mind coolly took in the situation. They were double-teaming her, but the narrow ladder on the fire hatch split their attack. They couldn't come at her at the same time. They would have to climb up separately. But they were moving fast. She only had a small window of opportunity to take the first one out before the other reached the landing. She dropped her foot and rested her weight on it, ready.

In less than thirty seconds, the first momerath was up, scrabbling the stairs. Alice saw its arms first, stained with rivulets of dried blood. The remains of its fingernails were jagged and yellow, giving its hands the appearance of gnarled claws. Her muscles tightened. As soon as the whites of its eyes came into view, Alice kicked, the tension in her leg cracking like a whip.

Her boot connected with its jaw as it cleared the landing. The force snapped its head back so far, she heard a terrible crack as the momerath fell to the pavement. It hit the asphalt underneath her with a loud thump followed by more angry chattering. She couldn't inspect the damage because the other 'rath was almost on the landing. Already kneeling low, Alice swung her blade in front of her, slicing the momerath with all her strength.

The screaming 'rath brought its arm in front of its body—to reach her or shield itself, Alice didn't know. What she did know was the deadly blade sliced straight through its wrist, neatly cutting off its outstretched hand before splitting through the sinew of its neck like a knife through butter. The 'rath tumbled to the ground, its body violently convulsing in broken pieces. Beside it, the large momerath snarled at her, bloody spittle dripping down the side of its mouth as it gnashed its teeth in rage. The momerath Alice kicked dragged itself to its feet, huffing in rage. It pulled itself up, its head hanging at an unnatural angle, barely connected to its spine. *Bad luck*, Alice thought.

Moving as a single unit, the remaining momerath backed away. Three pairs of filmy, dead eyes trained on Alice. She stepped away from the safety rail to center herself on the platform.

The 'rath launched themselves at her, arms outstretched and frantically clawing at the metal, tearing any piece of the landing they could. As one, they reached for the platform and pulled, using brute force to tear it from the wall. With a groan, the aging metal ripped from the side of Firm-Tech and crashed to the pavement, taking Alice with it. The best she could do was brace herself as she fell.

The fire hatch slammed into the street, crumpling under the force. One of the beams tore loose, and the sharp edge cut a huge gash in Alice's calf. She cried out as pain laced through her leg, followed by the gleeful howls of the momerath lunging at her as a synchronized, crazed team.

Biting through the pain, Alice scrabbled over the tangled hangar, hurrying to get onto flat ground and footing. The jagged mess of bars tore her clothes and her shirt snagged on another edge of the destroyed fire escape. She broke free with just enough time to square off against the momerath jettisoning at her torso. It slammed into her. The impact knocked Alice's blade out of her hands and onto the sidewalk, out of reach. The 'rath continued to attack, spraying blood with every lunge it took. She needed to get this thing off her. Fast.

With all her might, Alice launched herself up, forming a bridge with her body. Her unexpected movement flung the momerath off her, and sent it tumbling to the pavement. Alice swung her legs around, using the swift motion to stand before the other two 'rath could catch her. She almost stumbled when her injured leg buckled under her weight, but she gritted her teeth and pushed through the pain. She righted her body and reached to grab her lost blade, swinging it around in front of her.

The fallen momerath quickly regained its composure and flew at Alice again, trying to claw her face before she could stand.

Behind, the largest momerath let out another sharp growl and sent its other lackey into the fray. It ran full speed at her, falling in line behind its comrade. It was almost on top of her, a fresh road rash wound oozing blood down its other cheek. Alice couldn't let it near her. She took a desperate swing and felt its impact jar her arms as she chopped straight through the monster's neck. *Then there were two.*

Instantly, the other 'rath was on her. It was cleaner than the others, with no visible marks or wounds aside from its freshly broken neck. It had been recently turned, and didn't have any of the self-inflicted gashes so common on other momerath, but everything else about it was dead. It swung with wide, erratic grabs that were far from reaching her.

Its perception is off, Alice realized, as she watched its head dangle from its neck. It was obvious the spinal cord was severely injured, just not enough to incapacitate it. It wouldn't take much to finish it, only one good hit. Quickly, Alice moved her blade into her guard hand, holding it defensively. Dominant hand free, she threw the strongest cross she could muster, and hit it directly on the chin. There was a sickening pop as what was left of its spinal cord severed and its head fell limply to the side, held on only by its decomposing skin.

Now the only 'rath left was the leader. It roared in frustration as the last of its pack fell, then attacked, spit spraying everywhere as it screeched in rage. It came so fast, Alice only had enough time to awkwardly toss her weapon back into her right hand and make a desperate cut upward.

It worked. The machete tore a gash in the momerath's upper arm, severing its bicep. She stepped back, holding her sword firmly between the momerath and herself. Her tired muscles screamed in protest against the abuse they had taken and her head throbbed. Adrenaline flooded her body, and a sudden surge

66

of energy tore through her. She gripped the machete, and an eerie calm washed over her.

The lead 'rath lunged, and a guttural howl tore from its chest as it leapt to reach her. The moment its feet left the ground, Alice thrust her machete forward, stabbing its heart and cutting through its body.

Grabbing the hilt with both hands, she jerked it from the 'rath's chest and drew it over her shoulder, parallel to the floor. The 'rath's filmy eyes narrowed, and blood-tinged spit bubbles formed at the side of its mouth. It hissed and jumped at her, more like a wounded animal than any person. Resolved, Alice swung, following the strike through until her arms completely crossed her body and stopped, resting on top of her shoulder. In slow motion, the momerath dropped to its knees before its head slipped off its neck and down to the pavement, mouth open mid-cry.

Trembling, Alice took in the scene before her. Now the threat was gone, her heart relaxed, but every other part of her body protested vehemently. Her muscles and chest were on fire, exhausted from being overworked. Limbs that fought skillfully were now heavy and awkward. Her mind, focused during the attack, felt hazy and slow. She needed to rest.

She saw an empty planter in front of the Firm-Tech building and shuffled over to it. She leaned against it, her shoulder pressed against the smooth stone. Her legs were still shaking, a mixture of shock and exhaustion, and she slid to the ground, finally allowing them to relax. Her leg ached where the hangar had sliced it, reminding her of the wound. Gingerly, she pressed her fingers to her calf to check the damage. The metal had cut a neat gash in her pants and the denim felt sticky with blood. She was sure she would need stitches, but was shocked when her hand came back clean.

Unexpectedly, tears sprung to her eyes. They began as a

small trickle, then turned into full-blown, ugly sobs. She tried to stop, but just couldn't. Every time she started to calm down, something new would spring to mind—Dinah, losing the doctor, Borogove, Chess, crazy angry momerath—and the tears would come right back. She cried so violently, she was afraid she might drown in her own tears.

When she couldn't cry anymore, she sniffled weakly and took a deep, steadying breath. It was time to go. "But which way do I go from here?" she wondered, searching the unfamiliar city.

"That depends a great deal on where you want to go," a familiar voice said over her shoulder. She scrambled to stand, trying to wipe her cheeks clean at the same time. She bumped face-first into a faded leather jacket that smelled of cinnamon. She didn't even have to look to picture the face smiling down at her. Chess was back.

ADVICE FROM A CATERPILLAR

11

"You've got to be kidding me!" Alice's temper spiked at Chess's lazy grin. She couldn't believe he was sitting there like nothing had happened. Didn't he see what she had just been through?

How could he? He disappeared long before the momerath came around. Her brows knotted together as she seethed. *But still,* her inner voice countered, *the fight hadn't been that far away. Surely he could see the mess that got left between Firm-Tech and Borogove.* She glanced at the crumpled fire escape and blood-stained cement. There was no way he could have missed it.

Maybe he just doesn't care.

Based on his standing Houdini act, Alice was leaning towards the latter. But it didn't explain why he kept coming back. She looked at Chess, hoping to find an answer, but only saw his stupid grin widen as he watched her from the ledge of the planter with his legs kicking casually back and forth.

"What'd I miss?" He hooked his thumbs in his jacket pockets and crooked his head in feigned innocence.

Alice tried to bite her words, but she wasn't fast enough.

"What did you *miss*? What the *hell* is wrong with you?" she blurted, more an accusation than a question. Her fingernails dug into the palms of her hands as she clenched her fists to steady herself. She needed to calm down or she was going to completely lose it.

"Damn, it must have been good," Chess chuckled. A mischievous glint lit his eyes and he carelessly stretched his neck to scratch behind his ear.

Alice lost it.

"Good. *GOOD*? I was almost torn apart by not one—but four —momerath *and* a fire escape! Not to mention the random *Drink Me* bottle that magically appeared out of the wall. But you wouldn't know about any of it because you disappeared *again* and left me completely on. My. Own!" She jabbed her finger into Chess's chest after each individual word.

"Ow! Hey!" He raised his hands to block her attack. "Alright, alright! I get it, you have abandonment issues." He smirked.

Before Alice knew what happened, her fist swung. Chess let out a startled cry and his head whiplashed with her punch's follow-through. He rubbed his jaw where she slugged him, and Alice was fairly certain she had just caught him off guard for the first time since she met him. She was surprised too—but she ignored it, just like she ignored her throbbing knuckles.

Chess gently probed his inflamed jawline, shocked only a moment before his lips quirked and his infuriating grin was back. "You pack a pretty good punch, Butterfly." He appraised her with approval.

"Oh my God. Seriously?" Alice drew her fists. "I will hit you again."

"Come on. That was good." He tapped her lightly on the shoulder. "You know, 'Float like a butterfly, sting like a...'" Her dangerous expression gave him pause. "Never mind. It's alright. One punch is more than enough for today, Ali." He placed his hand over hers and gently examined it. "Besides, it looks like you could use some bandaging yourself." Alice followed his gaze and noticed she had indeed busted her knuckle. A trickle of blood ran down her hand. She would need to cover it so it didn't get infected—or worse.

"I'll be fine." Alice pulled away. She didn't want his concern. It would only make it worse when he disappeared again. "My sister is the one who needs help, not me." She stormed off, tired of his distractions.

"Hey, hold up!" he laughed as he trailed behind her. "Where are you going?"

Alice whirled around to glower at him. "I'm going to help my sister!" she said. "If you haven't noticed, the entire time I've been in this awful place, I've been doing the same thing. I'm not out here for kicks like you seem to be. I actually have things I need to do, and they need to be done *quickly*. If I'm not back in time—" Alice's voice cracked. Hating her vulnerability, she whirled around to stomp away.

"Whoa!" Chess grabbed her shoulder, holding her in place. She didn't look at him. "I know you're trying to help your sister. I get it." His voice softened. "I think it's really great you care enough about her to do something so dangerous." He sighed. "It's why I want to help."

"Help me?" she scoffed. "Is *that* what you call up and leaving me in places I've never been? I mean, I guess the van wasn't too bad, but Borogove? Come on, Chess, you might as well have stuck a *Fresh Bait* sign across my back for all the help you were."

Chess hunched guiltily in front of her, his hands stuffed in his pockets. "I'm sorry. It's just—I had to go. Okay?" He slowly pulled his hand from his pockets to press them to her shoulders while he stared into her eyes, searching for forgiveness. "I can't explain it, but trust me, I'm on your side."

Alice wasn't sure what to think. Though she hated to admit

it, having Chess around had come in handy. But he was hard to count on. That wasn't just frustrating—it could be dangerous later if she needed him and he wasn't there. She bit her lip as she weighed her options. She could walk away now, and be one hundred percent on her own, or she could accept Chess's apology and risk him bouncing again.

Neither choice was great. In the end, it all came back to Dinah—that's what she had told Chess. If she really wanted a cure, she would have to take any help she could get, even if it came sporadically.

She let out a heavy sigh. "I'll give you *one* more chance." She narrowed her eyes, making sure to keep her voice stern. "But if you ditch me again, we're done. I'll find some other annoyance to guide me through Wanderland."

Chess grinned from ear to ear, wiping any lingering remorse from his face. "That's my girl." He squeezed her in a giant side hug. "I knew you needed me."

"Don't make me regret my decision," she said through gritted teeth.

Chess laughed and released her. "Not a chance, Alice," he said, walking briskly in front of her, once again her personal guide.

Alice paused. "You said my name." She had been expecting another one of his stupid nicknames.

"Huh?" Chess waved back nonchalantly and kept on strolling. "Slip of the tongue. Don't worry, it won't happen again, Sugarplum."

Alice rolled her eyes, but couldn't fight the smile tugging at the corners of her lips. She was glad Chess faced the other direction. She didn't want to encourage his antics.

"Where are we going anyway?" she called, hurrying to catch up. The pain in her leg was practically nonexistent now, just a dull throb when she stepped, like she had worked out too hard the day before. She almost asked Chess if he would look at it, but thought better of it.

"I'm going to take you to my friend, Bug," he said, glancing at her over his shoulder. "If there's anything you need to know about Wanderland, he's the one who can tell you."

12

"You have a friend named Bug?"

"Sure. Why wouldn't I?" Chess asked. "I have another friend who keeps telling me to call her Alice even though I give her *way* better names—which is even weirder if you ask me." He gave her a pointed look.

"I didn't." Alice watched the ground as she walked, focused on her steps. She refused to be riled by his teasing. "So, were you the one who came up with 'Bug'? Considering how fond you are of nicknames," she jabbed.

"Nah." He shrugged. "Everyone calls him that."

"Everyone?" Her brow quirked. She wondered how many others constituted 'everyone,' but her next question rattled out before he could respond. "Why?"

"Because he looks like a bug," Chess answered without hesitation, ignoring her first question.

Alice tried to picture bug features on a person. *Probably not very cute,* she thought. She imagined a cross between man and mantis, creating a freakish green twig person with antennae sticking out of his head. *Nope. Not cute.*

She shook away the image. "Why do they call you Chess?" she asked, continuing her inquisition. "Is that a nickname too?"

"Yep. My real name is Eoghan, but no one ever spelled it right so I changed it." He spoke casually as he tiptoed through a spilled pile of garbage in their path.

Alice raised her brows. She wasn't sure she believed him. Honestly, she second-guessed about seventy percent of everything he said anyway, and she doubted spelling was a huge issue for *anyone* these days. "So how did you come up with Chess?" she prompted.

"That's easy," he said, turning the corner to a run-down alley. He paused for a minute, grunting as he pushed aside a stack of warped wooden doors. Alice was confused until she saw the hidden staircase.

"After you." Chess gave her a small bow and swept his arm gallantly in front of him. When she passed, he tugged the doors back to re-cover the secret entry. "They call me Chess because I'm six steps ahead of everyone else, like in the game." Alice heard the smugness in his voice as he trailed behind her. She fought to suppress an eye roll.

"Have you ever even played a game of chess?" she asked dubiously. The current state of the world wasn't exactly conducive to a loyal Chess Club following.

"Of course I have," he stated. "Rule number one: Always protect your queen." He flashed a sly grin followed by a quick wink.

This time, Alice didn't bother to conceal her eye roll. Though she was no expert, she had learned enough from the few games she played with Dinah that keeping your queen in the game was important. "Everyone knows that rule," she said, unimpressed.

"Well, next time we find ourselves a chessboard, we'll have a match. Then you'll see what a real game is, Miss Hoity-Toity." Chess stuck up his nose in mock superiority and stepped around

Alice to stand in front of the dingy door. He knocked in a series of patterns mixed with soft and loud thumps that she could never have remembered. By the time he finished, Alice actually was impressed.

"What was that?" She leaned in to whisper. She had to stand on tiptoes for her chin to reach over his shoulder. Even though her height was perfectly average, standing next to Chess made her feel incredibly short.

"Secret code. Lets Bug know it's me," he answered back, eyes glued on the door.

Alice felt the sarcasm on her face. "He wouldn't know when you used the secret door? I can't imagine he gets many visitors." Judging by the entrance, she honestly didn't think he got *any* guests besides Chess.

Chess shrugged his shoulders. "Bug's..." He paused and absently scratched behind his ear as he searched for the right word. "Different. You'll see." He stopped speaking as the door unlatched with a loud click. The heavy oak frame creaked and a plume of cigar smoke streamed from inside the dimly lit room.

Chess stretched an easy smile when a huddled figure peered through the crack in the doorway. "Bug! How are you, man?" He slapped his friend heartily on the shoulder. More smoke seeped from the room; the pungent smell filled Alice's nose and made her eyes water.

Between the smoke and Chess's barricade, she could hardly see the man inside, but apparently, he saw her. He scurried around Chess to glare at her, his blinking owl eyes magnified enormously behind a pair of coke-bottle glasses. He wore a green beanie on his head that clashed terribly with his dark purple shirt and bright orange cargo pants, making Alice wonder how blind he really was. Not one part of Bug's outfit flattered his physique. The beanie he wore flattened any hair he might have had, making his head look tiny compared to the rest of his bulky, oversized clothing. Even his shoes were cumbersome— too-big scuffed military-standard boots that provided him some extra height. The stolen inches still only left him at about five foot six, and standing beside Chess wasn't doing him any favors.

Chess was right. His exaggerated facial features combined with his exoskeleton of clothes really did make him look like a giant bug-man. Even the massive cigar he clenched between his teeth could have passed for some protruding mandible. A vivid scene of a massive boot chasing after him played through Alice's imagination and she had to bite her lip to keep from laughing. The image was forgotten quickly, however, when Bug grimaced and scuttled forward, inches from her face. She was in the middle of thinking he was the most intimidating insect she had ever seen when he fiercely demanded, "Who are you?"

13

A lice blinked, leaning slightly away as Bug peered in her face. She could smell the mixture of stale coffee and tobacco on his breath. "My name is Alice," she said, hoping he didn't hear the tremble in her voice.

Bug continued to examine her from behind his enormous glasses. "That may be so," he said, "but *who* are you?" He leaned forward, his nose centimeters from hers, completely disregarding her personal space.

"I'm sorry?" Alice shot a panicked glance over at Chess, silently pleading for help. She didn't know how to answer the strange man's cryptic question. She was Alice. That was it.

Thankfully, Chess rushed to her aid. "Bug! Back off, man! She's with me." He clapped his hand back over Bug's shoulder, gently prying him from Alice's space. He flashed another trademark grin and wrapped his free arm around Alice's shoulders, wedging himself between the two of them.

Bug chewed the end of his cigar as he scrutinized Alice. A moment passed before he grunted and shot a cantankerous glare at Chess then skittered back inside his den. "Bolt the door behind you. Make sure to get the bottom lock. It's new," he said, then scurried in to safety. Alice exhaled, only then realizing she had been holding her breath the whole time.

Once Chess securely latched all the locks—Alice counted six total—she fell behind him and together they followed Bug into his lair. Unfinished walls showcased exposed wires and wood beams in gaps of missing drywall. Hanging lanterns strung from a rope rigged to the ceiling gently swayed as they flickered in and out. The whole place smelled musty and dirty, like everything could have used a good airing out, but being underground, there were no windows to open.

Their shoes scuffed against the cement floor, sending ghostly echoes through the chamber. They walked farther, and soon the sound was drowned out by multiple CV radio tones clamoring for Bug's attention. Though most of the noise was static, every now and then, a tinny voice broke through, calling for listeners or rattling off nonsensical codes.

They continued on until the corridor opened to a small room. Although it was impossible to see everything clearly through the haze of cigar smoke, it was clear these were Bug's living quarters. A messy drop-down bed commandeered the corner of the room, surrounded by a mess of books and loose papers. The opposite corner made up his kitchen. An ugly lime green table with two mismatched plastic chairs sat next to a tiny pantry beside a small sink, piled high with dirty dishes.

The other wall made up a makeshift command center. An old teaching desk stood buried under a mound of CV radios heaped on top of each other. More papers scattered across the top of the desk, cluttered under an assortment of stained coffee mugs and ashtrays. An abandoned broadcasting microphone waited next to a pair of studio headphones. The wall in front of the desk was covered with a large, crooked cork board smattered with a jumble of newspaper clippings, old photographs, book pages, and scraps of paper that appeared to be Bug's own scrawled notes.

Bug dropped into the desk chair, causing it to squeak loudly in protest. He watched Alice shrewdly, puffing on his cigar while he adjusted to his visitors. He took in several deep draws of smoke before slowly exhaling, sending wisps sailing across the room in rings before they disappeared into the rest of the room's murk.

Without waiting for an invitation, Chess flopped on the lumpy bed and sprawled across it like a large cat, making himself at home. Alice stood awkwardly in the doorway before she wandered over to the collage on the wall, drawn to the mess of information.

"Don't waste your time, Chickpea," Chess said mid-yawn. "Bug's conspiracy wall will just give you a headache."

"Conspiracy wall?" Alice glanced back at him, too intrigued to even bother with his newest nickname.

"Not a conspiracy wall!" Bug screeched and shot a furious glare at Chess. He let out a cross huff, then rose to stand beside Alice. "It's where I collect my research."

"Research for what?" She scanned the board in amazement. Bold headlines proclaiming new outbreaks of the Plague dotted the board, scattered among articles hypothesizing potential cures. Everything centered around a slip of paper in the middle with the letters 'MR-V' scrawled in angry red.

"The outbreak of the Plague." Bug's features contorted in excitement, eager to share his research with a willing student. "The answers are here. I just need to find them." He gazed at the board intently. Alice could picture him standing the same way day after day, hunting for answers.

"Why do you need to know that?" Alice asked. "The Plague already happened. It's not like we can change anything." Her attention lingered on the board. Chess let out a small snort behind her, but she ignored him. She searched Bug's collection, and was surprised to find a pattern in the seeming chaos of the board. Although it was jumbled, there were definite sections to his research. It may have looked a mess, but it wasn't random.

"If we can't change anything, then what are you doing here?" Bug asked. "I've never seen you before, never even heard of an Alice. But here you stand." He gestured at her with a snap of his wrist and puffed fervently on his cigar. "I can't imagine you decided to take a walk through the desert and somehow ended up on my doorstep."

"I—" His argument stopped Alice short. He was right. If she didn't believe things could change, why *was* she here?

"So let me ask again, Alice. *Who* are you?" He turned to face her, exhaling another thick cloud of smoke.

"I already told you, I'm Alice. Just Alice." She shrugged helplessly. "That's all."

"Why?" Bug eyed her meaningfully, as if to communicate something she was missing. Alice glanced at Chess to see if he could clue her in, but he was sleeping soundly on the bed, mouth wide as he snored.

Alice's mind whirred, at a loss to what Bug was looking for. His questions didn't even make sense. She was starting to think everyone in Wanderland was mad.

Bug searched her face as intently as he had the board before. "*Why?*" he pressed, his eyes boring into hers. "What is your purpose?"

"I guess...well, my purpose is to help my sister." Alice spoke shakily as she reasoned her thoughts, but once she answered, she knew she was right.

"Your sister. I see." Bug nodded and brought his cigar up for another draw. "And what do you wish to accomplish?"

"I want—I *need*—to find a cure. Or an antidote, or something." Alice said. "She's sick, but I think I can still help her."

The annoying tingle attacked her nose again. She sniffed loudly, chasing unwanted tears away.

"If she has been infected, there is no cure," Bug said. There was no remorse in his voice. Just fact.

"She hasn't," Alice hurried to explain. "I think she's a Carrier. I don't know for how long, but she started getting sick the day before yesterday." Her voice wavered around the lump in her throat. "I don't think she has much time."

Bug peered at his board and puffed on his cigar in silence. He didn't speak, opting instead to exhale his smoke in another series of rings before pointing out an article. *Borogove Industries to Release New Miracle Drug,* it read in huge block letters. Underneath the bolded text was a faded black-and-white picture of two men standing side by side behind a neatly organized laboratory table. The man on the left was much taller than the man on the right. He stood proud, an arrogant smile resting comfortably on his face. He reminded Alice of someone she had seen before.

Unbidden, a memory washed over Alice. Mom had brought her in with Dinah to surprise Mr. Carroll for lunch. The secretary let them into the back rooms where he stood behind his desk, talking animatedly to a man Alice didn't know. He had his back to them, but she remembered watching him wave his arms around the air. She didn't understand what he was talking about, and thought adults talked funny. When he saw Alice and her family, the other man quickly excused himself and told Mr. Carroll he would come back later. He smiled and patted her fondly on her head before exiting hastily to the lobby.

It had been ages ago. Obviously, this doctor wasn't the same person, but Alice was intrigued how complete strangers could look so similar. Entertained by the idea, she glanced at the second man—*Dr. Abbott?*

Alice's heart fluttered nervously as she turned to Bug. "Do you know these men?"

"Not personally." He smoothed the picture against the board. "I know *of* them."

"Why do you have their picture?" Alice asked, now trying to piece together the information on Bug's wall to find her own answers.

Bug took another puff of his cigar. "Why is it relevant?" Bug peered at her. It seemed he already knew what she was going to say, but was waiting for validation.

"Dr. Abbott—the man there." Alice pointed at the shorter doctor's face. "He's the reason I came here. At least, I think he is. Back home, my friend told me there was a doctor working on a cure, and I...I think it's him."

Bug tilted his head, the corners of his mouth turned down in thought. "Those two men are Dr. Matthew Hatta, and, obviously, you know Dr. Waite Abbott. They were prominent scientists at Borogove Industries." Her eyes widened at the name. "More importantly, they are the men responsible for MR-V."

"MR-V?"

"Momerath Virus," Chess called sleepily from behind them before he yawned and flipped over to face the wall. Apparently, he needed some attention. Alice shook her head in amusement before she turned to Bug.

"How do you know?" Alice asked.

"He doesn't," Chess cut in. Bug ignored him.

"It's what all my research is about. MR-V originated here, in Phoenix. Before that, there were no recorded outbreaks. What's more, it happened right around the time this 'miracle drug' was set to release. The *only* pharmaceutical company headquarters here belong to Borogove. It's here. All here..." Bug placed his hands on the board as if the motion could draw the answer from the papers into his brain.

Alice hesitated. It seemed plausible, but he had no actual evidence—unless you counted a jumble of assorted notes on a corkboard—which she didn't. She studied the board again, feeling as lost as Bug looked. Her eyes fell on a small black-and-white photo of Dr. Abbott walking into Borogove. He glanced over his shoulder nervously. Alice could almost hear him saying "I'm late."

"Is it true Dr. Abbott is working on a cure?"

"Everything I've heard and seen suggests so," Bug said. "He goes into Borogove at least three days a week. Sometimes he'll stay there for weeks at a time. When he leaves, he's never gone for long before he comes back. I don't know what he's doing in there, but it must be important."

"Maybe he just lives there, like you live here."

"No. His patterns are too irregular. It doesn't fit." Bug paced away from the board. He didn't get far before coming back to search it again. When an answer didn't materialize, he began another circuit, muttering excitedly as he walked.

Alice still didn't know if she believed that, but it was clear Bug wasn't going to let the theory go. She stared at the board in front of her. Her attention jumped from one page to another, not resting until she saw a sketch of a charging momerath. Its eyes were whitewashed so the pupils could no longer be seen. The rest of the sketch was shaded with pencil lead to color the momerath's graying skin. The artist had sketched skin flaking off the monster's hands and face. Most unnerving, though, was the way the image captured the momerath's rage. The artist was clearly not a professional, but the care taken in preserving the emotion of the momerath was exceptional. Alice could almost feel hatred emanating from the page.

She smashed her index finger against the photo to cover the momerath's ugly snarl. "Why do they act like that? What's wrong with them?"

Bug dropped into his chair and rubbed his temples. "Why do snakes chase mice?" he asked wearily. Without his compulsive focus on the board, he looked very tired. "They are hunters and they are stronger than us. They are predators. We're the prey."

"Then why don't we just stop being the prey? Why don't we fight back?" Alice asked, put off by his defeatist attitude.

A sly smile tugged Bug's lips. "Now I see." He gave her his first look of approval since he laid eyes on her. He turned to Chess, who snored loudly on the bed. "Some people just don't have it in their nature. There are runners and there are fighters. In everything. A large part of who we are is determined by that simple fact. The question is, Alice: which are you?"

Alice considered the question. She'd like to think she was a fighter, but all her life she had been trained to run from danger. She warred over the answer, until she sadly admitted, "I don't know."

The gleam in Bug's eye faltered, but he gave Alice a small nod. "That's something only you can find out," he answered. "I cannot help you." He saw the despair on Alice's face and puffed thoughtfully on his cigar again before adding, "But I can tell you who might."

"Who?" Alice asked eagerly.

"The Red Queen."

"No!" In a flash, Chess was up and in Bug's face, anger blanketing his features. "You can't send her there! Those fanatics won't give her a chance, Bug! You know that! They shoot first and ask questions later!"

Alice pushed between Chess and Bug. "Who's the Red Queen?" She raised her hand to interrupt Chess's tirade and gave him a questioning glance. It was odd he reacted so vehemently, but if this "Red Queen" could give her answers, she needed to hear Bug out.

Chess jumped in again, responding before Bug could. "She's some crazy fanatic who got a big following by setting up a high security facility in the middle of the desert and then started destroying everything she came in contact with," he said. An angry flush crept across his cheeks. "No. You can't go there!"

Bug turned to Alice. "The Red Queen may have the answer you seek," he said. "Though her methods may be a bit...*unconventional*." He directed a scowl at Chess, "She has connections."

Chess gave Bug a sulky glare. Alice was unsettled by his reaction, but what choice did she have? She sighed. "How do we find the Red Queen?"

Chess let out an exasperated huff and stormed off to the tiny bathroom at the end of the hallway. Alice flinched as the door slammed, shaking the whole house. Bug ignored him. "She's not far. Chess knows the way." Alice doubted Chess would go for it, but Bug seemed unconcerned.

A million questions zipped through her mind. "What should I do when I find her?"

"Well, I would start by stating your name and business." Bug almost smiled, then turned serious. "Don't forget, Alice. Wanderland is a dangerous place. It is where the epidemic started—Ground Zero, if you will. Things are different here, beginning at the center and spreading like a ripple. I don't know how far it's reached, but I do know the Queen has secrets of her own."

A thrill of fear washed through Alice. "What do you mean?"

Bug didn't answer immediately. Instead, he pulled a worn journal from his desk. He removed the cigar from his teeth and discarded it before leaning back in his chair. Once he found his page, he cleared a cough from his throat, painfully reminding Alice of how Dinah sounded when she left. He paused dramatically, then, sure he had her attention, began to read.

"How doth the little crocodile improve his shining tail, and pour the waters of the Nile on every golden scale." His eyes flicked meaningfully from the book to Alice before he continued. "How cheerfully he seems to grin, how neatly spreads his claws, and welcomes little fishes in, with gently smiling jaws."

Bug set the journal on his desk and gazed at Alice intently. Unable to decipher anything, she felt dumb. Clearly, it wasn't the reaction Bug was hoping for. He sighed, then stood to pat her on the shoulder. "You'll figure it out. But remember to be vigilant. Momerath can show up any moment, and they'll be hunting you."

14

The journey to find the Red Queen was tense. Alice was keyed up after the strange warning Bug gave her. What was that weird poem? She accidentally kicked a crumpled soda can on the sidewalk and practically leapt out of her skin when it clanged against the pavement. The tension between her and Chess didn't help either. He stormed ahead, his neck and shoulders tense. He hadn't spoken a word since they left Bug's house.

If he wants to be mad, that's his own dang fault, Alice thought irritably. *He's the one who volunteered to come. It's not my job to make sure his feelings aren't hurt.*

They continued in awkward silence until Chess finally let out an impatient huff. "You shouldn't be doing this, you know," he blurted, his brows furrowed as he glowered at her.

"I don't have much of a choice," Alice clipped.

"Of course you do," he pushed. "You always have a choice."

"What choice is that exactly, Chess?" she asked, her voice shrill. "The way I see it, I can either go hunt down some crazy lady who calls herself 'The Red Queen' and see if she knows anything about Carriers, or give up because I'm scared and let my sister die." She paused to wipe the prickle from her nose before she continued her tirade. "Actually, she wouldn't even die. It would be *worse*—I would be leaving her to become one of those *things*! Great options. Really." She clenched her fists, trying to settle down before she lost control. "To be honest, I'm not particularly crazy about either choice," she said, "but I have to pick one, so I'm going to go with the one that sucks less and ends up with me not hating myself for the rest of my life. So, I'm sorry if it hurts your feelings, but they're not really high on my priority list right now."

Chess stood stunned, watching her with a strange, hurt expression. When he didn't say anything, Alice impatiently shook her head.

"Never mind." she pushed in front of him. "I don't expect you to get it. It's not like you stick around when people need you anyway." As soon as she said the last part, her stomach twinged with guilt. She had gone too far.

She stopped. Without looking back, she let out a heavy sigh. "I'm sorry." She wiped her hand across her face. "I just have to do this."

Chess didn't answer. She turned to face him and saw him staring past her, his expression laced with panic. Alice followed his gaze and her eyes widened when she saw a lone momerath crouching in the far corner of the alley. It watched them intently, frozen in place with the remains of a bloody rat carcass dangling from its mouth.

"Don't move," Chess commanded, his voice so low it came out in a rumble.

Alice's mind was a blur. Every fiber of her body fought Chess's directions. *Don't run? We need to get out of here as fast as we can! We've waited too long already! Why hasn't it tried to kill us yet?* Her sore muscles ached as they tensed, ready for action.

At least they still knew what to do. She gaped at the 'rath, its sights locked on them, body stiff as a statue.

As if reading her thoughts, Chess repeated again, more deliberately. "Don't move, Alice. Let it go."

Alice closed her eyes and took in a steadying breath. When she opened them, she saw the momerath had returned its attention to the rodent. It ravenously pulled at the skin of the dead rat, looking more like a starving dog than an undead monster.

Suddenly, a loud bang shot through the streets and echoed off the empty buildings. It startled the momerath, who shrieked and dropped the chewed-up carcass before facing Alice and Chess, wild panic in its eyes. It hissed loudly, then tore down the street, clawing its face as guttural cries wrenched from its throat.

Chess swore and grabbed Alice's hand. He pulled her with him as he took off the opposite direction the momerath had gone. "We need to go. *Now.*"

"What? Why?" Alice asked, incapable of piecing more intelligent sentences together as she hurried after Chess.

"That was a Flighter—a Runner. If it's moving, it's gonna bring more 'rath. Fighters. We gotta get out of here."

Not far behind them, another terrible cry rang out across the ghost of a city. Chess tightened his grip on her hand and sped his pace. "Sounds like it found them. Hope you're ready. We're about to have company."

Alice had no idea what Chess meant, but then, she didn't understand anything about Wanderland. She focused on running; keeping up with Chess was much more difficult than it was with Dinah. She felt herself slowing him down. She pushed until her lungs were on fire and her sides screamed with every breath. She still wasn't fast enough.

A bloodcurdling roar rounded the corner they just turned. Instinctively, she looked over her shoulder to find the noise and saw a pack of momerath scrambling around buildings into the street. They were different from the 'rath they found in the alley. It was smaller, its body streamlined and lean, designed for speed. These momerath were larger, built to attack. They were still obviously dead—or rather, undead—but as they chased her, Alice had no problem imagining them tearing her from limb to limb.

"Keep running! We're almost there!" Chess yelled.

How is he not tired yet? Alice wondered. He didn't even look winded. "I'm trying!" she screamed, regretting it instantly. She didn't have Chess's lung power, and her overworked muscles already clamored for all the oxygen they could get. She gasped, her heart pounding over the raspy breaths of the momerath closing in on them.

She risked another glance behind and saw the pack had grown. There were at least eight momerath pursuing them and they were practically on her heels. They wheezed as they gave chase, the sounds escaping their throats contradicting their unnatural speed. *They're supposed to be dead! How do they move so fast?*

The 'rath closest to her lunged and she felt its claws scrape against her backpack. They were so close. Too close. Her adrenaline surged, and a burst of energy coursed through her body. Suddenly, it wasn't as hard for her to breathe, and she pushed faster, her muscles instantly less fatigued. Her temper flared. *We shouldn't have to run.* She slowed ever so slightly, her mind assessing the best point of attack.

"What are you doing?" Chess's voice interrupted her thoughts. "Keep going!"

But running wasn't going to help. They were too far from where they needed to be. They hadn't even escaped the city yet. She reached for her machete and whipped it in front of her as she spun to meet the oncoming horde. Her blade skewered the momerath behind her, but still, it attacked. It snarled and swiped again, barely missing her cheek. With a sickening squelch, she ripped her blade from the momerath's belly and stepped back. It faltered, then launched at her in a single-minded attack. Alice had just enough time to flick her weapon up to slit the rath's throat as it fell. It was enough. The blade cut deep, severing the monster's neck, stopping it permanently.

That was only one. Alice blanched as the remaining horde approached her. It was larger than she thought. Dozens of momerath tore down the street, ripping their skin as they ran. Every few steps, another 'rath would howl, bouncing frantic yowls off the brick-and-mortar buildings. They swarmed, trampling the mangled body of their companion to reach their prey. Alice kicked the nearest momerath, dislocating its knee and dropping it to the ground. Still, it chased her, clawing to its feet, dragging its broken leg like some disfigured rag doll. Alice kicked again, this time striking it straight in the chest, sending it tumbling into the 'rath behind it.

The 'rath hissed and bit at it like a jealous dog, but it only slowed them a moment. They lunged, and Alice struck. She flipped and slashed her machete on autopilot as she fought the monsters. She took them out, chopping off their heads and kicking them down the street, spewing blood everywhere as they rolled across the asphalt. Still more came. Alice dodged and struck the next 'rath, severing its femoral artery. The gaping laceration brought it crashing to the ground, forcing it to drag its body along the cement to reach her. She stepped back, readying herself for the next attack. She glanced up to see what was coming, and her heart sank when she saw more momerath tearing down the streets. She gritted her teeth and tightened her hold on her blade. She wouldn't go down without a fight.

Alice rushed forward, shooting into the fray and tearing into as many 'rath as she could. She attacked with everything she had. In one smooth move, she tore the throat out of one with only her hand at the same time she slit the neck of another with the machete. She didn't know how she was moving so fast, but she felt wired, alive. She parried and dodged, anticipated and countered attacks. She thought she was going to make it until, from the back of the pack, four 'rath jumped her, pinning her against the asphalt. Her skull cracked as it slammed against the concrete. Her brain went fuzzy and her vision blurred out the world. The last thing she remembered was screaming for Chess before dozens of decaying bodies blocked out the sun.

THE QUEEN'S CROQUET GROUND

15

"Get her out of here! Take her to the van!" A muffled voice yelled over the cacophony of automatic gunshots. Alice opened her eyes. She tried to make out the scene in front of her, but her head swam, making it difficult to focus. Though her vision blurred, she was able to make out a dozen black figures running down the streets attacking larger, lighter-shaded figures. Through the haze, she heard the sounds of men yelling over bursts of shot rounds.

"You can't take her anywhere." A deep voice barked back at the first man she heard. "You know the rules!"

"We can't just leave her!" the first man shouted in a husky tenor. "There's another pack coming! We haven't seen this many 'rath in months!"

"Orders first. Our objective is extermination, not saving some chick with a death wish," the second snarled before calling to the others. "Complete the mission! Paint them red!"

After the command, all conversation stopped. Alice struggled to watch the battle in front of her. Eventually her vision steadied and she could make out more than blobs of colors dancing around her. The ground was littered with bodies, and Alice saw a few of the 'rath she had taken down on her own. Beside her were the four that landed on top of her. At least, most of them. Their heads were separated from their bodies; it looked like someone used a chainsaw on them. Bits of blood and gore flecked the street and splattered her clothes in a grisly mess.

Feeling ill, Alice tore her gaze from the mutilated bodies surrounding her. She tried to sit up, but searing pain laced through her skull, rocking her like a boat. She flipped onto her stomach and started crawling across the street, staying low to fight off her dizziness.

Keep moving, she urged. *You need to find Chess and get the hell out of here!* She lurched to a stop as she remembered her friend, feeling a pang of guilt that it had taken her so long. *Chess! Where is he?*

She racked her brain to remember when she last saw him, but couldn't think of anything. Panicked, she forced herself up to search for him, but another dizzy spell rendered her immobile. Though her body ached, she kept pushing, determined to drag herself away from the center of the battle.

Shots rang across the street, and Alice tried to pinpoint where they were coming from. Almost all the momerath had been killed —and the rest were surrounded by a group of heavily armed soldiers. Alice watched one of them, a monster of a man, step forward with a massive axe and hack each one, removing their heads with ease. From the center of the bloody remains, he towered over everyone, at least a head taller than the rest of the soldiers. Alice supposed the armored suits added some extra bulk to the people who wore them, but no suit could add that much muscle. It was intimidating.

After all the momerath were incapacitated, the circle broke and surveyed the damage. Soldiers gathered the bodies of the dropped momerath, collecting them in a huge pile. All except the man with the axe. He sauntered towards Alice, singing in a deep baritone. "Painting the momerath red, we're painting the momerath red—"

His song cut short when he reached Alice. He pulled off his helmet and dropped to his knees to observe her. "What do we have here?" He ogled her with dark brown eyes that were almost black in the dusky evening light. She imagined his twisted smile was intended to be friendly, but his leering only made her uncomfortable.

A secondary soldier approached, rescuing Alice from the monster-man. "Found her in the middle of the horde," he said. She recognized his voice as the soldier who argued to help her earlier. Like his counterpart, he also removed his mask, revealing a figure every bit the opposite of the man hulking over her. Concern covered his face, softening the edges of his strong features. Paired with his bright blond hair and sky-blue eyes, he could have passed for a real-life knight in shining armor.

"She was practically in the middle of that nest," he said in disbelief. "I don't know how she got here, but she's lucky to be alive." He flashed Alice an incredulous smile. "You put up a hell of a fight." The admiration in his eyes sent a wave of pride thrilling through her.

"We'll see about that." The large man snatched Alice up and dumped her unsteadily on her feet. She was still woozy from smashing her head against the concrete. The sudden movement made the world teeter dangerously before she balanced herself. "Are you infected?" he barked, searching her for puncture wounds, indifferent to whether she was stable on her feet or not.

"No, I—Hey!" Her temper flared as the hulking man lifted her shirt, exposing her stomach. He had examined her arms and legs and apparently had no qualms about checking other areas as well. She slapped her arms against her stomach, smashing her shirt to her skin. Her defiance only earned a mocking look from the massive soldier before he dismissed her and stomped away to bellow at the others.

"Skin's clean. Run a check on the rest of her system!" He shoved his axe into a black tool belt on his hip, not sparing Alice a backwards glance. "Take anything we can use. Get rid of the rest."

Alice watched in shock as the men scrambled to follow orders. The soldier who complimented her remained by her side, his hand outstretched to hers. Alice looked at him. He was close to her age—maybe three or four years older—and handsome, with statuesque features made even more striking by the uniform he wore. He was taller than Alice, and although he wasn't quite as tall as Chess, he had a sturdier build. Where Chess was lean muscle, the "knight" was strapping. Explicitly aware of his attention, Alice hurried to move. She took a step toward the van, but stumbled as her vision blurred.

"Oh geez." He rushed to catch her, grabbing the crook of her elbow to steady her before he gently set her down. "That's a good-sized gash you've got there. You're gonna have to get that checked out." He prodded the side of her head at her temple. Though his touch was gentle, it sent jolts of pain searing through her body, making her wince. He sucked a breath, then pulled his hand away. "Here, take this." He handed her a small towel and guided her to the wound. "You'll need to keep pressure on until we can get you back to camp. Then the Doc can fix you up."

Alice gave a small nod. She delicately pressed the towel against the cut, feeling it dip in where the skin was broken. He was right. It was deep. It would probably need to be stitched—if she could find anyone who actually could do that here. "Thanks," she said meekly, feeling silly for having to be taken care of.

"It's my job. To protect and serve. Besides, it looks like you've been taking care of yourself for quite some time," he said, still kneeling in front of her. "That was some pretty impressive fighting back there."

Alice's cheeks burned. She was saved from having to respond when the brutish man strode back over, yelling. "Nate! Have you run the test yet? We're losing daylight!"

"Not yet, Ace." Nate stood to address the other man. Alice couldn't help but notice he didn't respond to Ace the same way the other soldiers did, scurrying around to follow his every whim. "She took a pretty good hit to the head. She needs medical attention."

"Not without checking out, she doesn't," Ace growled, sneering at the gash on Alice's head. "No one comes into camp without verification."

"I don't know if she'll make it that long." Nate lowered his voice to a whisper. "She's already lost a lot of blood."

Ace ignored Nate's attempts at discretion. "Then you'd better hurry so she doesn't lose more."

Nate's jaw tensed, but he nodded and kneeled, holding a small vial to Alice. "You're going to have to drink this," he apologized, handing her the bottle. The bright blue liquid was familiar. It was the same mixture in the bottle at Borogove. Alice quirked her eyebrow, wondering where he had gotten it.

She feigned ignorance. "What is it?"

"It's a tonic that will let us know if you're carrying the Plague." There was a shadow of guilt in his expression, indicating there was more than he was letting on, but the throbbing in Alice's skull kept her from pushing it. Besides, she'd drank the concoction once before and nothing had happened. At least now she knew that was the general idea.

"What if I don't drink it?" she asked. Regardless of whether or not she'd had the potion before, she didn't know anything about these people. She wasn't about to blindly do everything they told her—even if the one asking was gorgeous.

"Then we leave you to die," Ace cut in. He paused, then reconsidered. "Well, you might not die, but you'll be left." He crossed his arms over his chest, glowering as he waited for her to take the flask.

Nate shifted uncomfortably, then politely offered the vial to Alice once again. "It's not that bad," he promised with an encouraging smile. "It just tastes terrible."

Alice glanced at the tiny bottle, then at Ace. He stood with his mouth drawn in a hard line, waiting. She wasn't going to get out of here without drinking the contents of the bottle.

Slowly, she accepted the potion. She uncorked the vial, and drew it slowly to her lips before quickly braving the mixture. After the glass was empty, she wiped her mouth with the back of her hand, grimacing at the bitter taste on her tongue, and waited.

Again, nothing happened. Alice drummed her fingers impatiently against her thighs. When nothing happened after a few minutes, Alice broke the silence. "Now what?" she asked, handing Nate the empty vial.

Nate glanced from Ace back to Alice. She didn't miss how his eyebrows raised when he glanced at the empty jar. It was the only crack in his armor revealed before he was back to business.

"Put her in the van," Ace ordered before addressing the rest of the troops. "Move out, men." He spared Alice one last questioning glare before stalking to the van.

"You heard him." An amused smile played on Nate's lips as he directed her to the vehicle. "Looks like you passed."

"What would have happened if I hadn't?"

"If you were a Carrier, the potion would have activated the virus in your system and accelerated the change. You would have turned on the spot, and Ace would have chopped off your head."

Well. At least he was honest. For all his gentlemanly concern, he didn't have a problem stating the facts. "It is strange you didn't have any response at all, though." His voice was thoughtful. "I've never seen that happen. Usually, folks don't take the serum so well."

"What do you mean?"

"Think of it as an aggressive allergen. Even if the person who takes it isn't a Carrier, usually, their body freaks out, like it's rejecting it. It makes them really sick. Sometimes they expel everything in their system. Some get the shakes real bad. Some people even break out in hives. Heck, I saw one guy who had all three happen at the same time—it wasn't pretty. Either way, there's always at least *something*. You're the first person I've seen who's taken it like it was no big deal."

Alice didn't know what to say. While she was glad she didn't have some horrific reaction to the serum, knowing she was the only person he'd ever seen not have *any* sort of response wasn't reassuring either. Her expression betrayed her and Nate put his hand on her shoulder. "It's okay, though," he said. "You're clean. We all saw it. Now we just gotta get your head checked out."

He led her to the van and offered his hand to guide her. She crawled in the middle row and scooted over as far as she could. Nate followed, clicking his seatbelt in place. "You might want to do the same." He indicated Alice's strap. "Ace is a terrible driver."

Alice glanced at the large man in the driver's seat. He made a rude gesture at Nate before winking suggestively at her through the rearview mirror. She tried not to gag and hurried to click her seatbelt in place. "Where are we going?"

Ace shifted the car into gear, peeling out the tires as he accelerated. He barreled through the streets, lazily picking his teeth with a playing card Alice recognized as the Ace of Hearts. "We're taking you to home base," he leered at her suggestively. "We call it Tulgey Wood."

16

U nsurprisingly, Tulgey Wood didn't resemble its name in the slightest. Not many areas in the greater Phoenix areas had been woodsy before the Plague, and even less were now. Arizona's deserts had spread, covering neatly manicured lawns and parks long since forgotten. In their place, wild cacti and mesquite trees sprung up, reclaiming their territory. One landscaping anomaly newly introduced to most parts of the city were the Joshua trees that sprouted after the Plague killed off the other plant life. The spiked, menacing plants thrived in the harsher environment, uprooting the weaker foliage in an impressive show of evolutionary force. If Alice had to guess, it was the barren trees that gave Tulgey Wood its name. The area was absolutely covered in them. They shot from the ground, growing out of the parched earth in twisted angles like something from a warped Dr. Seuss book. The van careened through a good ten miles of vast desert filled with nothing but the strange trees for landscaping until a camp appeared in the middle of the strange forest.

Alice had to admit, Tulgey Wood had a solid setup. Whoever this "Red Queen" was, she took defense seriously. A massive concrete wall wrapped around the settlement and bright flood-lights lit the entrance like a beacon. The base of the wall had whittled-down wooden spikes protruding out to skewer anything unfortunate or stupid enough to approach uninvited. If that wasn't enough, a group of armed soldiers patrolled the top of the wall, providing an additional layer of security. Alice wouldn't have been surprised if more safeguards were in place behind the fence as well. The impressive defense made Alice question how the Sector had survived so long.

The van ground to a halt as they approached the entrance. Ace impatiently flashed the headlights to signal the gates, like some modern-day castle. They waited a moment until a loud buzz resonated through the quiet desert air, and the gate slowly slid behind the wall. Once the path was cleared, a row of men armed with assault rifles surged forward to surround the vehicle. The uniform for these soldiers was different than the gear worn by men in the van. They were all in full battle rattle, including a heavy-duty helmet to protect their faces. The men circling them simply wore standard issue military ACUs with armored vests strapped to their chests and a camouflaged cover for their head. What was odd was that every one wore a large metal contraption resembling an electronic dog collar around their necks. On each collar, underneath the soldier's right ear, a tiny green light flashed on and off in a steady rhythm.

"Who are they?" Alice whispered. She leaned into Nate and glanced nervously around the men encircling the car. It seemed each man that passed was larger than the first. A couple of them even made Ace seem small. Alice vaguely wondered if the Queen was putting something extra in their Wheaties.

"They're the Queen's Guard, but everyone else calls them her Jokers," Nate murmured conspiratorially, following her gaze. He peeked at one of the collared men, then quickly added,

"Don't let her hear you say that, though. Sometimes she can be a bit...*temperamental*."

Ace snorted loudly from the front of the van. "Is that what you're calling it these days, Pretty Boy?"

Nate stiffened at the jibe. Alice didn't blame him. She knew all too well how aggravating nicknames could be. The thought reminded her of Chess, and she briefly wondered if he was all right.

"She's got a lot to deal with. It would make anyone irritable," Nate said. "Especially dealing with you as one of her Marshals. I know it annoys the hell out of me."

"Don't sugarcoat it. She's a bitch." Ace smirked as he picked his teeth. The other men in the van laughed with him, but Alice noticed how nervously they watched Nate's reaction.

"Bitch or no, she's still your superior—a title she has more than earned—and I doubt she'd take too kindly to your tone." Though he wore a genial smile, there was a bite to his voice and his eyes betrayed a glint of anger.

"Whatever." Ace barked out a cocky laugh at the rearview mirror. The glass reflected Nate's severe expression and he dropped his gaze back to the empty stretch of asphalt in front of him. He let out a forced cough, and didn't say anything more. The rest of the passengers hurried to busy themselves and the van fell into an awkward silence. Some checked the safeties on their weapons. Others wiped mud off the soles of their shoes. The man next to Alice rolled himself a cigarette.

Alice shifted uncomfortably. She noticed the tension between Nate and Ace since their first interaction, but now it could have been cut with a knife. She had no desire to engage in the battle of wills or whatever was going on between the two of them, so she retreated into her own thoughts. There was more than enough to keep her busy. Mostly she thought about Chess.

She couldn't even remember when she had seen him last. *Was it before the 'rath showed up or after?*

After, she decided. She remembered Chess yelling at her to keep going, and then... nothing. The momerath had caught her and—*what happened to Chess?*

Frustrated, she bit her lip to keep from yelling out. She didn't exactly feel like explaining him to the Queen. *So much for his promise,* she thought, angry that he had gone back on his word and even more irritated that it surprised her. She stared out the side window and let her thoughts wash over her.

The base unfolded before her as they drove farther into the camp. Once the sun fell behind the mountains, the beautiful orange and red hues quickly turned to the dusky grey of night. In the dim, Alice saw large groups of tents, some with small campfires set in front with groups of people gathered around, curiously watching the caravan of soldiers driving through Tulgey.

Finally, they pulled into a dirt patch that served as a parking lot for the commune. Eight more vans waited in the area, each decked out in combat weaponry. Looking closer, Alice recognized the paint job from the van she spent her first night in Wanderland in.

So, it had been one of the Queen's vehicles. That explained the weaponry. She wondered what happened to the people inside, then remembered the empty *Drink Me* vial and decided she probably didn't want to know.

"Alright, men, that's it for tonight. Back to your quarters," Ace shouted at the men as he cut off the engine. "Everyone except her." He jerked his thumb toward Alice. Her stomach churned. "The Queen'll want to meet you." He pulled himself out of the vehicle, rocking it sideways as his bulk transferred from the van to the desert floor.

"Unfortunately, he's right," Nate said, though Alice wasn't sure if that was because she would have to meet the Queen or because he didn't want to admit Ace had been right about something. She decided to go with the latter. The irony wasn't lost on her that she had been trying to find the Red Queen to begin with. Granted, this wasn't the way she had intended to arrive, but the end goal was the same, right?

Nate rested his hand on the small of her back and carefully led her through the camp. The Queen's Guard silently flanked them on both sides as they walked, always watching, never interacting. There were six Jokers in total, each dressed the same down to the creepy collars wrapped around their necks. Alice did her best to study them without openly gaping at them.

"What are those for, anyway?" Alice asked Nate in a hushed voice.

Nate took a few more steps without saying anything, then answered, "It's the Queen's insurance policy."

When he didn't elaborate, Alice probed deeper.

"For what?"

Nate had the decency to act embarrassed. "All the members of the Queen's Guard are Carriers, Alice." He looked at her meaningfully. Alice thought she understood, but her mind wouldn't quite process the answer. He waited another minute, and when she didn't say anything, he sighed. "Everyone who enters the camp is tested. If their test comes back clean and the Queen thinks they can help the camp, they're offered a place to stay. If their test comes back showing the MR-V virus, they're escorted off the premises." He didn't look at her as he spoke.

"It still doesn't explain the collars," Alice pointed out, refusing to let him dance around the subject.

"The Queen is all about strategy," Nate said. "If she thinks someone can be useful to her cause, and they're willing to volunteer, she'll use them. Sometimes," he spoke in slow, measured tones, "Carriers can be useful too."

Alice jerked her head, gaping at the guards surrounding

them. "You mean, *they're momerath?*" The question burst from her, much louder and higher-pitched than she intended. She dropped her gaze to the ground, blushing furiously, horrified they had heard her. To their credit, the Jokers ignored her outburst and continued to stare straight ahead as they escorted her through the camp.

"Not yet," Nate hissed in her ear. "Right now, they're only carrying the virus. They volunteered their service to the Queen. In exchange, they've been given a place to sleep and food to eat every night, instead of getting stuck out in Wanderland, cut off from the rest of society. They could be much worse off." He spoke with conviction, defending his Queen. It was evident he respected her leadership. Alice wondered how far his loyalty to her would take him.

"Then what about the collars?" Alice prompted. Dread filled her gut as she studied the sinister-looking metal pieces.

"It's how the Queen guarantees the rest of Tulgey will be safe. The Guard are allowed to move around camp freely, but if something happens and they start to turn..." He trailed off as they arrived in front of a large building, the door barricaded by two more collared guards. Nate settled his grip on the handle, eyeing the stoic Jokers surrounding them before leaning into Alice and whispering quietly, "—it's off with their head."

17

B efore Alice could respond, Nate pushed the door open and strode into the room, leaving her standing there, blinking like an idiot. The Jokers kept walking, filing behind him, not missing a beat. One of the men, a large Samoan with a friendly face, cleared his throat loudly as he passed, startling her to attention. Sheepishly, she hurried to catch Nate before he reached the Queen.

The room was much larger than it appeared from outside, giving Alice plenty of time to fall in line. It was also much nicer. Panels of crimson curtains ran down the lengths of the room, contrasting dramatically against the whitewashed concrete walls. Centered between each panel was a potted rose tree. They were in full bloom, showcasing beautiful bouquets of blood-red roses that filled the room with an almost overpoweringly sweet scent.

In front of the Queen, Nate dropped to one knee in a formal greeting. "You wanted to see the refugee, Your Majesty?" he asked, head bowed low.

Alice remained standing, uncertain of Tulgey etiquette. She found herself facing a surprisingly pretty older woman with curly auburn hair drawn into a loose ponytail at her neck. A few strands escaped at the crown of her head, framing her face and highlighting the hard lines etched around her eyes. Everything about her was harsh. From the angular shape of her face, to the prominent freckles dotting her nose, to the stiff posture she kept, it was clear the Red Queen was a fighter, not a lover.

The Queen gazed intently at Alice, face hidden behind her hand as she studied her. "No accounting for manners, I see," she said curtly, leaning against the gray high-backed chair behind her desk.

From where he knelt, Nate gave Alice a small, meaningful tilt of his head. Understanding dawned on her and she stumbled into an awkward curtsy in front of the Queen. "How do you do?" she asked, hoping she said the right thing. It was more formal than anything she would normally say, but clearly this woman was accustomed to being treated like royalty. She figured it would work best in her favor to entertain her, even if she thought it was crazy.

Appeased, the Queen straightened and flashed Alice a haughty half smile as she appraised her. "So you're the girl my men found taking on a nest of runners on her own." Her fox brown eyes searched Alice's for hidden secrets. She touched her hands to her lips as she considered. "Either you're very good, or very stupid." She paused. "Maybe both."

Alice's eyes narrowed. She didn't like the way this "Queen" was speaking to her, but she forced her mouth shut. The Queen continued, unconcerned by her animosity. "Either way, you may be useful." She nodded at Nate, still kneeling obediently in front of her, and motioned for him to stand. "Is it true nothing happened when she drank the elixir?" Though her expression remained neutral, curiosity burned behind her carefully arranged mask.

"Yes, ma'am," he answered, standing at attention.

"Interesting." She swiveled her attention back to Alice. She rose from her desk and strode around to Alice, circling her like a vulture. Alice forced herself still as the Queen scrutinized her. "There's never been anyone who hasn't had *any* response to my Unveiling Serum."

"So I've heard." Alice focused straight ahead, purposely avoiding eye contact with the older woman.

Her impertinence earned a small huff from the Queen, but the older woman pushed on. "I'd love the opportunity to examine *your* reaction," she said. "Or rather, your lack of one." She smiled, but there was no warmth in it.

Alice balked. She had no desire to drink the potion a third time, but she doubted the Queen would take refusal kindly. She'd already had it twice with no adverse reactions. Still, she couldn't bring herself to physically say yes, so she just gave a stiff nod of her head.

"Excellent." The Queen clapped her hands together, letting out a girlish giggle. "Nathan, bring me two vials of Serum for our guest."

A question flit across Nate's face, but he obediently approached the cabinet at the back of the room, obscured behind the Queen's desk. If Nate hadn't walked to it for the serum, Alice would never have noticed it. He drew a key from a chain around his neck to unlatch the cabinet and retrieve a tiny bottle. From where she stood, Alice made out an assortment of small glass bottles and syringes neatly arranged on the shelves before he snapped the door shut and dutifully turned back to the Queen.

"Would you like to see what happens?" the Queen asked coquettishly as she accepted the vials from Nate. Alice had no desire to witness the serum's effects firsthand, but apparently, it had been a rhetorical question. The Queen gestured to one of the Jokers beside her, and he hurried forward, eyeing the bottle warily.

"Majesty," Nate began, but stopped when the Queen raised her hand to cut him off.

"Not now, Nathan," she snapped. "Some things can't just be explained." She turned to the Joker beside her. He was a large man, though not quite as big as Ace, with several web tattoos running up the sides of his neck ending with a sprawling black widow inked on the back of his cleanly-shaved head. He didn't look like he could be scared by anything, so it caught Alice off guard when his face went white.

"But, Your Majesty," the Joker's gruff voice broke as his lips quavered. "I'm not sick—"

"Of course you are, Lyons. That's why you're in a Contra-Band." She raised one of the serum bottles to examine its contents. "Your service has been greatly appreciated, and now I need you to do one last thing for me." She smiled sweetly at the terrified man.

"I can be of better use to you! I will fight harder, work more shifts," Lyons begged, his hands trembling at his sides.

"This is what I need you to do," the Queen clipped, retrieving a small box from her pocket. It looked like the remote control to Alice's old television, with a hundred different buttons to press.

Alice didn't think it was possible, but once Lyons saw the clicker, he lost even more color. He didn't say any more, but his head shook in silent protest. The Queen didn't pay any mind as she pressed one of the serum bottles into his trembling hands. She clasped her tiny fingers around them, forcing him to grip the bottle tight. Once she was sure it wouldn't drop, she took several large steps back, putting a healthy distance between her and Lyons. Nate and the other Jokers followed suit, pulling Alice back with them. Lyons stayed put, still pleading with the Queen to stop.

"Lyons, show Alice what happens when a Carrier takes the Unveiling Serum," the Queen ordered, a hard glint in her eyes.

Lyons glanced around the room, searching for someone willing to help him. The other Jokers lowered their eyes, refusing to meet his gaze. Nate stood beside the Queen, silent as his grip tightened around his sword. Ace guarded the Queen's other side, grinning and weighing his axe in his hands. Perturbed by Lyons' hesitation, the Queen raised the remote and rested her thumb against one of the buttons.

Lyons blanched once more, now completely void of any color. His mouth gaped open and shut like a fish out of water as he brought the bottle to his lips. His hands shook so violently, he almost dropped the vial twice before the glass reached his mouth. He paused once more, silently pleading with the Queen, but she merely narrowed her eyes at his disobedience. Lyons' tongue darted nervously across his parched lips, then with a jerky motion, he gulped down the contents of the bottle.

Once the vial was empty, Lyons dropped his arm, finally letting the glass fall to the ground. It clattered to the floor, rolling away slowly from where Lyons stood. Before it stopped, he was doubled over, crying out in pain as he clutched his stomach. He stepped backwards, smashing the bottle under his boots as he writhed in agony.

His muscles spasmed, contracting violently, making Lyons' arms thrash as if he was swatting an unseen assailant. Alice watched in horror as, before her eyes, his skin decayed, turning from pale white to dusty gray, as if he was smoldering from the inside. His silent pleas were gone, replaced by gut-wrenching howls as he twisted in agony. The transformation lasted only a few minutes, but it seemed an eternity. She tried to look away, but she was mesmerized.

Suddenly, Lyons stood straight up, back arched as let out one last scream. Before his cry finished, it morphed into a haunted howl, wild and ravenous. The change was complete. He lunged forward, swerving his head around the room, staring down his potential victims. His filmy eyes locked on the Queen, and unadulterated fury covered his face. He let out another screech then launched himself across the room at the Queen, who firmly pressed the button she held.

The small orange light on the side of Lyons's collar flickered rapidly and a high-pitched beeping shrilled from it. A loud crack echoed across the room, sounding like a muffled gunshot, and Lyons' head was gone, replaced with a bloodied stump. What was left of his body slumped to the ground, covered in bits of flesh and blood, twitching uncontrollably as his nerve endings died.

"Take care of the mess," the Queen ordered the Joker nearest to her, dismissing Lyons' body as she returned to her desk. Alice gazed at her, numb with disbelief, terrified by what she just witnessed. She dared a quick peek at Nate, who stood at attention, gaze unwavering from the Queen.

"It's an interesting little potion," she said delightedly, leaning back in her seat. She held the bottle to the light, examining it as she swirled the contents inside. "My head scientist brought it to me when he joined my camp. We don't generally use it at home base. Too...*messy*. Although, it has been particularly helpful for my men in the field. But I guess there is an exception to every rule." Her eyes gleamed as she handed the vial to Alice.

Still in shock, Alice weakly gripped the bottle. The glass was ice against her clammy skin, and she fought the urge to vomit. She stared defiantly back at the Queen and downed the contents. She finished the drink, gulping dramatically as she dropped the bottle in the Queen's hand.

The Queen accepted the bottle, but her attention remained on Alice. Furious at being put on display, Alice crossed her arms in front of her chest while she waited for the Queen to accept nothing was going to happen. She tapped her foot, feigning boredom.

"Fascinating," the Queen remarked. She walked full circle around Alice before returning to lean against the edge of her desk. She tapped her fingers against her lips as she thought. "I have a proposition for you..." She looked at Alice expectantly.

"Alice," she supplied with an eye roll.

"Yes. Alice." The Queen airily dismissed her slip. "I have a proposition for you, *Alice*, if you would be so inclined."

"That depends," Alice answered. She wondered what the Queen could possibly want from her.

"Clearly, you have experience as a fighter, and I can always use skilled soldiers. Especially female soldiers. Tulgey has an exceptional combat force, but it is tragically lacking in female representation. And I wouldn't be truthful if I didn't admit I find you most entertaining." Her lips curled in a devilish grin. "But more than that, there are benefits we can offer. Most obviously, a high security facility where you are free to pursue your own interests—so long as they further the interests of Tulgey. You would be welcome to stay and make it your home if you agreed to work for me."

Alice couldn't think of anything that sounded worse, but she tried to remain diplomatic. "I'm flattered, but unfortunately, I can't," she said. The last thing she needed to do was offend the temperamental dictator.

Confusion covered the Queen's face. It was obvious she was not used to her "propositions" being denied. She recovered quickly, arranging her features back into her casual mask, covered by her smug half smile. "You enjoy roaming the wilderness on your own? Want to keep it a one-woman act?"

"Not exactly." Alice bristled at the condescension in the Queen's voice. Beside her, she heard Nate's sharp intake of breath and looked at the Queen, whose lips pursed in disapproval. More level-headed after her brief temper flare-up, she realized it probably wasn't in her best interests to piss off the woman she wanted to help her. "I'm working for myself right now," she amended sheepishly.

"Really." The Queen brought her hand underneath her chin, eyes gleaming. "Do tell."

Alice glanced at Nate, who smiled encouragingly. She didn't like the way the Queen was eyeing her, but her plan had been to get the Queen's assistance. It was unlikely she could do so without disclosing any information.

"My sister's sick."

The room shuddered. Nate stiffened, almost a mirror image of the Queen. Even the Jokers took an almost-imperceptible step away from her. Alice ignored it. "I need to find a cure."

"There is no cure." The Queen turned up her nose. "You'd be better off putting her out of her misery." She sniffed haughtily, dismissing the idea.

"What do you know about 'better off'? From what you just showed me with that Joker, you don't seem to care too much about anyone," Alice snapped before she could stop herself. She really needed to keep her attitude in check. To her surprise, the Queen started laughing, a robust sound, nothing like her sly giggle. She thrust her head back, holding the desk for support. When she calmed, she peered at Alice.

"You are a fighter, I'll give you that," she said. Her eyes narrowed, and her honeyed purr turned into a growl. "I haven't been spoken to like that in a very long time."

Alice didn't speak. She waited for the Queen to continue.

"You see, my dear, there are actually two different tests to identify Carriers. The first you have already seen and experienced—several times, I may add. This particular test is the nastier of the two, either resulting in the subject getting disgustingly ill or transforming into a momerath, with you being the sole exception.

"The other test is exclusively for my base, also developed by my head doctor. He has a certain...*brilliance* when it comes to the Plague. He discovered the Carrier gene is unique to one specific blood type, as the antigens in that particular strand do not register the virus as a threat. If someone has that antigen, they have the potential to be a Carrier." The Queen stood and took a step forward, closing the distance between her and Alice. Her eyes gleamed as she spoke.

"However, the only way to test this without triggering an immediate reaction is through a complex series of blood work. When my men are out in the field, they don't have the time or resources for this test, so the Unveiling Serum is sufficient to identify potential threats. Generally, if someone is invited to my camp, they are required to complete the blood screen before they are allowed in. There is also a generic screening process they must pass to see if they are worth my physicians' time and supplies. If they're valuable, then I run the blood work. If they are clean, they can stay in Tulgey and come and go as they please."

"If they don't pass?" Alice noted the omission. The Queen pressed her lips together in a small laugh, amused by her audacity.

"If they *don't* pass, they are still welcome to stay, but they must agree to my terms." She dragged her finger along the collar of one of the guards standing beside Alice. She was surprised to see a pretty Indian girl with kohl black hair and intelligent brown eyes. She was tall compared to Alice, and looked like she could easily hold her own in a fight, but her lovely features set her far apart from all the other hulking male Jokers. She stiffened when the Queen walked past her, eyeing the control she carried nervously.

"How does that work?"

"It's simple, really. The collar has a detonator installed, controlled by a device only I have access to." She waved the clicker she held. "In the event one of my Carriers turns, I have a way of *expediting* their expulsion from my camp."

Alice fought to keep her face neutral, but the Queen had no qualms about the barbaric system she had established. She actually seemed proud of herself. Her face rebelled at the thought and the Queen's haughty grin fell into a frown.

"Don't look at me like that," she pouted. "It's not as bad as it sounds. The Carriers under my employ have a much higher quality of life than any other Carriers in Wanderland. Better even than non-Carriers in outside sectors, I'd wager. They can continue to live normally until they turn, and in the unfortunate event it happens, I have a safety net in place to protect my other citizens. And honestly, at that point, if they could, they'd thank me. It's sad, but necessary."

Explained that way, the theory made sense, but Alice couldn't help bringing her hand to her throat as she imagined being forced to wear a death collar each day, knowing it was only a matter of time before it exploded. She shuddered at the thought, then jumped when the front door slammed open. A harried man in a white lab coat came scurrying in. Alice knew who it was before she even saw his face. She could have recognized Dr. Abbott's frenzied walk anywhere. He hurried in, feverishly checking his watch as he crept towards the Red Queen.

"Doctor. So nice to see you." The Queen smiled. Up close, Alice was able to get a better view of the anxious man. Although his snow-colored hair was disheveled, the doctor wasn't as frantic as when he ran from her in the city.

"Majesty." He inclined his head in a respectful bow. He was calmer than the last time Alice saw him, but she could still see a slight tremor running through his hands.

"We have a guest who needs your assistance." The Queen indicated to Alice. "See to her wounds, then return to your research."

Dr. Abbott nodded and turned to Alice. His eyes widened in recognition, but he gave no other sign they had met before. "How were you injured?" he asked, directing one of the Jokers to bring a chair for her to sit in.

Before she could respond, Nate chimed in. He rattled his report like a proper soldier, providing succinct details and nothing more. "She hit her head in a scuffle with a group of momerath in the city. One of them took her down pretty hard."

"It would seem that way," the doctor responded absently, focused more on Alice's wound than Nate's report. "How are you feeling now?" He held two fingers in front of Alice. "Can you see how many fingers I'm showing?"

"Two," Alice said, unconcerned with her injury. She had more pressing questions for the doctor. "I'm fine. My head just hurts a little."

"Any dizziness? Blurred vision?" the doctor questioned further, dabbing antiseptic on her head. She flinched at the sting as it disinfected the wound.

"Not anymore," she answered. That had long passed, leaving only the remainder of a headache. "Some aspirin would be awesome, though, especially if you're going to keep poking me." She pulled away from the doctor's prodding fingers.

"No. We're all done here," Abbott said briskly. "The wound isn't that deep. A couple of butterfly bandages should hold it together nicely."

"Band-Aids?" Nate asked incredulously. "Doctor, she needs stitches! Can't you see how much blood she lost?" He pointed to her heavily stained clothes. "There's a huge gash in her head!" Alice was touched by his concern, but squirmed uncomfortably when she noticed the Queen watching the exchange with interest.

Dr. Abbott appraised Nate, clearly irritated at being questioned by a soldier. "While I admire your concern, Marshal, I can assure you, the wound on her head is minor. Head traumas generally have more blood loss, so it makes sense you would think the injury more severe. But I can assure you, a simple bandaging will be sufficient."

"But I saw it!" Nate yelled. He ground his teeth in frustration, making the strong chisel of his jaw even more prominent.

"Nathan, that's quite enough." The Queen's harsh reprimand declared the conversation finished. Cowed, Nate fell back to where he originally stood, arms clasped behind his back. Alice could see his muscles flexing tight against his black T-shirt, most likely imagining strangling the doctor with his bare hands.

At the Queen's command, Dr. Abbott straightened his jacket, ignoring the hostility emanating from Nate. "Is there anything else I can help with, Majesty?"

"As a matter of fact, Waite, there is," the Queen said, the silk back in her voice. "My guest is here looking for something for her sister." A smile danced on her lips, as if she had a secret no one else knew. "A cure for the Plague."

Abbott paled, but Alice had to give it to him, he maintained his composure pretty well for a guy known for mental instability. "A cure, Majesty?"

"Yes, a cure." Her lips twisted in a disappointed pout. "But I informed her it was just not possible, as there *is* no cure. Isn't that right?"

"Y-yes, Majesty," the doctor stuttered apologetically, his tremor more pronounced. "Unfortunately, we have been unable to manufacture an antidote. We're still trying," he hurried to add, seeing the Queen's derisive expression. He glanced nervously at his broken watch. Behind her, Nate let out a frustrated sigh at the doctor's crumbling composure.

"Oh, calm down, Doctor." Irritation laced the Queen's features, but she gently set her hand on the doctor's shoulder. "You still have time," she said firmly. The doctor visibly settled.

He breathed a relieved sigh and turned back to Alice, then straightened his glasses.

"There is no cure for the Plague." He spoke to Alice with more authority than when he addressed the Queen. "If someone has contracted MR-V, it is already too late for them. I'm sorry," he said sympathetically, "I can't help you."

"What if they don't have the Plague completely?" Alice grasped pitifully for some way he could help. "What if they are a Carrier?"

Dr. Abbott sighed. "It would be highly unlikely. Less than fifteen percent of the population have the ability to even *be* Carriers, and you wouldn't know for sure until they turned." Focused on the science of the Plague, Abbott's apprehension vanished completely. There were no nervous tics, and even his tremor disappeared. Like this, it was easy to picture him as a skilled physician.

"What makes a Carrier?" Alice inquired, determined to learn as much as she could from the doctor now that she didn't think he was a total nut job.

"That has more to do with the person than the disease. Carriers are people who have been exposed to the Plague and have a combination of a particular antigen paired with a substantially lowered immune system. Unless someone has a B-blood type, they don't even have the capability to be a Carrier. It's the *antigens* that don't recognize the Plague as a threat to the system. For some reason, they accept it. Because of this, the pathogen is able to make its way in, cozy up in the Carrier's body, and hibernate until conditions become ideal for it to emerge. Once that happens, it's only a matter of time from when symptoms emerge until they turn. Has your sister been exhibiting any symptoms?"

Alice's heart sank. She already knew Dinah was a Carrier, but having it confirmed felt like a punch to the gut. "Yes, a couple of days ago. That's why I need to hurry."

Pity flashed through the doctor's eyes, but he maintained professionalism, using Dinah's case as an opportunity to glean more information. "Let me ask you, before your sister started showing symptoms for MR-V, did she have any other illness? Something that could have lowered her immune system and given the virus the chance to take over?"

Alice thought to before Dinah got sick. "Yes." She remembered the Petersons. "She went to check on a neighbor's baby. They thought she might have been sick."

The doctor shook his head sadly. "Then in all likelihood, your sister is a Carrier for the Plague. It's impossible to diagnose without examining her myself, but it sounds like she doesn't have much t—" He choked on the last word before gulping away the rest of his sentence.

Alice shook her head, refusing to believe it was over. Tears formed in the corners of her eyes. She balled her fists. She would not cry in front of these strangers. "You don't know that," she said adamantly. "I just need some medicine. Something to fix her. You have to have something. That's what doctors *do*: they *fix* people." Her nose pricked and she rubbed her hand against it angrily until it went away. She tossed her hair in frustration and stared at Abbott, who watched her with a blank expression, which made her even more upset.

"Dinah's not even a nurse yet and she fixes more people than you do!" she yelled. "What do you know about the Plague anyway? You're just some crazy old man!" She was ranting but didn't care. She was furious nobody was going to help and even angrier that disobedient tears streamed silently down her cheeks.

Dr. Abbott's shoulders slumped. "I wish I could help you," he said. "If you could bring her here, perhaps I could examine her," he tried to offer helpfully.

"There's not enough *time!*" Alice saw the doctor's eye twitch, but at this point, she was too worked up to bother censoring herself. "I've already been away from home for almost two days, getting sent on wild goose chases and hunted and forced to drink these god-awful concoctions, and it's all been just a huge waste of time!"

As soon as Alice finished, she realized she had gone too far. Everyone in the room watched her in shock—everyone except Dr. Abbott. He was waging a battle with himself, muttering incoherently under his breath as he compulsively ran his hands through his hair. Every now and then, he would stop to glance at his broken watch before reverting back to unintelligible speech.

"Calm down, Doctor," the Queen began, but it was no use. Abbott ignored her and rocked on his heels as he stared at his wristwatch.

"Late. I'm late!" He stared around the room. His eyes glazed over everyone, not actually seeing them. One of the Jokers stepped forward to subdue him, but was stopped by the Queen.

"Don't touch him!" Her command didn't come fast enough. The Joker tapped Abbott on his shoulder and the doctor spun around to face him.

"I'm late!" Abbott smacked the Joker's outstretched hand. "So very, very late!" He pushed the soldier back and tore down the hall, sprinting to the door, screaming, "I'm late! I'm late! I'm late!"

"Wonderful," grumbled the Queen. "He's absolutely useless when he gets like this."

"I'm sorry, I didn't mean to," Alice apologized. "I didn't think—"

"Clearly." The Queen pursed her lips. Anger rolled off her in waves, washing over everyone in the room. She brought her hand to her forehead, rubbing the pressure points above her brows. The Jokers held their positions, but cringed from where she waited in the center of the room. Nate's jaw clenched as he awaited his orders. Even Ace looked uncomfortable.

"Nathan," she clipped, continuing her massage. "Take our guest to her quarters for the evening. Ace, monitor the doctor and make sure he doesn't hurt himself. Perhaps if he snaps out of it, he can still get something worthwhile done tonight." She waved her hands, dismissing them.

Alice felt a light pressure on the small of her back. Without another word, she let Nate guide her to the doors as they hurried to escape the Queen's wrath.

18

Outside the Queen's room, Alice stared at Nate, wide-eyed. "Nate, I'm so sorry, I—" she started, but Nate stopped her.

"It's alright. It's not your fault." He smiled, but his voice was filled with anger.

"No, I shouldn't have," she tried to argue, but Nate grabbed her shoulders and looked directly into her eyes.

"Alice. It is *not* your fault." He gave her a small shake for emphasis. "That doctor is seriously unbalanced. He's a genius, but he's like that *all the time*. The smallest thing sets him off, and the Queen is the only person who can ever calm him down. Even then, that doesn't always work. You saw," Nate said. He ran his hand through his hair, frustrated. "I honestly don't know why she keeps him around. He's more dangerous than anything."

Alice kicked the dirt guiltily. Sure, the doctor was unstable, but she shouldn't have pushed so hard. She could see he was getting upset and she kept pressuring him. Even if Nate didn't think so, it was her fault.

"Can I go apologize?" she asked. She felt bad about causing

Dr. Abbott's freak-out, and secretly, she hoped for a chance to talk to him without an audience. She doubted she would get another opportunity. After what just happened, she wasn't sure if the Queen would let her see him again at all.

Nate hesitated. "That's probably not a good idea," he said. "The doctor is going to be out of commission for a while, and my orders were to escort you to your tent."

"Please, Nate? I feel *really* bad about what I said. I'd like a chance to tell him I'm sorry," she pleaded. "You can escort me back afterwards, I promise." She clasped her hands together and brought them under her chin as she begged.

"That's not fair," Nate said.

"What?" Alice dropped her hands, confused.

"The eye thing!" He gestured at her face. Realizing what he meant, Alice blushed furiously, but played along, giving an exaggerated flutter of her eyelashes. Nate groaned. "You fight dirty."

"So you'll take me?" She flipped her ponytail playfully. Nate laughed.

"Yes. But it has to be quick," he said. "I don't want to get in trouble. Being on the Queen's bad side is not a good time."

Alice beamed. "I'll be fast," she promised. "Thank you!"

"I can't believe I let you talk me into this," Nate groaned, but he smiled as he led her through Tulgey. He took the long way, making complicated twists and turns and even doubling back a few times. When Alice asked about it, he said he wanted to make sure Dr. Abbott had calmed by the time they arrived. "There's no point in getting him all riled again. Then we'll never get anything done." He ducked around the wall to the water station and held out his arm to stop her.

"We're here. You stay outside until the coast is clear," he whispered, straightening to enter the doctor's makeshift lab. He hurried inside, and Alice crept to the door to listen in.

"What are you doing here?" Alice heard Ace's snarl from within.

"I came to ask the doctor a question about one of my guards," Nate said coolly.

"Oh yes, your Jokers," Ace snorted. " 'Jokes' is more like it. Everyone knows that 'Guard Marshal' is just some bullshit title the Queen made up to give you something to do," he sneered.

Filled with curiosity, Alice crept closer to the door and peeked in as far as she dared. Though she couldn't see the whole room, she could make out Dr. Abbott sitting uncomfortably at a table against the wall, watching the soldiers nervously. They stood in the middle of the room, less than a foot apart. Although they weren't fighting yet, it certainly looked like it could come to blows at any second. Nate's jaw was clenched so tight, Alice was afraid he was going to crack his teeth.

"Yes, because 'Battle Marshal' is a job that can be found in all the historical records," Nate countered, forcing his voice even. "Come on, Ace, we're all just doing the best we can here."

"*Most* of us are doing the best we can." Ace took another step towards Nate. "Others are taking handouts." Nate opened his mouth to retort, but was cut off when the doctor interrupted.

"Gentlemen." Abbott stood to address the two of them. "Primitive as it may be, this *is* a research facility, and as you both know, the Queen is very keen to find an antidote. So, if there is nothing else pressing, I really must return to my work." He motioned to the door, politely hinting they leave.

"Ace, did you have anything to ask the doctor?" Nate's voice was smug. "No? Then you don't mind if I have a moment."

Ace glared at Nate then stalked out the door. Alice almost didn't have enough time to hide before he burst from the building, muttering murderously under his breath. She held her position until Ace was out of sight, then scurried in to join Nate.

"I really do have important business to attend if you don't

mind, Guard Marsh—" The doctor stopped when Alice ducked through the door. "What is she doing here?" he asked angrily.

Alice hurried to answer as Nate stepped outside to stand watch. "I came to apologize," she said. "I'm sorry about earlier. I didn't mean to upset you."

"Never mind that." Dr. Abbott shook his head, dismissing her. "If that is all you have to say to me, you may go." He rubbed his eyes tiredly before turning to continue his work.

"There is one more thing," Alice quickly added. The doctor's shoulders sagged. He swiveled his chair to face her.

"I figured as much." He sighed. "What else do you need?" He removed his glasses and cleaned them while he waited for her answer.

Alice thought for a moment about what to ask. She didn't want a repeat of earlier, so she decided to avoid asking about the antidote. Instead, she opted for a different question.

"How do you know so much about the momerath?"

The doctor sighed and ran his hands through his hair. He was quiet for a moment, then he carefully pulled out a small piece of folded newspaper from his lab coat pocket. It was torn and faded with age, but Abbott held it like a priceless artifact. In the dim lighting, he looked much older and more fragile than when Alice had first encountered him running through the streets of Wanderland.

Alice waited silently while Dr. Abbott studied the page. Slowly, he passed it to her, and she recognized the same newspaper clipping of Dr. Abbott and his partner from Bug's conspiracy board.

"This photo was taken less than a week before the outbreak," Abbott said quietly. "You probably recognize me. That man is Dr. Matthew Hatta." He tapped the photo, covering the image of the other man with his finger. "He is the man responsible for the Momerath Plague."

Alice studied the picture again. Dr. Abbott looked much younger in the picture, his hair a dark chestnut brown instead of its current stark white. His only wrinkles were small creases that sprouted from the corners of his eyes when he smiled. Hatta was young and vibrant, like he had the whole world at his fingertips and he knew it. These men were excited, determined to change the world. Abbott's confirmation made her dizzy. "How?"

Dr. Abbott sighed and leaned back in his chair, removing his glasses to fiddle with them while he spoke. "Matthew Hatta and I met in medical school at Dartmouth. We weren't in the same social circles. I got in on academic scholarship and several student loans. Hatta had his expenses paid in full with a trust fund set up by his parents. But don't mistake that for him simply taking a free ride. Hatta was driven by a need to be successful and soon earned his place at the top of the class.

"We first encountered each other in a secondary biology class when we were designated lab partners. I guess you could call it fate. During this time, we got to know each other. His area of study was Neurology and I was interested in Paralysis. We worked well together and soon became friends. We partnered through med school, and when he was offered a job at Borogove Industries after graduation, he told me about an opening in a sister department, and I was offered a job too."

Alice's brow furrowed as she thought about the picture celebrating the doctors' partnership. "But if you both studied different things, how did you end up working on the same project?"

A grim smile turned Abbott's lips. "You are the observant one, aren't you," he mused. He straightened in his posture and continued his tale.

"I loved my work at Borogove. It was an established company with a name for being at the forefront of pharmaceuticals. And of course, my best friend was there with me. That doesn't mean we always got along. Hatta was brilliant and he knew it. Because of this, his ego often got the better of him. He quickly advanced the ranks of Borogove, but sometimes I wondered if he wasn't being reckless in his achievement. Although we weren't in the same departments, we often shared working lunches where we would sit together and discuss our projects. Matt enjoyed having someone listen as he talked through his ideas; it gave him an opportunity to hear the sound of his own voice. As I listened, I would posit questions and give a different perspective to problems he encountered. In some ways, you might say I was his voice of reason.

"There were several occasions where I tried to temper his experiments. He would listen to what I had to say, but it was obvious he didn't share my opinion. However, due to strict company guidelines and, I like to think, a respect of our friendship, he never crossed the boundaries of the Hippocratic Oath.

"He also never had any major results. As more time passed with no notable progress, it was obvious he was getting frustrated. Then he had a breakthrough. It was an experimental drug aimed at combating depression in young adults—MNX-A, given the market name Manxoma. Hatta had recently been promoted and was working as a co-lead with one of Borogove's senior pharmacists. They struggled with the formula for years until they finally cracked it. Of course, Matt was immensely pleased with himself, and considering the sizable profit Manxoma brought in, so was Borogove. He was instantly granted approval on his next proposal —an attempt to regenerate dead and dying cells. Borogove couldn't wait for its next big payday. Hatta didn't care about that; he wanted the notoriety. Regardless, he was given full access to any and all company resources and was allocated an obscenely generous budget to assemble his team.

"It wasn't long after that Hatta requested I join his team. My background in the nervous system and paralysis was of specific interest to him, and he didn't mince words in his offer when he told me I was practically working for him anyway. As I said, he had an ego. But he also had a point, so I agreed. Secretly, I was also fascinated at the prospect of working with Matt. He was a visionary and I knew he would be a pioneer in the Neurology field, along with anyone else he chose to join him."

Dr. Abbott paused and leaned towards Alice, lowering his voice to a whisper. "I'll tell you a secret: if you ever meet a doctor who tells you they don't want recognition, they're lying." His eyes twinkled as if he was letting her in on something he shouldn't be. "We do lots of things for the greater good in our profession, but they are also things that make us more impressive. Nobody goes through twenty-plus years of schooling to be selfless. All doctors are egotists in some form, myself included." Alice nodded her head, uncertain of what response the doctor wanted. The acknowledgment was enough, and he leaned back in his chair, making the hinges squeak under his shifting weight.

"We worked on Hatta's concept, MR-V—'Mass Recovery'— for years with no viable results. The idea was to find a medication capable of reversing paralysis using regenerative cell therapy. During this time, I discovered Hatta requested me specifically because of the method in which he wanted to apply the medication. His theory was to inject the serum directly into the spinal cord to repair the paralyzed areas of the patient's nervous system. He hypothesized that randomly generating stem cells was not a workable method of therapy or else there would have already been a cure. Matt believed we needed to be thinking outside the box. So, we did.

"After four years and eight trials, we finally began to make some progress. We were able to utilize our findings and improve them to be increasingly effective with each new serum. Our most exciting discovery was that our idea of integrating the serum through the nervous system *was* feasible, and it increased the effectiveness of all trials. Utilizing this method, our best serum, MR-19, was able to regenerate enough healthy cells to reverse paralysis in ninety-three out of one hundred lab specimens. Those findings were practically unheard of. After that, we were promptly given the green-light to begin human trials."

Dr. Abbott paused to run his thumb over his image on the clipping once more. When he returned his gaze to Alice, his expression was filled with regret.

"Our trial was administered on a recently paralyzed subject. She was a twenty-two-year-old gymnast slated to participate in the upcoming Olympics. During a routine practice, she lost her footing and broke her neck, paralyzing herself from the waist down. Otherwise, she was in perfect physical health. She was devastated and desperate to regain her body—an ideal test subject. The required paperwork was filed, and 'March' was set up as our first patient. I didn't know her real name. Hatta insisted test subjects be strictly anonymous. He was probably right. It's easier if trials fail when there are no personal attachments. But I could never work long-term with a patient and not have at least a name to associate them with. I called her 'March' since her birthdate—one of her few personal details listed—was March 14th, 1991.

"It was evident from the beginning Hatta thought the MR-19 was going to be an unqualified success. At first, it truly seemed he was right. The first week, we had excellent results. With treatment, March was showing signs of nerve repair within her spinal column and had even regained mobility in her feet up to her ankles. Matt was so excited, he immediately scheduled a meeting with the board of directors, all of whom agreed to come see Hatta's newest miracle drug, expecting a revenue boom.

"Then, on the eighth day of testing, March stopped improving. Her regenerated cells began to deteriorate. Matt did not take it well. I tried to remind him things like that were bound to happen in clinical trials, but he wouldn't listen. He was preoccupied with his exhibition for the board. He refused to reschedule, claiming it would make him seem less credible. It was his pride talking, and we all knew it, but nobody was willing to say it out loud. For three days, we worked tirelessly, praying the serum would turn out, but each day, March regressed further and Matt got increasingly frantic.

"The day of the board meeting, Hatta was a mess. The trial was crumbling, and he was not taking it well. He refused to accept the project was a failure, and clung to the initial improvements recorded. He insisted we were just experiencing a hiccup. He was so irritable, he picked fights with everyone on the team and eventually kicked them all out of the lab, save me. I tried my best to reason with him, but he was too agitated. He was fixated on dosages and insisted the ratio of the serum we were supplying to March was not equivalent to the ratio we used inititally. I assured him it was, referencing our extensive notes and even working out the formula composition for him again. He refused to listen. We quarreled, and finally, I left the lab to clear my head."

Dr. Abbott took in a large breath, exhaling loudly. He wiped his hand over his eyes before he continued, his voice broken.

"I don't know what happened in the laboratory while I was gone. It couldn't have been more than an hour. After I calmed, I returned to support Hatta when he told the board the trial had failed. Failure was never something he took gracefully. Imagine my surprise when I entered the lab to find the entire board of directors gathered eagerly around March's bed hours earlier than the scheduled time.

"She was prepped for trial administration, lying flat on her stomach with her medical gown open at the back, exposing her spinal cord. Hatta stood beside her, giving one of his grand speeches. The board members listened intently, excitement evident on their expressions. It wasn't surprising. Hatta was a captivating speaker. His charm and passion for his work were infectious. I might have been drawn in too if, as he spoke, I hadn't noticed the massive fifty milliliter syringe he held filled with the MR-19 mixture he kept gesturing to. The standard dosage we administered during the trial was only five milliliters.

"Realizing what was about to happen, I rushed to stop him, but I was too late. Hatta had seen me and knew I would try to interfere. He winked at me then plunged the syringe into the base of March's neck, deep into her medulla oblongata—what you would call the brain stem."

Alice's heart raced. She knew what happened next, but given the chance to hear a first-person account thrilled her inquisitive mind. She watched Abbott with rapt attention, not wanting to miss a single detail.

"As soon as the needle pierced March's skin, the world froze. I remember it like a photograph: Hatta's arm extended out to March's back; the semicircle of business professionals hovering greedily around the hospital bed, practically salivating with excitement; and myself at the back of the room, reaching out like a fool as if I could actually do something to stop him.

"At first, nothing happened. Everyone in the room just waited, fixated on the woman in the hospital gown for what seemed an eternity. It wasn't until I started feeling lightheaded that I remembered to breathe. Suddenly, the room exploded.

"March had been lying face down on the center of the bed since Hatta had punched the syringe through her skin. But then, without warning, her body jerked violently, as if she had been electrified. When she sat up, the first thing I noticed was her eyes. She had the most beautiful dark almond brown eyes I had ever seen, that now were filmed in smoke, storming behind a terrifying sneer. Through the trial, I had seen March display many emotions: happiness, anger, hopefulness, despair. But I had never seen this. It made my blood run cold. She scanned the room, glaring at the board members in front of her as a terrible cry ripped from her throat. It sounded more like the snarl of a wounded animal than a person. In a flash, she jumped to her feet and perched on top of the table, staring down everyone in the room with dead eyes.

"For a moment, nothing moved. A mixture of terror and excitement scattered among the board members. It was obvious the MR-19 had worked. March was no longer paralyzed. But nobody knew what to make of the adverse side effects. Beside her, Hatta stood in triumph. He had reversed paralysis. Max Recovery was a success. Nothing else mattered.

"Until March jumped on the Chief Financial Officer."

Dr. Abbott's voice broke, pulling Alice's attention out of the world his story had woven together and back to him. He looked awful. He brought a trembling hand to his brow, face pale and sunken. He cleared his throat so he could continue.

"She attacked with a force I never thought possible. Although she had an athletic body, March was a gymnast—she was tiny. The CFO easily had two hundred pounds on her, and he didn't stand a chance. She tore into his face, clawing the skin on his cheeks and gouging his eyes. He defended himself with a cross of his fist, breaking her nose. The fracture started gushing blood, but it didn't slow March at all. Blood poured from her face, covering the CFO and seeping into his open wounds while she slashed at his neck until she ripped out his throat. He fell, a sickening gurgle escaping his throat as he choked on his own blood.

"While one coworker died on the floor, another board worker let out a terrified scream, pulling March's attention from her victim to the people watching in horror. She growled and dove, landing on the Senior Marketing Advisor. After that, it was chaos. Everyone tried to escape, terrified for their lives. Everyone but Hatta."

Abbot swallowed and slowly returned his glasses to their resting place on the bridge of his nose. His eyes were misty, and they fogged the lenses as he continued.

"*He* stood in the middle of the room, shouting victoriously. 'It worked! She can walk,' he laughed maniacally. I tried to snap him out of it, but he was gone. I think that was the moment he truly went mad. Who knows? In the chaos, nobody else paid Hatta any mind. The CFO had also been forgotten, until he stood, searching the room in a frenzy. Like March, his eyes were white-washed and his expression contorted in rage as he screeched and attacked the man standing closest to him, ripping off his ear with his teeth—"

The story stalled as Dr. Abbott trailed off, his features twisted as he gazed into ghosts of the past. His hair stuck up at different angles where his fingers tore through it during his story. His hands trembled uncontrollably and he glanced anxiously down at his watch before muttering, "Late, I was too late."

Alice couldn't help but feel sorry for the doctor. He had been trying to make people better and instead created a monster. She couldn't imagine living with the awful things he had seen. She tried to comfort him, but when he felt her hand on his shoulder, Abbott shoved her away and screamed. "Too late! It can't be fixed! Too late, too late, too late!"

"Dr. Abbott, calm down!" Alice yelled, trying to settle the frantic man. Nothing worked. His shouting grew louder, and soon a small group of soldiers swarmed the room.

"Alice! Get out of here!" Nate ordered. He grabbed her and pulled her away before rushing to where Abbott stood. He tried to calm the doctor, but the older man kept howling about time as he paced erratically around the room. Nate approached him again, but Abbott cried out and swung, punching him square in the jaw. As soon as the doctor turned violent, two Jokers rushed in from behind and subdued him.

"Take him to his sleeping quarters. Make sure he's secure, then let the Queen know he had another of his episodes," Nate ordered bitterly over the doctor's frenzied shouts, then he turned his attention back to Alice. He placed his hand firmly on her shoulder and led her briskly through the camp, not slowing until the doctor's deranged screams disappeared into the night air.

"That was exciting," Alice said when he finally slowed. She glanced nervously at Nate, who grimaced as he rubbed his sore cheek. They continued in silence until her questions burned through her. "What was that?"

Nate sighed. "The Queen thinks it's post-traumatic stress," he answered roughly, guiding her through the camp. "Sometimes he's calm and a decent doctor, and then other times, well, you saw what happened." Nate shook his head, his jaw tense with frustration.

Alice nodded. Nate was right. Interactions with Abbott were like flipping a light switch—two extremes. But after hearing his story and what he had been through, she wondered if she would be any different if it was her.

Yeah, she thought. *You'd probably be full-on crazy, not just half.*

They walked quietly another moment, lost in thought. Nate was first to break the silence. "The Queen requested to see you tomorrow morning," he announced, back to business. "She wasn't happy you ran out on her." His expression was serious, but a smile played at the corner of his eyes. Alice blushed, hoping he couldn't see in the dim lighting. "I wouldn't worry about it too much," he continued. "Her bark is worse than her bite."

"Is it really?" Alice asked before she could stop herself. Nate glanced at her, surprised. She bit her lip, not wanting to speak badly about someone he obviously admired. Unfortunately, she'd already opened her big mouth, and now had to explain herself.

"Those collars she puts on her guards are just so awful." She hesitated, unsure how to explain the rest of her thoughts.

"The Queen does what she has to," Nate said firmly. "Her decisions keep everyone in Tulgey safe, and take a lot of potentially dangerous people off the streets. Instead of killing them or forcing them to roam the wild, the Queen gives them their lives back."

"Until she kills them," Alice said softly.

"What is she supposed to do?" Nate asked. "Let them go and hope they don't bother anyone else? Lock them in a cage? Feed them bits of people in the camp who pass away? Alice, you know what we have to do with someone once they turn! How many people did *you* kill this afternoon?"

Alice didn't respond. *That was different*, she thought. Putting collars on people and forcing them to do your bidding until they were no longer useful was flawed. She didn't know how to say it though, so she kept quiet. They continued in silence until Nate stopped in front of a small single-person tent.

"You must be tired." He flashed a gentlemanly smile. Clearly, he'd moved past their argument. "It's been a long day for you." Alice nodded and yawned. She was exhausted. "You can stay here for the night. There's a bed and a change of clothes if you'd like. I'll come pick you up for the Queen in the morning. Don't worry, we'll get breakfast first." He winked, and her stomach fluttered wildly. "Sweet dreams," he said before turning to go.

Alice waved goodnight and walked wearily into the little tent. She flopped onto the small cot and snuggled into the lumpy pillow she'd been given. Nate was right. It had been a crazy day, and she was beat. She yawned, stretching her stiff muscles and telling herself she would just relax a minute before she got ready for bed. She didn't last that long. Finally given the chance to rest, she was asleep before she kicked her shoes off.

19

A lice woke the next morning to sunlight streaming through the small mesh screen in the roof of her tent. She lay flat on the bed staring at the sky, ignoring the soreness in her arms and legs. *Two days. I've already been here two days*, she thought. Though it felt much longer. It seemed she'd been stuck in Wanderland for weeks. She didn't have weeks, though. She didn't even have days. She needed to hurry.

That meant she had to get out of bed.

Groaning, she willed her sore muscles to stand from the relative comfort of the cot. She looked down at the sad state of her tattered clothes and was thankful she had thought to pack a spare set. Soon, she was freshly clad in a dark tee and a worn pair of black skinny jeans. She shrugged into her light, military-style fitted jacket and tugged on her boots. Once they were laced, she opened the flap of the tent and ran her fingers through her hair to pull out any tangles worked in overnight. She didn't have anyone to impress. She was busy teasing a stubborn snarl as she hurried outside, and didn't notice Nate until she almost barreled into him.

"Whoa!" He held her shoulders to steady her when she bounced off him. He was more solid than he looked, and holding onto her with his arms flexed tight against a dark gray T-shirt, he looked pretty darn solid. Suddenly, Alice wished she had done more with her hair. She flipped it behind her shoulders to hide the mess and blushed furiously. She was completely out of her element. She had never had to deal with anything like this before. In the Sector, the closest thing she even had to a romantic option was Lewis, and he was, well, *Lewis*.

Not the time to lose it, she scolded. *Focus, you idiot.*

"Sorry!" she exclaimed. Her cheeks burned as she chased away her inner monologue. "I didn't see you."

"Don't worry about it. I should have announced myself. Are you hungry?" he asked. An easy smile played on his lips. It lit up his whole face and brought out the bright blue in his eyes. With his chiseled features and halo of golden hair, he could have been a Renaissance angel.

Alice nodded, thankful for the topic change. And truth be told, she was starving. She'd packed some food in her bag, but had rationed it strictly. Breakfast sounded wonderful.

"Great, follow me," he said. He walked quickly, and soon, they were in a large common area set with dozens of wooden picnic tables. Wrapped around the seating area, canopy-covered rectangular tables arranged in a large U formed an assembly line of sorts. A team of workers stood behind them, prepping and serving food to the people of Tulgey. Alice's mouth watered at the heavenly smell. She was glad the commotion of people laughing and eating masked her rumbling stomach. Eagerly, she followed Nate to the buffet line. While they waited, he pointed out the different parts of Tulgey and explained how it ran. She hated to admit it, but she was impressed by the Queen's command of her base. Although the buildings were not state-of-the-art, it was obvious they were well tended. The camp itself was maintained and clean, following a clearly established sense of order. There were easily five hundred people living here and they all had food, water, and shelter. Not to mention access to showers and recreation, if they wanted.

Unlike the Sector, Tulgey Wood was all about efficiency. There was no "Main Street" or pop up shops with vendors bartering for themselves. Walking through the organized workstations without being yelled at or haggled with made her a little homesick.

"You okay?" Nate asked when Alice didn't respond to the question he asked a second time.

"Hm? Oh! I'm fine," she said quickly, covering her flushing cheeks with her hand. "Just tired." She forced a yawn, hoping it was believable.

"You didn't sleep well?" He led her to a long picnic table in the middle of the common area. He set his tray down across the table, facing her. She wondered how he didn't have every girl at the camp falling all over him, then remembered his attentiveness to the Queen. She wondered if that had something to do with it.

"What? Are you kidding? I had the best sleep of my life. Like, ever." She bobbed her head and pitched her voice high as she answered.

Nate laughed again. "Our cots are top of the line." He winked at her conspiratorially. "Imported directly from Germany. I would know. I've been here a lot longer than you have."

Alice raised her brows. "And how long is that exactly, Mr. Expert?" She fought a smile, but couldn't force it down. Even when she bit down on her lips to push them flat, the corners tugged up in rebellion.

"I've been with the Queen since before she founded Tulgey." He paused dramatically, taking a swig of the watered-down orange juice offered with breakfast. "She's my aunt."

If Alice hadn't swallowed her swig of juice, she would have spewed it all over him. Her eyes goggled as millions of questions about Nate and the Queen warred in her mind, leading to her eloquent response.

"What?"

An undignified snort escaped Nate's nose at Alice's stunned reaction. It was the most ungentlemanly thing she had ever seen him do, but even that was endearing.

"The Queen is my aunt. She's my dad's sister," he explained. "Before the Plague, I used to live in Houston. Aunt Rose lived in Tucson, but she would come and visit every spring break to celebrate Brody's and my birthday. She had just arrived when the Plague hit Phoenix. After reports of the attacks spread, my dad said it wasn't safe to travel, so she stayed with us a little longer. Unfortunately, you know what happened. Plague spread everywhere, Houston included. We followed the orders the government issued, and it worked for a while, but then the city got overrun. Mom, Dad and Brody all got infected. I would have too, if it weren't for Aunt Rose."

"Aunt Rose." Alice's food sat forgotten, her fork suspended between her plate and mouth as she gaped at him, mystified. She was having a hard time reconciling the Queen she knew as Nate's "Aunt Rose." *Although it does explain the flowers,* she mused, glad to make sense of *something* in this upside-down place.

Nate laughed again. "Don't look so shocked. Everyone had a family at some point before the Plague. The Queen is no different. Her family just also happened to be mine." He shrugged as if it explained everything.

Alice raised an eyebrow. She still wasn't convinced, but she wanted to hear the rest of the story. "Mhmm..." was all she said as she gestured with her fork for Nate to continue. He let out an amused huff, but then a shadow fell across his face. Before Alice had time to register it, he flashed a brave smile.

"After the attack on my family, Aunt Rose decided we needed to leave Houston. She said it wasn't safe. She was right, but then, nowhere was safe. You know?" He glanced up at Alice, and she nodded through a mouthful of pancakes. Her cheeks blazed, and Nate shook his head good-naturedly, his smile finally reaching his eyes as he watched her.

"I think she wanted to go back home to Tucson, but we didn't make it all the way." He continued, picking at the bits of egg left on his plate. "The death of my family hit her hard. Harder than I thought it would." His eyes were haunted again.

"Whenever she saw a momerath, she did anything and everything in her power to kill it. It became an obsession. She would even go off on her own to hunt them out. As we made our way west, she found other people, hunters like her, who decided to come with us. That's how she found Ace." The thought of the hulking menace made Alice's face scrunch in distaste. When Nate looked up and saw her expression, he snorted.

"That's what I thought too," he said. "But it wasn't all killing," he added quickly, as if he realized he was painting an unfavorable view of his Queen. "We also helped people who were in trouble. And after Aunt Rose saved them, they decided to stick with us too. By the time we made it to Phoenix, we had a group of twenty following us. It made mobilizing harder, so she gave up on Tucson and set up camp outside the city. That's how we ended up in Tulgey."

Nate took in a deep breath. "Ancient history." He took a bite out of his scrambled eggs. "And *that* is why I'm the expert." He winked, erasing any trace of sadness from his face.

Alice was stunned. She still couldn't believe Nate was the Queen's nephew. Instead of answering her questions, it only gave her a million more.

"Relax," Nate laughed. "You're going to hurt yourself with all that thinking. It's not like I said I was an alien visiting from another planet."

I might have had an easier time believing that, Alice thought. Nate was so different from the Queen. Hearing she was his aunt *and* she had practically raised him just didn't make sense. Her next question was out before tact caught up with her.

"Then why are you so nice?" As soon as the words were out, she realized how rude they sounded, setting her cheeks ablaze. She was mortified when Nate stared blankly at her, but then, to her relief, he laughed.

"My dad was big in politics and my mom was a debutante before she met him. Etiquette was practically drilled into me before I could walk. Aunt Rose was more...

freethinking. Just because she was related to State Representative Hart didn't mean they were the same person."

Alice considered that for a moment. She of all people should know blood didn't matter in family. She was thoughtful as she picked at her breakfast, all but forgotten during Nate's story. Still hungry, she scooped up a bite of eggs and couldn't believe she had waited so long to eat. She scarfed the rest down, ravenous. Nate let her eat, keeping polite conversation going while giving her time to swallow the spoonfuls of food she shoveled into her mouth.

"Are you finished with breakfast, or should I give you two a minute alone?" he asked, chuckling after she licked her syrupy plate clean. He had a nice laugh. It rumbled all the way from the bottom of his chest like he wasn't trying to hold anything back.

Alice slowly set down her plate and attempted to daintily wipe her face clean. "Do you know the last time I had pancakes?" she asked. "Because I don't." She leaned back against the chair and placed her hands on her finally full stomach. "Oh, I ate too much," she groaned happily.

"So, that's a yes?" Nate asked, even more handsome with his mischievous grin.

Alice crumpled her napkin into a ball and tossed it at his head. "Yes, I'm done."

Nate dodged the napkin ball easily and walked over to where Alice sat to pull out her chair for her. "Then, my lady, it's time to go see the Queen."

Alice dropped back onto the table bench. "I changed my mind. I'm not done." She reached for her fork again. "Are there more pancakes?" She craned her neck, searching for the pancake lady. She was gone. Her shoulders sagged, defeated.

Nate let out another soft chuckle. "No. Cook's fresh out. You ate them all." He patted her on the shoulder. "Come on. Aunt Rose really isn't that bad. She's a little rough around the edges, but it's only because she has to work so hard to keep everyone safe."

Alice groaned. "It's too early to deal with cranky dictators," she whined. "Even if they are family."

"She's only difficult when people don't follow her instructions," he countered, gently pushing her towards the Queen's quarters.

"Is that all?" Alice asked offhandedly. She tried to come up with a more intelligent response, but got distracted by the warmth of his hand on her back.

"Yes," Nate said, his smile widening at her impertinence. "Now come on, we'd hate for the Queen to get cranky." He laughed again at Alice's eye roll.

"Fine," she huffed, only slightly irritated he had thrown her own words back at her. She followed him back to the large building in the center of Tulgey. She resisted going in until she felt Nate's hand press firmly against her spine. She stepped tentatively into the dimly lit room without the slightest idea what to expect.

"Alice, dear, come in," the Queen purred. Perplexed, Alice glanced at Nate, but his attention was no longer on her. He had gone formal again, standing stiff beside her, focused on the Queen. She noticed his hands resting at ease, and her back felt cold where he had touched her.

Why are you surprised? It's not like he's going to choose you over her, she fumed. *He's her freaking nephew and he met you what, yesterday? Get a grip.* Her personal tirade did nothing to improve her mood as she approached the Queen. The only thing she could do was hope she wasn't scowling as much as she imagined she was when the Queen addressed her.

"You caused quite the commotion in my office yesterday," the Queen stated. "It upset the doctor terribly, I'm afraid." Her voice was calm, but Alice noticed the Jokers surrounding her twitch uncomfortably as she spoke.

"I'm sorry for my rude behavior." Alice decided the best strategy was to appease the Queen—whatever mood she may be in. "I'm just so concerned about my sister..." She didn't have to fake her sincerity. Her voice broke, and she had to pause to clear the lump caught in her throat.

"I understand," the Queen said sympathetically. "That's why I'd like to help you."

"Really?" Alice breathed. Relief flooded her body, but her inner analyst took over. "Why?" she asked doubtfully, and instantly regretted it. If she could have done so without looking insane, she would have slapped the shit out of herself.

The Queen's face puckered before she turned on another brilliant smile. "Because I like your spunk. And I think in the future, we could make a good team." Alice wavered. She needed the Queen's help, but she didn't know how she felt about working for her. Behind her, Nate cleared his throat. Even if she didn't trust the Queen, she trusted him. She glanced at the Queen, her smile plastered on her face while she waited for a response.

"I would have to take care of my sister first—"

"Of course, of course," the Queen said loftily. "You think I would send you to get an antidote and then not let you give it to the person you were chasing it for? What kind of person do you think I am?" She smiled sweetly at Alice, and she wondered how often she got what she wanted by using this behavior. The Queen was older, but she was still an attractive woman. It wouldn't surprise Alice at all if she used her appearance as part of her diplomacy tactics.

When Alice didn't answer right away, the Queen's expression tightened. "Well? What would you like to do?" The Joker closest to her shifted nervously. Clearly, they had experienced her temper before.

"I would like to accept your offer," Alice decided.

The Queen beamed. "Excellent," she said. "I was so hoping we could come to an arrangement. I'll assemble a team, then you may leave promptly."

"Thank you," Alice exclaimed, eager to be on her way. "I can't tell you how much I—"

"There is just the matter of your end," the Queen interrupted. "I hate to seem petty, but I did not get to where I am today by simply doing favors for everyone out of the goodness of my heart."

Alice bit her tongue. Now that she knew the Queen was willing to help, she didn't have much patience for posturing. "I understand."

"After you have retrieved your antidote, you are to return to Tulgey Wood. From there, we will discuss your role in my camp. Agreed?"

"Agreed," Alice said. "As soon as I get the medication to my sister, we will come back to stay with you."

"So optimistic." The Queen let out a small giggle. "It seems we have a deal." She leaned back in her chair and waved her hand at Ace, who stood obediently beside her. "Fetch the doctor. He has some instructions our Alice is going to need for her mission." She waved him off with a flip of her wrist. "And make sure his wits are about him this time," she called. "He's *so* infuriating when he gets worked up. Don't you agree, dear?" Her eyes gleamed as she pulled her fingers along the base of her cheek as she watched Alice's expression.

Alice bristled. The Queen owned her, and she knew it. *It's for Dinah. Dinah is worth it,* she coaxed herself, fighting to remain calm.

The Queen let out a smug giggle. "Yes, well," she sighed. "Though some good did come from it last night, *do* try to not agitate him so this time."

Alice didn't understand what the Queen meant about good coming from Abbott's distress, but she didn't care. *You would be the expert on agitation,* she raged in the only rebellion she could. She was saved from further taunting when Ace barged in, Dr. Abbott in tow.

"Ah, Doctor," the Queen purred. "So nice to see you looking well rested this morning."

Abbott's eye twitched, but he bowed respectfully to the Queen. "Your Majesty."

The Queen's predatory smile widened. "Oh, come, Doctor. I should think you of all people would be excited about the opportunity. After all, you've been working so hard to find a cure." Her face twisted in faux sympathy. "Unless, you *haven't* really been looking..." She covered her smile as she watched Abbott fidget. She had him trapped.

"No! I mean, I would never deceive you, Your Majesty." His hands started trembling again and the Queen silenced him with another careless wave.

"Yes, I know." Her words shot out in barbs. "That's why you're still here." She smiled, but the threat behind it was thinly veiled. She cleared her throat. "I need you to tell Alice what you told me."

The doctor swallowed. His eyes flicked from the Queen to Alice, and back. When the Queen's eyes narrowed dangerously at his hesitation, he rushed to comply. "Though I have not been able to find a cure yet, there may be one hidden in Borogove."

A jolt shot through Alice. *A cure. There may actually be a cure.*

The doctor looked to the Queen hopefully, but she merely urged him on. His shoulders sagged. He turned to Alice. "There is another doctor in Borogove. His name is Matthew Hatta." Alice remembered his name from last night. She didn't understand why Abbott was telling her the same information, but when she saw his gaze flit anxiously to the Queen, it made more sense.

He's afraid of her, she thought. Not that she blamed him. She inclined her head to show Abbott she understood.

"On one of my recent excursions, I happened upon his research. He is still in Borogove, and he has been busy." He looked ominously at the Queen, but she ignored his gaze.

"Don't be so dramatic, Doctor." She examined her blood red manicure. "Really, for a scientist, you're *very* high-strung."

Abbott's eyes narrowed, and Alice saw a shadow of the proud scientist from the photograph. Before the Queen noticed, he fixed his expression and busied himself cleaning his glasses. "I believe Hatta has found a way to alter the virus. It could be the key to finding the cure." He sniffed and slid his glasses on, deferring to the Queen.

"Fantastic, isn't it?" the Queen asked Alice. Her voice dripped with honey, but there was danger in her eyes. "And such *excellent timing.*" She passed a suspicious glance over Alice before turning her attention to Abbott.

"That will be all, Doctor," she said airily, directing Ace to his side again. "For now."

Abbott's cheeks lost what little color was left, but he stood tall. "Yes, Your Majesty." He tilted his head and allowed Ace to escort him from the room. When he passed Alice, she noticed his thumb rubbing absently across the face of his watch.

The Queen cleared her throat. "So, my dear." Her voice was crisp, electric. "Are you willing to brave Borogove for your sister?"

Alice's brow furrowed, confused. She had already faced the horrors of Wanderland for Dinah. *How could one doctor in a dusty old building be any worse?* "Absolutely."

"Excellent." The Queen's smile slithered across her face. "Let's get you ready."

In less than an hour, a team was assembled and packed to leave Tulgey. The Queen offered to send five soldiers along with Alice and Dr. Abbott to Borogove Industries. She directed Ace to lead them, and Nate volunteered to go on his own. "It looks as if you will be getting two of my best soldiers." She spoke as if she was a fairy godmother bestowing a miraculous gift. Personally, Alice would have preferred she kept Ace, Battle Marshal or not. He could have been the best fighter in the whole world and she still would have wanted him to stay. He gave her the creeps.

The rest of the team was filled by three Jokers. Alice had seen each of them in the Queen's chambers, but hadn't taken much notice of them until they were in the car. Away from the Queen, they were much more relaxed and personable. They talked and joked with each other, and even exchanged friendly banter with Nate.

One of the men, the Samoan she had seen earlier, had to be the largest man Alice had ever seen. He stood around six feet five inches tall and was easily three hundred and fifty pounds. His name was Big Mike, and he was probably the funniest person she had ever met. It didn't matter what the topic was, he could make it comical. He even made a joke about how the Queen had to special order his ContraBand from a Big and Tall store.

Indi, the pretty girl she had seen earlier, was the only female Joker in the Queen's Guard. Her real name was Inderjit, but she insisted Alice call her by the same name as her friends. She had been chosen for her skill with a blade. Her father had grown up in London and had a passion for fencing. He had passed on everything he knew to his daughter and she excelled in the sport. After the Plague, it was an easy enough transition for her to go from a sabre to a real sword. Compared to the other Jokers, she was delicate, and her proper British accent only reinforced what a lady she was. But she made it clear the only person allowed to say anything about it was Big Mike, and that was because he could crush her with one leg if he wanted to. When he heard that, Big Mike dissolved into a fit of laughter, tears streaming down his chubby cheeks.

Last to join them was a boxer named Juan, who went by Johnny. Alice pegged him at about five foot eight, and solid muscle. Every movement he made caused some part of his arms or shoulders to ripple. Even his neck, which had a rose shaped like a skull on it, was all muscle. He had quick feet and a quicker temper, reverting into his native Spanish when he got worked up. The only soft spot he seemed to have was for Indi, who he lovingly called "*Querida.*"

Watching them joke back and forth made Alice homesick for Dinah. She missed having someone understand her sense of humor and personality. She also couldn't help but wonder if maybe Nate was right about the Queen. Even though all three of the guards wore those awful collars, outside the Queen's chambers, it didn't look like they minded. They seemed comfortable, as if they had acclimated to the situation they had been put in. They had even found their own adopted family of sorts. She continued to watch them kid with each other as they prepped to leave.

"We're ready to head out," Nate announced after Big Mike slammed the back door of the van. "Everyone in."

To Alice's dismay, Ace was driving again. She crawled in the very back seat, trying to put as much distance between Ace and herself as she could. It didn't keep him from leering at her from the rearview mirror, though. Indi hopped in next to her and gave him the finger, whispering in her lilting accent, "We girls have to stick together." She nudged Alice then called to Juan, "There's room back here for one more, Johnny." He waved and nodded before hurrying to join them.

Dr. Abbott, Big Mike, and Nate were the last ones to pile into the van. Nate motioned for the doctor to sit up front, giving up the better seat to the older man and sliding into the middle seat of the van himself. When Big Mike stepped in, the whole van rocked sideways, pulling to the ground. He squeezed in next to Nate and shut the door.

"Could you be any bigger?" Ace sneered from the front as he watched the large man try and squish in, but Big Mike didn't care. He clicked his seat belt into place and tapped his belly proudly with both hands. "Just means there's more of me to love. Isn't that right, Indi?"

"Absolutely, Mikey," Indi leaned forward to pat him on the shoulder. Ace rolled his eyes and muttered something under his breath before shifting the van into gear.

The ride to Borogove flew by. For as quiet as the Jokers were in their ranks, they made up for it on their "field trip." Big Mike cracked jokes the entire ride—no topic was off limits. Especially Ace, who turned surlier each time his name made it to one of the punch lines, which was fairly often. Even the doctor eased up around their banter. Watching Nate was Alice's favorite part of the trip, though. He was so reserved when he was around the Queen, seeing him relaxed and natural endeared him to her. Before she knew it, they were in front of Borogove Industries.

"Alright, Dr. Abbott is going to get us into the facility," Nate instructed, huddling the group for debriefing. "Once we're in, everyone follow me. We only have an idea of what to expect from the information the doctor has given us, and even he has warned us things have changed in there. We're going to take it slow, and quiet. That means you too, Mike." He slapped the large man on the shoulder. He needn't have said it, though. It was amazing how quickly the Jokers switched gears. One second they were laughing and fooling around like there were no worries in the world, and the next, they were cool killers. "Any questions?"

Alice had about a million, but when nobody else asked any, she figured it was best to keep them to herself. She would just do what she always did: watch and follow along. Once the briefing was over, they crept to the side of the door. Nate led the line, followed by Ace and Indi. Behind them, Alice was sandwiched between Dr. Abbott and Johnny, followed lastly by Big Mike. Nobody spoke when they reached the door. Nate gave a signal and Indi escorted Dr. Abbott to the front. He must have had instructions of his own because he knew exactly what to do. At the door, he pressed his finger against the same scanner Alice had used in her botched attempt to break in. Her stomach twisted as she remembered the terrible alarm that sounded and the momerath it brought out after her.

"*Borogove personnel. Dr. Waite Abbott,*" the detached female voice chimed after the scan registered the doctor's fingerprint. "*Access granted.*" The door swung open, finally revealing Borogove Industries.

A MAD TEA PARTY

20

Walking through the dimly lit access hall was a bit of a letdown after all the effort it had taken to get into Borogove. The corridor was empty and still; the only sign of life a small emergency light next to the door, setting a blue sheen to the narrow hallway. The troop crept slowly behind Dr. Abbott, footsteps and voices hushed as best as possible, but the stainless steel walls and tiled floors turned every step into an echo. They passed several closed doors and one open one leading to a tiny kitchen. An upturned bowl of fruit lay scattered across a small table in the middle of the room, broken to pieces. The smell of stale coffee saturated the room, escaping from a torn bag of espresso roast spilled all over the floor. It didn't look like anyone had used the room in a very long time.

They continued down the hall until it opened to the front lobby of Borogove. Whoever designed the space had attempted to give it a warmer feel than the unwelcoming hallway. Plush carpeting blanketed the floors, muting the horrible echo haunting the group. The walls were painted a calming green and adorned with softened geometric artwork. Directly in front, an oversized mahogany receptionist's desk waited, with papers strewn across the top and scattered on the floor below. The large room was clear with no seating area in sight. Alice thought it strange for a company sure to have visitors until she noticed all the cushioned lobby chairs piled high on top of each other in front of a set of double doors to the left of the receptionist's desk. Every chair had been smashed against the doorway, including the rolling receptionist's chair. Some had toppled when the doors behind them were forced open. It wasn't a large gap, probably only a few feet wide, but big enough for a person to squeeze through. Only the bloody marks on the metal and glass windows indicated it wasn't a person who had escaped. An involuntary shiver flew down her spine and she huddled closer to Indi.

Dr. Abbott was unbothered by the eerie lobby. He toured them through the building, using his thumbprint to open an identical set of double doors to the right of the receptionist's desk. They trailed after him, once again assaulted by the harsh chorus of echoes in the tiled hall. This walkway was dimmer than the other had been, with fewer emergency lights spread farther apart.

"This hall leads to the pharmaceutical research laboratories," Abbott said, his hushed voice resonating down the sterile corridor. "At the end, there is a guest lobby that branches into different research rooms. The trial for MR-19 was conducted in Research Room Five." He anxiously checked his watch. The farther they ventured in, the twitchier the doctor got. Alice watched his eyes shift from Nate to Ace to the bloodied walls of the hall. The way they bugged behind his glasses made him resemble a scared rabbit in a trap.

They walked along until they reached another steel door, the glass in the middle shattered and tinged with blood. Alice saw Indi give Johnny a meaningful glance before they both tightened hold on their weapons. Behind her, Big Mike jerked his head left, and then right, releasing a terrible crack from his neck as he loosened his shoulders.

Dr. Abbott unlocked the door, granting them access. The guest lobby was a disaster. Chairs leaned against blood-spattered walls, splintered into millions of pieces. The few paintings that remained on the walls hung crooked, looking down at their brothers shattered on the floor. Shards of frames scattered across the patterned tile floor, crunching to dust under heavy combat boots. A bloody handprint covering the emergency button beside the door caught Alice's breath when she saw the bloody trail smeared down the wall beneath it. On the opposite wall, the doors were flung open, their heavy metal dangling from loose hinges.

"Late, I'm late," Abbott started to mutter from the front of the line. She peeked around Indi and saw him run his hands through his hair, pulling the strands up at different angles around his head. He glanced around the room nervously, his body crackling with anxiety as he continued to murmur. "My fault. Late. I was too late."

"Somebody shut him up," Ace growled, responding to the doctor's unsettling nerves. Nate leveled an impatient glare at him and stepped forward to calm the doctor.

"Dr. Abbott, it's alright," he mimicked the Queen's soothing tone. "Keep your voice down. No one is late."

It was the wrong thing to say. The doctor whirled around to glower at Nate, his eyes blazing. "You're wrong! I'm late! I'm late! I'm late!" His voice rose each time he repeated the word "late." The sound bounced off the walls of the small room, ricocheting through the open doors and down the abandoned hallways.

"Nate! Shut him up or I will!" Ace snarled, aiming his handgun between Abbott's eyes. As he did, the three Jokers jumped to synchronized action, pointing their weapons at the Battle Marshal.

"Whoa!" Nate jumped in front of the barrel of Ace's gun. "That's not your choice to make, Ace. We have orders!"

"Screw orders!" Ace said. "If he keeps screaming like that, he's going to get us all killed!" Alice hated to admit it, but he had a point. There was no reason to put all their effort into slinking through the building if the doctor blew their cover in a crazy outburst.

"I'll handle it!" Nate hissed, still trying to take control of the situation. He turned to the doctor again, but this time, Abbott wasn't going to listen. He swung, sending Nate stumbling into Ace before he tore down the hall, back the way they came. His voice echoed, growing fainter the farther he went, until all Alice heard was the ghostly traces of, "Late...too late."

The quiet only lasted until a raspy growl rang down the hallway Dr. Abbott had escaped through. The Jokers sprang to action, leaving Alice in the center of the room, waiting. She peered down the corridor, attempting to calculate the distance between them and the monsters.

"Back in formation! This way!" Nate's yell startled her from her thoughts. "Indi, Johnny, watch Alice. Keep her safe. Let's go!" With that, she was swept off, pushed forward by the Jokers following their Marshal's orders. They ran until they reached a small corridor opening to a collection of closed doors. They split up, everyone struggling to force a different exit open to escape.

"They're all locked!" Indi slammed her shoulder against the doorframe in an attempt to force it open. Behind them, the grating cries were magnified as the swarm gathered outside. More momerath were coming.

"What are we going to do, Nate?" Alice asked. Nate searched the room, grim-faced. Before he could answer, Ace spoke up.

"Mike. Up here. Now," he demanded. Big Mike looked confused by the command, but hurried to comply. "Go down to Room Five." Ace pointed to the doorway at the end of the lobby.

Mike hustled to the room, surprisingly fast for such a large man. He waved to Ace to signal he was ready for his next orders.

Ace pulled out a small controller resembling an old television remote. "Sorry about this." Nate gasped in outrage and sprang forward to grab it, yelling unintelligibly at Ace to stop. Before he could reach him, Ace pressed down on a large red button and a high-pitched beeping shrilled from the remote. Indi and Johnny stared in horror at the little black box before turning to their friend.

"Mikey!" Indi yelled. She took a few steps towards where he stood, but Johnny yanked her back to where he stood. Mike's smile fell at the same time the beeping stopped. Then his head was gone, splattered across the room like a burst watermelon. The force of the explosion knocked everyone else to the floor and cracked the seal on the doorframe of Room Five.

Ears ringing, Alice lifted her head off the floor, propping herself on her elbows as she surveyed the damage in a daze. Spots danced across her vision and her head throbbed where she hit it the day before. A sharp ring whined in her ears, blocking all other noise from the room.

Disoriented, she watched the others shakily pull themselves off the floor. Ace, having been more prepared for what was about to happen, had braced himself and stood, brushing dirt and debris off his clothes. Nate leaned against the far wall, clutching his head as blood flowed from a wound above his ear. Alice hurried to help him to his feet, and leaned him against the wall for support. Indi and Johnny were tangled on the floor, struggling to stand. Indi's eyes blazed with rage as she scrambled up and rocketed herself at Ace. Shouts rang out as Nate and Johnny tried to stop her, but nothing could drown out Indi's tortured cry.

"You *bastard!*" she screamed, slamming him against the wall.

Ace choked as Indi's forearm crushed his windpipe. "I didn't have a choice," he gasped, fighting for air. "The momerath are coming. He was as good as dead anyway. He went out saving us. It's what he would have wanted."

"How do you know what he would have wanted?" Indi demanded through clenched teeth, pressing harder against his neck. "You didn't even know him," she seethed, pulling a knife from her back pocket.

"Indi, stop!" Johnny gripped her round the middle, fighting to pull her off of Ace. "*No tenemos tiempo, Querida.*" Indi struggled against him, holding tight against Ace's neck. "We don't have time, my love," he said, voice low. Alice watched from across the room, propping Nate on his feet against the wall. Her breath caught as a gravelly shout rang through the room. The momerath were almost there.

Nobody moved until Indi dropped her gaze and pulled away from Ace's windpipe, freeing him to gulp for air. "You aren't worth it," she hissed, spitting at his face. Angrily, she wiped away the tears in her eyes with the back of her hand. "Let's move," she said bitterly. "We owe it to Mikey."

"Come on, Nate," Alice said as she braced his unsteady feet. They struggled along until Johnny wrapped Nate's arm around his shoulder.

"Go with Querida," he told her. "I'll take care of him." Alice nodded and turned to meet Indi, but it was too late. The momerath had caught them.

The first one burst through the broken doorframe, screeching with unadulterated fury. Specks of saliva sprayed from its mouth, dripping onto its ripped and bloodstained lab coat as it howled in rage. Behind it, two more momerath followed close, arms flailing as they ripped and tore their skin.

Behind her, Johnny let out a roar of his own and screamed at the momerath. Alice didn't speak Spanish, but she was pretty sure whatever he said wasn't very nice. "We got company." He reverted to English as he cocked his rifle with his free hand.

Nate still wasn't steady on his feet, but when the momerath arrived, his face set in determination. He pulled his arm off Johnny's shoulder and pushed off the wall, slightly swaying as he regained his balance.

"Protect Alice," he said. He unsheathed an old broadsword from the hilt on his side, holding the heavy weapon in both hands.

Indi shoved Alice behind her, sandwiching her between Room Five and her defensive stance. Three more 'rath joined the ranks, bringing the total to seven monsters versus two Jokers and an unsteady Marshal. Her throat caught as she watched them prepare to defend her. She reached for her own sword, ready to jump in. Before she could join the fight, Ace's deep voice boomed across the room.

"Let's even the odds." He stood to full height and fell in with the others' battle formation. He brandished his massive axe, glaring with contempt at the decaying 'rath in front of him. He lunged forward, wrenching himself between the 'rath that launched itself at them, crashing forcefully into it.

After the initial attack, the rest of the 'rath burst through the door like a dam. They surged forward, bloody stains streaking the disfigured remains of their past lives.

Johnny yelled in Spanish once more as he gunned the momerath down, riddling them with bullets. It didn't kill them, but it did slow them enough to give the Marshals time to swoop in and finish them off.

Without missing a beat, another momerath charged, disheveled hair escaping from a tight bun at the back of its head. It wore an expensive-looking pair of heels, though one had broken, making it walk with a forced limp. A wired headset hung around its neck, leaving the cord dangling in front of its chest. It must have been the receptionist. It bared its teeth with a hiss and dove for Nate's throat, but he was too fast. He dodged back, pulling out of its reach. His sword swung skyward, splitting its skull in half. Alice cringed as blood sprayed the room with each pulse of its temple. It wasn't enough. The former receptionist howled in agony and charged, its cries morphing into a gurgle as they fell out of the 'rath's mangled face. Before it could get any closer, Nate slashed again, decapitating the mutilated monster. It stumbled forward a few more steps before slumping to the ground, no longer able to function.

Without pause, two more momerath launched themselves forward, drawing Indi and her sabre into the fray. Though she was smaller than Ace and Nate, she fought the momerath just as efficiently, immobilizing them with a graceful swish of the sabre across their femoral arteries, and severing their thigh muscles. Another flick of her wrist expertly aimed at their necks ended them.

Now only one momerath remained. This one had been through the ringer. Several fingers were chunked or missing alto-gether from its graying hands. One of its eyes had been violently gouged from its socket, leaving only frayed ends of remaining optical nerves poking from the gaping hole. If the scars running across its face were any indication, it probably tore it out on its own. It pulled angrily at its ears as it stalked towards them, drawing attention to butchered body parts more closely resem-bling blobs of flesh than actual appendages. It wore a mainte-nance jumpsuit with the name *Bill* stitched in the pocket, complete with a set of keys that jangled each time it thrashed its body. "Bill" threw back its head and let out an angry roar before glaring at them through its singular glassy eye, chest heaving through garbled, raspy breaths.

Indi's attack on the last two 'rath had helped clear the room, but it also left Alice exposed and in Bill's direct line of sight. It staggered towards her, its cruel snarl turned gruesome as Alice registered a chunk of skin caught dangling between its rotting teeth. She took a frightened step back, and her shoulders pressed against the wall. Her heart raced as the feeling of being cornered gripped her, shooting panic through her body.

She tightened her grip on her machete. Her mind raced with maneuvers she could use to neutralize the threat. "Let's get this over with," she mumbled, sinking into a low squat, preparing to fight.

Suddenly, a loud yell rang out beside her, and before she could react, a large figure rocketed in front of her, brandishing its sword threateningly at Bill.

"You need to go, Alice," Nate yelled. "We'll handle these guys." He inclined his head, telling her to move. He glanced at her, tossing her a brave smile. That was a mistake. The minute Nate's eyes pulled away from Bill, the momerath charged, hurdling across the room. The momentum of the attack, combined with Bill's bulk, hit Nate full force and knocked him to the ground, pinned beneath the furious 'rath.

Bill sneered at Nate, saliva dribbling from holes in its mouth where teeth should have been. Alice watched in horror as Bill hungrily eyed Nate then raised its arm, pushing back its jumpsuit sleeve. It grinned evilly and brought a razor-sharp nail to its flesh, digging in to puncture its skin. It brutally slashed its arm, drawing a bloody line from wrist to elbow. Bill raised it tauntingly over Nate, watching sadistically as blood pooled in the open wound. Alice's ribs contracted. She couldn't leave him like this.

Ignoring his directive, Alice threw all of her weight against Bill's midsection. She caught it off guard, flinging it off Nate before it could do anything with its tainted blood.

Furious, Bill swung and backhanded her across the face. Her cheek burned as the impact of the slap stung her skin. Bill hit her so hard that her whole body twisted, following the force of the attack. She brought her hand to her face to soothe the wound and felt warm liquid under her fingers. Trembling, she pulled her hand back so she could examine what it was, and saw her fingers were stained with blood. Frantically, she wiped her face, desperate to clear possible contaminants from her skin. She scrubbed until her face was raw, then raised a trembling hand to check her cheek for wounds. If she was cut, she was as good as dead. Her heart raced, threatening to beat out of her chest as her hand brushed smooth, unmarred skin. She exhaled a huge sigh of relief, followed by a small disbelieving laugh. Realizing she was okay, she turned her attention back to Bill, all but forgotten during her momentary panic attack.

Her maneuver with the momerath must have given Nate enough time to regain his bearings because as Alice turned around, she saw Nate and Bill square off, each watching the other with unbridled hatred. Alice tried to stand, but the blow to her head had been aggravated again, and she had to fight to stay on her feet. Nate's eyes darted quickly to her before his glare darkened murderously at Bill. He let out a loud cry and surged forward, hacking at Bill's disfigured body with his broadsword. He moved so fast, Bill only had time to lunge forward, which assisted Nate in completely severing its head from its pudgy body. Bill's head slid from the neck and fell, rolling softly to land at Alice's feet. She kicked it away in disgust and scrambled off the ground, hearing more angry screeches rushing through the halls.

Resounding footsteps thundered down the corridor, followed by a gut-wrenching wave of snarls. There had to be at least twenty momerath pushing and climbing over one another to get to the small room. From where she stood, Alice saw Johnny cross himself and quietly whisper, "*Ay Dios mio.*" Beside him, Ace let out a string of curse words, and Nate clenched his teeth in determination.

"Alice, get out of here, *now*," he commanded, his gaze fixed on the army of momerath in front of him.

"No, I want to help—" she argued, but Nate raised his hand to silence her.

"Fighting is our job." He gripped his sword so tight, his knuckles turned white. "You're here to find a cure."

"But what about you?" Alice's voice trembled.

"Help your sister." His stormy eyes pierced hers. Her stomach lurched, and she wasn't sure if it was fear, adrenaline, or him. Maybe all three.

"While I hate to break up this touching moment," Ace sneered from his corner, "we have a big, nasty problem staring us in the face, and I'd like to take care of it before it bites us in the ass."

Alice's cheeks blazed, but she agreed. This was not the time for sentimentality. She waved meekly to the team as she hastily retreated. "See you guys soon," she said, then pushed her way through the blasted door and into Research Room Five.

21

A lice hurried through the door, closing it after her as best she could. The heavy metal muffled the sounds from the fight taking place in the room she left behind. The stark difference made the dark space feel even more eerie. Slowly, she crept over the large tiled floor, hands outstretched to feel her way through the shadows. The room was musty, and the smell of dirt covered the sterile bleach odor. Everything was quiet except a soft buzzing noise from across the room. Alice followed the sound, a vibration of electricity. Maybe it would lead her to a light or generator.

She followed the buzz until her hands brushed another cool wall. It was windowed at the top with metal paneling on the bottom. Two doors stood next to each other, both with a keypad sitting outside the frame. Peering through the glass, Alice could make out the shapes of what appeared to be rows of shelves and large cabinets in the first room and a series of doors in the second. She didn't expect either to be open, but tested the handles anyway. Locked.

"What now?" She considered entering a code into the keypad

but didn't want to trigger another alarm. She groaned and pounded the door in frustration. The clang of her fist on the metal reverberated softly through the empty room.

Over the echo, the sound of muffled footsteps approached from behind. Alice tightened her grip on her blade and spun to face the threat. Her heart pounded as the shadowy figure approached, shuffling closer until the form of Dr. Abbott was revealed.

"Dr. Abbott! How did you get here?" she hissed. She distinctly remembered him losing his mind then running off in the *opposite* direction. Abbott didn't answer. He stood before her, gaze empty as he brushed his hair behind his ear. His hands trembled so badly that instead of smoothing the white tuft as intended, it only got more tangled. He reached into his pocket and pulled out a small keycard. He offered it to Alice with the same glazed look in his eyes. Cautiously, she moved to take it, but it fell from his violently shaking fingers onto the floor. He looked at it blankly, blinking his eyes as if trying to clear his mind from a daze.

"Shouldn't be here." He stared absently at the card. Without any other notice, he turned to walk away. He raised his wrist to inspect his broken watch. "I was too late," he whispered. "It's not safe."

"What's not safe?" Alice called after him, but the doctor didn't turn back. He ran his hands through his disheveled hair again, mussing it even more.

"In that direction is Hatta, and in that direction..." He shuddered. "March lives there. Visit either you like; they're both mad." His voice trailed off as he disappeared into the Research Room. Alice stared after him, waiting for him to return. When he didn't, she dropped her attention to the keycard lying forgotten on the floor.

She knelt to pick it up. It was a simple identification card with the Borogove Industries logo stamped across the top and a picture of Dr. Abbott in the upper right-hand corner with his name underneath. On the back, there was a special holographic seal in the lower left corner beneath a standard magnetic stripe. The seal shimmered and flashed from green to purple as she flexed the card to examine it. Intrigued, she brought it to the scanner for the door labeled Exam Room A. The card passed over the pad with a small beep and the door let out a loud click before sliding open.

Alice peeked into the room, readying her blade against any unseen threats. She inched forward, heart trapped in her throat. The thrumming generator powered the area, flooding it with white fluorescent light. She squinted her eyes shut, momentarily blinded by its brightness. It had been a long time since she had seen an electrically powered room, and it took her a minute to adjust to the harsh artificial light. When she finally did, she noticed the room was filled with rows of steel tables, and along the back wall were dozens of shelves. Each table held a large metal cage at the end of a long, cleared workspace, and the shelving units were filled with more vacant enclosures.

Alice shivered and crept forward. She didn't realize how cold the room was until a cloud of her own breath puffed in front of her. She rubbed her arms and hurried on, burning with curiosity. Her mouth gaped as she walked through the brilliantly lit room, scouring each cage for signs of life. Each was prepped for inhabitants, but all were empty.

She continued on until, at the end of the third table, she noticed a labeled metal cage. A bright yellow plastic tag was attached to the roof of the enclosure with the word "Dor-Mouse" scrawled across the top in nearly illegible doctor's print. The cage was open. Alice jerked away from the table, hunting for whatever belonged inside. Nothing there. Good.

Worried, she searched for the loose critter. The floor was

clear, so she peeked in the cage again. A picked-over bowl of food lay abandoned inside, along with a full water bottle. She did a double take when she noticed the murky brown shade of the liquid. Alice leaned forward and saw another scribbled label. *Tea?* That couldn't be right. She scanned the table, but it was empty except for an old porcelain teapot.

"Well, I hope the Dor-Mouse is gone—whatever it is," Alice said to herself. "I left my guard cat at h—"

She didn't get to finish her thought. The teapot exploded. At least, that was the best way she could describe it. A loud squeak ricocheted from the spout, followed by a giant white ball of fur bursting from inside. The dramatic motion sent the fragile porcelain crashing to the floor and shattered it into hundreds of pieces.

The thing inside scurried across the table in a frenzy of squeaks. Alice shrieked and jumped away from the demented furball. It slowly settled, revealing an oversized rodent with freakish violet eyes. Still agitated, it scuttled around the table until its mutated gaze landed on Alice. It let out another furious squeak and beelined toward her, claws extended.

Alice cringed and shielded her face, praying her long sleeves would protect her arms. Her eyes squeezed shut involuntarily as she braced for impact, but nothing happened. Slowly, she peeked one eye open, then the other, blinking in surprise at a new red-patterned porcelain teapot in front of her. A large pair of olive-skinned hands clasped the lid shut, struggling as it jerked around with angry squeaks escaping from the spout.

She glanced up at her mysterious savior. A middle-aged man in a white lab coat studied her curiously. He was much taller than her, and she supposed attractive, for an older man. He was also familiar. She racked her brain, trying to pinpoint how she knew him. Before she could place him, he spoke, considering her seriously as he asked, "Why is a raven like a writing desk?"

"Huh?" Alice asked dumbly. Her brain fought to understand

the question, but it was nonsense. She wanted desperately to make *some* sense of the freaky rodent, random teapot, and peculiar stranger, but she only succeeded in giving herself a headache.

"Why is a raven like a writing desk?" the man asked again, over-enunciating each word as if he thought she was slow.

Alice's expression fell into a blank stare for half a moment before she burst into a fit of laughter. She couldn't help it. Over the past few days she had seen and survived things she could never have even imagined and now this eccentric man armed with a porcelain teapot had the nerve to look at her like *she* was crazy. Maybe she was.

Once she regained her composure, she wiped a loose tear from the corner of her eye and exhaled, clearing her throat. "I'm sorry about that." She straightened her shoulders and tossed her bangs from her face to indicate she was calm. "I thought you asked me about a raven and a desk." She let out another small chuckle to show how strange she knew it sounded.

"I did," the doctor said. He set the teapot down on the metal table. It had stopped rattling, and the furious squeaking noises had finally ceased. Alice eyed it warily, wondering if the "Dor-Mouse" had suffocated to death. She wasn't willing to lift the lid to check. The doctor twisted his head, studying her like she was some new discovery he'd stumbled upon. It reminded her of the way Chess looked at her when he thought she said something odd.

She cleared her throat again, this time out of embarrassment. "Oh. Um..." she fumbled, unsure what to say. She noticed the man eyeing her blade and quickly hurried to sheathe it. Even if he was a little kooky, she felt she owed him some courtesy for saving her from the Dor-Mouse. She considered his question, attempting to puzzle out the riddle.

"Both can come in contact with a pen?" she guessed, fully aware the answer was a stretch. Feathered quill pens hadn't been regularly used in ages, and technically were used on paper, but she couldn't think of anything better to offer.

The man frowned as he mulled over her response. "That is incorrect," he said, as if he were administering a diagnosis. He turned from the table and walked towards the shelves at the back of the room. "The answer is there is no answer."

Alice's brow furrowed in disappointment. She liked puzzles that were tricky to solve, but being presented with an intentionally impossible problem irritated her. Still, she trailed after the strange man, drawn to the quandary he provided.

"You seem upset," he observed. He walked along the various cages on the shelving units, trailing them with his fingertips. White rabbits, mice, and even a small kitten were housed in individual cages, bodies tense as they watched him with unnatural electric violet gaze.

Alice paused in front of the kitten. It curled in a tight ball, tail twitching in agitation as it glared back at her. A low growl rumbled from the back of its throat when she peered in to look closer. Remembering the Dor-Mouse, she stepped back to check the latch on the cage. She realized the man had moved on and hurried after him, almost slamming into his back when he stopped abruptly in front of another cage. He looked at her, his head tilted to the side while the corner of his mouth quirked in an amused half smile.

Alice self-consciously dropped her gaze to the floor. Her bangs tickled her eyelashes and she tucked them safely behind her ear. "I just feel so off here," she said evasively. Something about the man unsettled her. Her brain couldn't quite grasp what it was, but even her body reacted to it. Her muscles twitched, itching to move away.

"Oh, you can't help that. We're all mad here," he said. "I'm mad. You're mad—" He reached for the latch to the cat's cage.

His extended arm exposed another Borogove badge, identifying him as Matthew Hatta, M.D.

Recognition flashed through Alice's mind as she remembered the picture on Bug's conspiracy board. Now that she had his name, she felt stupid that she hadn't made the connection sooner. He looked exactly the same as he did in the photo, except he had aged a few years. Even his aloof disposition was the same.

"Wait," she put her hand on his arm to stop him from moving any farther. Disbelief laced her voice as she confirmed. *"You're Matt Hatta?"*

22

U pon Alice's recognition of his name, Hatta's whole demeanor changed. He beamed at her, practically bubbling with excitement. "You've heard of my work?" He leaned in close for her answer.

"Yeah." She edged away from him. "I mean, I saw the article in the newspaper."

Hatta laughed, a mixture of glee and victory. "I knew it was only a matter of time," he murmured. "So, what do you think of my creation?" he asked, watching her like a stray Sector dog begging for scraps.

"Um," Alice stalled, trying to figure out what he was referencing. Abbott had told her he had worked on several successful projects. Was there a different article he was featured in? "Which one?"

The doctor's face scrunched in a frown, marring his handsome features. "Why, the Max Recovery, of course. It's my greatest success."

Alice hesitated. "It was life-changing," she replied honestly, hoping the noncommittal phrasing gave the doctor freedom to take her response however he wanted.

Hatta smiled in approval and she let out a small breath of relief. "That it was, my dear," he agreed. "Do you understand the implications of the findings of my research?" he asked enthusiastically. Her gut twisted. She didn't know how much longer she could evade his questions. Luckily, she didn't have to. Hatta seemed to have asked this merely for dramatic effect. After a brief pause, he continued. "Spinal regeneration, stronger instincts, faster motor function, and that's just the beginning. The improvements made on the human body by the MR-19 are spectacular."

"MR-19..." Alice's blood ran cold.

"Yes." He smiled at her as though she was a confused toddler whose ignorance was endearing. "MR-19 was the clinical name for Max Recovery, but of course that information was not featured in the paper. The press is always more concerned with the ends of a product rather than the actual means taken to accomplish them."

"Was it worth it?" Alice prodded, attempting to align Hatta's concession with the story she had been told by Dr. Abbott. So far, the details matched, but if what Dr. Abbott told her was true, she couldn't understand why Hatta was so proud of the Max Recovery.

"Of course it was!" the doctor exclaimed. A tenuous madness laced his voice. "The MR-19 bonded with the human body in ways we could never have imagined. The potential for advancement is undeniable. There's so much we can learn!"

Did Hatta realize the consequences of the Max Recovery? she wondered. If he did, would he acknowledge it? "What about side effects?" she pressed, trying to decide whether he was overly optimistic or delusional. "Are potential advancements worth so much risk?"

The doctor scoffed. "What risk?" He pretended to examine

the cat in front of him, but Alice saw the spark of anger in his eyes.

She hesitated. It was obvious Hatta was becoming agitated, and she wasn't sure how he would react when confronted. After spending a few days with Dr. Abbott, she wasn't sure if she could handle any more volatile tantrums. She needed to tread carefully. She wished she hadn't put her machete away earlier. It would have been nice to have its comforting weight in her hands. She steadied her breath. "The virus...the momerath..." She trailed off, unwilling to complete the thought once she saw Hatta's stormy disposition darken.

"That's what made the MR-19 so successful!" Hatta exclaimed, pretense forgotten. The cat let out a frightened mew and hunched in the corner of the cage when Hatta's voice rose in passion. "It propelled humanity into an advanced state of being. My serum began the first evolutionary stage the human race has had in a million years!" He raised his hands in the air, celebrating his imagined victory while he watched Alice hungrily for her reaction. She tried to force a smile, but her willful face wouldn't cooperate. Hatta's arms drooped. His hand fell heavily on top of the cage, rattling it and earning an angry hiss from the creature inside. "You disagree." His posture stiffened to stone.

"No!" Alice hurried to mollify his ego. "I just wonder if it's what *everyone* would think. Whether they would choose to be 'advanced' if given the option."

"Who wouldn't choose to be the best version of themselves possible? People, by nature, are narcissistic." He straightened his tie and jacket as if to support his argument.

Alice pursed her lips in thought as she tried to compare his statement to people in her own life. But Hatta hurried on, keen to prove his point.

"Consider this," he said. "Women starve themselves trying to squeeze their curves into size zero dresses. Men pump steroids into their bodies in an attempt to double and triple their muscle structure. Teenage honors students abuse prescribed medications to give themselves an edge when studying for advanced placement tests. All in an unending attempt to fit some unspoken ideal. An ideal I have found and merely need to share."

Alice nodded slowly. She needed Hatta to think she was playing along. Though some of the ice in his demeanor had thawed, he still scrutinized her as if she was a potential threat instead of the adoring ally he had hoped for. She needed to choose her next words carefully. She didn't trust the underlying tension in his posture. It reminded her of a rattler coiled in the underbrush of the desert.

"What if the ideal is not what's best?" she asked. "What people want is not always the same as what they need."

"Yet another benefit of the Max Recovery." Hatta flashed another disarming smile. It was easy to see how he garnered so much support from Borogove. Even though she was slightly terrified of him, his charisma still made her want to understand him.

"People don't know what they need anymore. Desire overshadows basic survival necessities. Mothers can't afford to feed their children, yet they carry designer handbags. Fathers work countless hours of overtime to pay for fancy televisions and cars they have no time to enjoy. The Max Recovery overrides the desire for frivolity and refocuses the brain on what basic instinct requires."

Alice thought about it. Logically, Hatta presented a valid argument. But it seemed too black and white. It seemed flawed. She considered her own past. What would have happened to her if she hadn't been adopted by the Carrolls? As an infant, what control did her basic instinct have to provide her needs? Even if she would have known she needed food and shelter to survive, she couldn't have done anything about it. She thought of all the sacrifices her mother and Dinah made for her. That wasn't self-serving or narcissistic. It was something else entirely. Something Hatta needed to consider.

"What about family?" she asked. "And love?"

A wistful look flitted across Hatta's features before he carefully arranged them back in place. "People get too invested in emotions," he said briskly. "It hinders them from processing information objectively and responding accordingly."

"But without emotions, what's the point?" she asked. Though she rarely got caught up in emotion, it didn't mean she didn't recognize their value.

"Survival!" The doctor pounded his fist against the shelf. The cages resting on top of it rattled, sending the trapped animals in fits of distress. "Meeting our full potential! Embracing the advancements of science!" The doctor got more keyed up with each phrase, until at last, he turned to her with a wild look in his eyes.

Alice took a careful step back to put some space between her and the flustered doctor. Playing on his humanity was obviously not working. Ironically, he responded emotionally, a contradiction that made Alice nervous. She combed her thoughts for an argument, for something to help him see reason.

"If advancement is your ultimate goal," she asked, deliberately choosing each word, "then why haven't you...*evolved* too? Don't you want to experience the progression of humanity yourself?"

"Someone must see in this new era." Hatta spoke like a teacher explaining a challenging concept to a struggling student. "I must maintain my current mindset so I may further my work by analyzing the full effects of MR-19. Only then may I assist the human race in continued advancement." His chest swelled with pride at his imagined destiny.

"Then is this stage really that advanced?" she puzzled. "If they don't have basic reasoning skills, isn't that a step backward?"

Her features twisted into a disbelieving stare. Immediately, she tried to neutralize it, but it was too late. The damage had been done. The doctor had seen through her facade.

Hatta hardened again, his golden eyes flashing with anger. The rest of his body stiffened, reminding Alice of the calm before a storm. When he finally spoke, his voice was terse. "I see. It seems you are not as enamored by my work as I believed." He reached for the agitated kitten and pretended to stroke its back. *What was with all the crazy people in this place?*

"I so hoped to have a protégée," he said mournfully. Her eyes widened in horror. The doctor's eyes narrowed when he saw the look on her face. "But I can see that's not an option." He sighed and scratched the back of his head thoughtfully. Then, without warning, he shot his hand out to grab Alice's arm, locking her in a vise-like grip.

"What are you doing?" she shrieked, furious she had been naive enough to leave her machete in its sheath.

"It seems the only way I can get you to appreciate the advancements I have provided is to have you experience them firsthand." He dragged her to the back of the room where a huge stainless steel counter covered the width of the wall. Medical cabinets hung above it filled with various equipment, vials, and syringes. Alice struggled against the doctor, trying to pull her arm free, but the more she fought, the more his grip tightened around her wrist. He searched through the cabinets with his free hand, muttering to himself as he clumsily knocked its contents from the shelves onto the tile below. The tinkling of shattering glass created a chilling soundtrack to his fervor.

He continued to ramble, but between her frantic attempts to escape, Alice only heard pieces of what he was saying. "Don't understand...brilliant...simple..." Finally, the doctor found what he was searching for. He held it to the light, illuminating a bright indigo serum.

"What is that?" Alice was momentarily paralyzed as she scrutinized the needle. Her arm ached where Hatta's hand circled her wrist. If she lived through whatever was about to happen, she was going to have one heck of a bruise.

"It's a modification to the MR-19 serum I have been working on." Hatta gazed at the liquid in the syringe with adoration. "It is quite impressive. I'm sure you will agree once you experience it for yourself." A maniacal smile distorted his features as he prepped the needle, destroying any trace of his handsome build. Pushing forward on the syringe to dispel excess air, he expelled the smallest drop of the violet liquid.

"The time has come," Hatta murmured, turning to face Alice. He tightened his hold on her arm once more, and she yelped in pain as he pulled her towards him. Her hand throbbed as his hold cut off her circulation. He pressed the needle to her skin, muttering incoherently while his features twisted in glee at the prospect of his newest experiment. "The time has come," Hatta rambled, "to talk of many things—"

Alice couldn't listen to his gibberish anymore. If she did, she would go mad. Her heart beat so hard, she thought it might burst. Blood rushed through her veins carrying a surge of energy with it. She gave her arm one last frantic twist and wrenched it free from Hatta's hold.

Hatta spoke so softly, Alice could barely make out his next words. "No matter," he said, then plunged the syringe into her chest.

Pain seared her chest as the needle pierced her collarbone. She jerked her body to rip the dangling syringe from her chest and smashed it against the floor. She burned with rage as she moved to strike the doctor, but something in his expression stopped her.

Hatta's smile remained plastered on his face, but it was a sculpture crumbling under its own weight. He stared dumbfounded at her collarbone, whispering to himself. "Failed. It failed."

Alice edged away, searching for an escape route. Her mind scrambled as it tried to make sense of all the thoughts swirling inside clamoring for her attention. *Serum, escape, pain, fear.* She was going to be sick.

"Why did it fail?" Hatta demanded, advancing on Alice. "I have tested it extensively, and the modified MR-19 has never failed. What have you done?"

"What?" Alice asked clumsily. Her usually nimble mind was bogged down in information overload.

"Are you deaf? Why do you keep making me repeat myself?" the doctor snarled, his initial shock replaced with searing hatred. He glowered at Alice as if she had personally affronted him. "Why haven't you changed?" he demanded. "The process should have triggered by now!"

"I haven't done anything," Alice whimpered. She could see the doorway she had originally come through. If she could distract Hatta long enough, she could make a break for it. "I don't know what you're talking about."

"Liar!" He surged toward her. Alice flinched back against the wall and her head smashed into solid titanium paneling. The thunderous clang of metal reverberated through her skull, amplifying the pain of impact. *What could possibly be so important to make Borogove reinforce the room like this?* she thought in a dizzy haze. Her stumbling cost her. Unable to defend herself, Hatta clamped his hands around her shoulders, trapping her in his grip once more.

"You have left us in a rather large predicament, my dear," Hatta said, looking as though the "predicament" they were in didn't bother him in the least. "You have made it explicitly clear you do not agree with my work, and unfortunately, my gracious attempt at enlightening you has failed." His features twisted into an expression of forced sympathy as he steered her towards a metal door she hadn't noticed before. She dug her heels against the floor to slow him down, but only succeeded in scuffing the white tile with the rubber sole of her boots.

"Now," he growled ominously, "I have no choice but to get rid of you."

23

Alice struggled against Hatta as he attempted to enter the access code in the paneled locking system. She stomped on his foot as hard as she could, hoping to distract him. Hatta jerked in pain and hit the wrong button, invalidating his entry. It only slowed him, though, and soon, he punched in the code, leaving Alice to watch in terror as he deliberately typed in each number.

3...5...1...6...6...4...8

Alice froze. It was the same number she tried to enter the first time she came to Borogove. How did she know it? Distracted, she abandoned her struggle. The mad doctor used it to his advantage to hustle her quickly into the secondary laboratory.

Motion sensored lights flickered on silently as they entered the adjacent room. Like its neighbor, the air was freezing. Huge puffs of Alice's breath wisped in front of her each time she exhaled, and her nose ached from the frosty air. The layout of this lab was much different from the one next door. Whereas the first room was more suited for research and study, this space was clearly designed for clinical trials. Small sections broke up the larger space, dividing it into individual compartments. Hatta continued to push her through the room, flickering automatic lights to life in each compartment to reveal the contents secured behind the double-sided glass. Each one had an identical layout, complete with hospital bed, curtained changing area, and vital sign monitoring equipment. Otherwise, they were vacant.

Alice continued to fight as Hatta forced her farther into the room, but she was starting to tire. She was physically and mentally exhausted. Her body was quickly reaching its breaking point. "Please don't do this," she begged, unable to hide the fear in her voice.

Hatta spoke through heavy breaths. "I weep for you, truly. I deeply sympathize," he said. Apparently Alice wasn't the only one whose energy was getting used up. Beads of sweat formed on his brow, and his previously immaculate hair had fallen into disarray. Still, he forced Alice forward. Once they reached the final compartment, he pushed Alice in front of him and sang, "Marchie, I have a surprise for you."

In response, something slammed against the metal door, *hard*. The sheer force made it sound like another ContraBand had detonated. Alice sucked in her breath. "You don't have to do this," she whimpered.

"Unfortunately, I do," Hatta answered. The pity in his voice didn't match the smile on his lips. "You should take solace in the fact that you are about to come face-to-face with my greatest creation."

The crashes from behind the steel door grew more frenzied as they neared the compartment. The thing behind the door beat against it repeatedly, trying to break free.

"Calm down, Marchie, I'm almost there," Hatta scolded, but leaned closer to Alice and laughed, whispering gleefully, "She always gets so impatient when I visit."

Alice responded by jerking her neck to smash her forehead against his skull. Hatta was quick, though, and pulled away, smiling and and *tsking* at her as if she were a naughty toddler. They were finally close enough for the sensor in the miniature room to flicker the florescent light to life. It illuminated the compartment and Alice immediately wished it hadn't. She stared in horror at the grisly scene unveiled before her.

The tiny space was a funhouse mirror reflection of the others they had passed. The other compartments were pristine, neatly organized clinical rooms. This one looked as though a bomb had gone off inside. The bed in the center had been forcefully overturned, its metal siding twisted and jutted out at unnatural angles from the base, as if someone tried to use the bars for origami. The bedsheets were shredded and scattered around the room, littering the floor in a disturbing patchwork quilt. The vitals machine was flipped on its side and had a fist-sized hole punched through the plastic monitor screen. Fist marks crunched the metal side paneling, indicating it had been used more frequently as a punching bag than medical equipment.

Most unsettling was the blood. Bronze stains covered every surface of the otherwise white room. Streaked handprints climbed up the walls and across the ceiling. Alice didn't even want to think how they reached that high. The floor was evidence from a nightmarish crime scene. Pools of dried blood turned the floor into sinister lakes, with floating pieces of shredded bedding glued in place by the sticky substance. Footprints led in and out of the bloody mess, spreading gruesome crimson stains around the room. Alice dry heaved at the sight.

Hatta didn't notice. He gazed beatifically into the compartment, staring at the figure inside with pure adoration. "Isn't she beautiful?" he breathed in rapture. Against her better judgment, Alice turned to follow his stare. She instantly regretted it, swearing her curiosity was going to be the end of her. If possible, the figure pounding against the door was even more repulsive than the massacred room.

"What is *that?*" Alice pressed against Hatta's body as she backpedaled away from the figure. Momerath were awful, but they had nothing on this...*thing.* Panic seized her, making it hard to breathe. Her muscles revolted and shot searing pinpricks of fire twitching through every fiber in her body. Her brain screamed to get away, but her eyes latched onto the nightmare in front of her, afraid if she let it out of her sight, the monster would snatch her.

And it was a monster. Worse than anything even Alice's overactive imagination could have dreamed. It crouched naked, revealing a humanoid body that had mutated into an amorphous figure. She wouldn't have even known it was a she had Hatta not just described her that way. Her whole torso was smooth; even her belly button was missing. The only thing that could be seen in her midsection was her bony, protruding ribcage.

Her skin looked like the sludgy algae that grew in the abandoned backyard pools of the Sector: a dirty, mottled gray. Her figure was so emaciated, every edge of every bone could be seen, making her body appear disjointed and angular. Especially her skull. It was massive, swollen like an overfilled balloon floating above a narrow strand of string. Her face, like the rest of her body, was unblemished, completely smooth. Her brows and eyelashes had all fallen out, and her ears had merged into slits on the sides of her head. Even her lips were indiscernible, their soft pink flesh replaced with the same sickening gray skin that covered the rest of her body.

She glared at Alice through pitch-black orbs and let out an earsplitting screech, howling like a rabid coyote. She slammed her fists against the window, keeping her forehead pressed against the glass while her face moved from side to side, staring down Alice like a hungry hawk.

"This is what mankind can be once we unlock everyone's full potential," Hatta said proudly, pulling Alice's attention from March's grotesque figure. He squeezed her shoulders reassuringly. "Don't worry, my dear, the glass will hold."

On cue, March kicked her bony leg against the wall, rattling the entire compartment. She hovered against the glass in the same predatory stance, salivating. Hatta was unconcerned. "This lab was made with state-of-the-art material," he explained. "Knowing the... *intense* nature of the clinical trials, Borogove was very supportive in equipping my research facility with high level security equipment. It has come in very handy."

Hatta's smug demeanor was almost too much for Alice to handle. She wished she could close her eyes and scream until everything disappeared. *Not likely,* she thought, supplying a much needed reality check.

She was the only one who could get herself out of this, but she needed time to form a plan. She had to keep Hatta talking. For once, she was glad her inquisitive nature constantly bombarded her mind with questions. She blurted out the first that came to mind. "Borogove knew about this?"

"In a matter of speaking." Hatta smiled. "The CEO of Borogove and I had an unspoken agreement when I began the Max Recovery project. Although I suppose it began sooner than that."

"How much sooner?" Alice prompted, working hard to sound interested.

"When I began working for Borogove. They sought me out directly after I graduated medical school, you know," Hatta said arrogantly, as if it explained everything. Alice tried to force an awed expression. Her face obeyed for once, and Hatta continued his story, delighted to have an audience. "They read my dissertation on ethics in medicine and felt I would be a good fit for the company. Soon after, they assigned me to my first project, a trial drug for eradicating terminal cancer. That particular project had been under evaluation for some time already. I was simply tasked with working underneath the head scientist for the project, Dr. Ian Carroll."

Alice choked. Hatta couldn't have just said what she thought he did. It was impossible. *Dad didn't work for Borogove. He had his own practice in Fountain Hills. We visited him there...*

Memories swam in her head as pieces of a puzzle she didn't know existed fell into place. *The familiarity she felt when she saw Hatta's picture for the first time... Manxoma, the funny name she had heard the stranger mention at her father's office...the stranger who was actually Hatta, not just someone who looked like him... knowing the access code to the Research Room without realizing it...*

It was too much. Her knees gave out underneath her and she sank to the floor, turning to dead weight in Hatta's arms. She almost hit the ground before he caught her.

"My dear, are you alright?" Hatta asked. "You look positively dreadful."

Funny he cares, Alice thought, *seeing as he brought me here to kill me.*

"W-what did you do with Dr. Carroll?" She forced the words from her desert-dry throat.

"At first, not much. Though my dissertation impressed some bigwigs at Borogove, I was still new to the field. I was assigned the task of administering medication and observing reactions. The drug, Vorpal, had already passed its initial testing phase and had just begun human trials. Per company policy, all candidates chosen had to be legal adults suffering from the ailment being tested. It made for a very dreary work environment.

"Day after day, I observed husks of people, waiting for any reaction from their bodies. Any will to live. None of them tried hard enough. After two years of insufficient results, Borogove was ready to pull the project.

"Throughout this time, I worked closely with Dr. Carroll, and we built a rather strong rapport. Although I was still technically his junior, he realized we were very similar in our ambitions and took me in, an apprentice of sorts.

"When Carroll got the final word the project would be shut down, I was the one he informed first. Naturally, he was displeased. After investing so much time and energy into a project like that, failure is never really an option.

"It was during this conversation I brought an idea to Dr. Carroll's attention. Initially, I was hesitant to share on the off-chance that he would oppose. But once the funding was pulled, what else was there to lose?

"My hypothesis was that our test subjects were too tired, too used up to be of sufficient use to our research—their bodies simply could not regenerate enough, even with the assistance the medication provided. I theorized that utilizing younger test subjects with newer, fresher cells might be the missing piece to completing the clinical trial. However, because of the restrictions provided by Borogove, it was virtually impossible."

Alice didn't want to listen anymore. She felt nauseous, like she had gotten punched in the gut and everything sitting in her stomach was fighting to come back out. Her hands were clammy and a cold sweat covered her entire body. She started to shiver—whether from the cold or what Hatta was saying, she couldn't tell. Hatta either didn't notice or he didn't care.

"Dr. Carroll was intrigued. He knew what we were trying to accomplish was bigger than individual lives. We could not allow simple-minded reservations of bleeding heart programs to hinder the progress of science, so we took matters into our own hands. Unfortunately, this presented some...*unique*...circumstances for our research, as the program had officially been disbanded and the Vorpal resources reallocated to other Borogove projects. We took it upon ourselves to overcome the situation and found test subjects not sanctioned by the company. This gave us the opportunity to further our research, but our methods were somewhat restricted.

"It was a very frustrating time. Lack of sufficient assets dramatically slowed our progress, and the test subjects did not take to the trial very well. Children had the ability to regenerate their cells quicker, but it seemed the cocktail of chemicals that formed the medicine did too much damage to their organs for their cells to rebuild fast enough. After each failure, we had to recalculate the chemical composition and start again. Of course, once that happened, we also had to find a new subject. It was exhausting."

Hatta sighed as if to portray just how much the effort put him out. She couldn't have cared less. She was too concerned with the "failures" he mentioned—each one a dead child. She wondered how many there had been. Rage replaced her queasiness and she felt a fire burn in the pit of her stomach.

She was going to kill this man.

"I have to admit," Hatta continued, oblivious to the rage coursing Alice's veins. "Dr. Carroll's fervor for success was even greater than my own. He made a particularly strong effort to procure test subjects and convinced his young wife to adopt a child. It hadn't been terribly difficult. Apparently, they had been having some difficulty with conception. Regardless, he procured another healthy specimen, and when she was old enough, he used her as a test subject for our most recent trial."

"You're lying!" Alice exploded. The scream burst from her lungs before she could reign it in. She jerked her elbow back into Hatta's gut as hard as she could. He doubled over, gasping for air, giving Alice the opportunity to put some distance between them.

Finally free, she ripped her sword from its sheath, swinging it around to the front of her body in a promise to defend herself. Before, she would have run. But now, she was going to fight.

"That's a lie," Alice snarled, her voice deadly quiet. "Dr. Carroll would have never done that. There's no way he would have used some experimental drug on Dinah."

"Dinah. Why, that was her name, wasn't it? How did you—" Hatta paused, slowly straightening his posture to full height. Recognition dawned on him and he gaped at Alice, wonder in his amber eyes as he searched hers. "It couldn't be." His features lit with glee at his newest discovery. "You certainly look the same. I never would have considered. But then, why wouldn't you be—"

"Yes. Dinah was her name," Alice snapped. "She was—*is*—my sister. But that doesn't matter because you're *lying*. My father would have never done anything like that to her."

Hatta watched Alice thoughtfully, uncharacteristically silent. He seemed more amused than concerned by her ire, which only angered her further. "Wouldn't he? How much do you really know about *your father*? Biologically, that statement isn't even accurate." A smile flitted across his face at the opportunity to gloat his superior knowledge.

"I know he wouldn't do *that*! He loved us." But even as she said it, Alice felt doubt. *Did he really love you, Alice?* her traitorous conscience goaded. *He left before you even had a chance to remember anything about him. That doesn't sound like love to me.*

Hatta's smile widened at her turmoil and he took a cautious step toward her. Registering the threat, Alice tightened her grip on her sword and commanded as much authority as she could muster. "Don't come any closer."

Hatta raised both hands in a non-threatening gesture as he fell back. "Loved you, didn't love you. It is of no concern. The fact of the matter is that it happened. Dinah almost didn't make it, but soon she recovered. Come to think of it, *she* was the first real breakthrough we had in the Vorpal experiment for quite some time. However, as luck would have it, not long after, Dr. Carroll and I had a bit of a disagreement and—you will be pleased to note, I'm sure—we parted ways."

Alice's eyes narrowed to slits at the complete tone of disregard Hatta had for her family, but she held her tongue, refusing to entertain the conversation further. When she declined to reply, he let out a disappointed sigh.

"But you're not really interested in any of this, I can see. And I have yet to answer your original question." He spoke briskly, his interest piqued again. "You asked about March." He gestured back to the monster behind them. She still leaned flat against the wall, scrutinizing them like a curious, disfigured puppy.

"I don't care about your train wreck of a science fair project," Alice sneered, still furious at the doctor's accusations.

"That's too bad." Hatta pouted. "Because she cares about you." He took two more steps back, reaching the door to the front of the room. Alice hadn't noticed he had been slowly stepping away from her the entire time they had been talking and had let him distance himself too much. Before she could stop him, he escaped out the front door to the Research Room and slammed it shut, locking her inside.

Alice swore as the mechanical female voice she had come to hate chimed, *"Auto-lock override engaged. Doors secured."* She was stuck. She searched the room, looking for something she could use to break open the door. She was interrupted when static crackled overhead then tuned into Hatta's smug croon.

"It's too bad you didn't want to work with me, Alice. That is who you are, isn't it?" She clenched her teeth as Hatta's gleaned knowledge of her life echoed off the titanium walls of the research room. "You were the second adopted Carroll. What an interesting development for me to have stumbled upon. It isn't going to matter much longer, though, I'm afraid. Marchie is hungry and she has been waiting so very patiently."

As her name echoed around the empty room, March attacked the wall with renewed vigor. Her fists clanged against the reinforced windows, dulled by a layer of Plexiglass. Her screams were distorted by the heavy plastic, but they still shrilled in Alice's ears. She shuddered.

"You should have been nicer to her, Alice. She really is an exquisite creature. She didn't start out that way, but as time passed, her evolution was perfected. Granted, it took some additional work on my part, but I was more than willing to put in the time and attention required to help her meet her full potential. There have been sacrifices along the way, some greater than others..."

Another roar from March's room made Alice twist to stare at the worked-up beast. Her eyes fell on a large pile sitting in the corner of the room where March's compartment met the front wall. The white heap stood as high as Alice's hip, formed by disheveled lab coats stacked on top of each other in disarray. Scattered among the pile of coats were a handful of blue maintenance jumpsuits like the one Bill wore. Streaks of blood dotted the garments, leaving few recognizable from the others that had been completely stained and ruined.

Following her gaze, Hatta amended his statement. "Yes, well, *most* sacrifices were greater than mine," he said when she raised a trembling hand to her mouth to stifle her scream. "Marchie's metabolism just increased so much since she first tried the Max Recovery, and nothing seems to satisfy her. It's intriguing. She can go for months without sustenance with no adverse side effects, but given the opportunity, she will gorge herself unceasingly. And it has been several weeks since she last ate. She must be starving."

Hatta's cruel laugh rang through the room, all but covering a high-pitched electronic keening through the speaker system. Inside the room, Alice heard the tinny clank of the heavy latch click open followed by the creak of the large metal door. The muffled roars and bangs coming out of March's enclosure for the last five minutes were suddenly louder and clearer, no longer suppressed behind reinforced steel. March was free.

WHO STOLE THE TARTS

24

A lice scoped the room, sizing up the space she had to work
with. It was mostly empty, an observation bay for the
cluster of exam rooms. On the upside, there was nothing in the
area for her to trip over. The downside: there was nothing she
could use as a barrier between her and the monster careening
towards her. She choked her grip on her machete, holding it
steady as her arms trembled with excess adrenaline coursing
through her veins.

In a flash, March shot at her at full speed. A terrible shriek
ripped through her vocal chords, piercing Alice's eardrums. Alice
winced in pain but held her position, lowering to a crouch.
Energy crackled through her body, heightening all her senses.
The cool air of the room swept over her face, counteracting the
flush of heat covering her body. The smell of blood permeated
the death-room, saturating the air and leaving a tinge of copper
on her tongue. Alice heard each pounding step March took as she
approached; the scraping of her overgrown nails across the floor's
surface sent shivers down her spine.

Time seemed to stop as Alice focused on March. Her grimy

skin, razor-sharp teeth, and soulless eyes were those of an unholy demon: a monster that should never have been created. But as she confronted the beast, a strange calm swept over her conscience.

Closing the distance between them, March dove for Alice's throat. But Alice was ready. Her counterstrike forced March to dive to the side and abandon her attack to avoid getting sliced in half.

That was different. Apparently, Hatta's modification gave her a greater sense of self-preservation than ordinary momerath. But her temper hadn't improved any. Infuriated by being deprived of her prey, March let out a savage cry and lunged again, throwing her entire body into the maneuver.

Alice expected her rebound. She struck again, splitting March's arm in half. Sludgy blood poured from the wound and March howled in surprised agony. Incensed, she attacked with more fervor, furiously slashing at Alice to reach any part of her she could. March arced her spine, striking like a rattlesnake, her body a blur as she lashed at Alice's face. Alice barely kept March's bloodstained nails from clawing her eyes out. But she didn't escape the attack completely. March hit her machete, splintering it into tiny shards. She was completely defenseless.

A metallic whine whistled through the room, interrupting the battle. "You'll have to do better than that, Alice." Hatta's gloating crackled over the speaker. "March is the height of evolution. And you're just...you. Come to think of it, that's not really a fair fight at all. Too bad," Hatta said, not sounding sorry at all.

"Abbott was right. You really *are* a prick," she muttered. She didn't have time for Hatta's running commentary. She needed to find a weapon, fast. The sound of her master's voice had given March momentary pause, but once the loudspeaker clicked off, her wrath returned to Alice. She glared wickedly, her eyes unmoving as she dragged her tongue across her wounded forearm, licking clean the clumpy, blackened blood oozing from the gash. A hissing laugh escaped from behind her broken, jagged teeth as her lips curled in a sadistic smile.

She launched at Alice again, vaulting the space between them. Alice dropped back, but March's reach was too long for her to escape unscathed. She raked her fingernails against Alice's collarbone, from shoulder to sternum. An agonized scream ripped from Alice's throat as fire seared through her wound.

Alice saw red. From where she stood, she had a clear view of the abandoned exam room and March's destroyed hospital bed. The metal bars from its side panel welding jutted in the air, their splintered ends glinting dangerously in the dim light. If she could break one of the pieces loose, it could work as a weapon. March stood between her and the door, obstructing her path. Without considering the repercussions, she dove for the room, somer-saulting across the floor between March's legs.

Alice's reckless charge caught March off guard, leaving her only enough time to slash wildly at her as she tumbled by. Her reach was too high. Alice swept clear under her outstretched arms and slid safely into the exam room.

In her rush to reach the bed, Alice stepped in the middle of one of the massive pools of blood covering the floor. It was fresher than she thought, and she slid through the red liquid. She almost fell flat on her face, but narrowly caught herself, supporting her body with her forearms, mere inches above the blood puddle. She tried not to gag as her nose was assaulted by the heinous odor. Taking a deep breath, she urged herself to reach the bed. Grip-ping the twisted frame, Alice yanked the railing to wrench it free. Behind her, March's heavy footsteps scraped closer. Alice pulled again, disjointing the metal weld. It bent under her weight, but she wasn't strong enough to force it apart. The metal remained firmly attached to the bed. March charged nearer, close enough for Alice to hear her gasping breaths over the violent drumming of her pulse.

Come on, come ON! Alice yanked desperately on the frame. *If you can't break this free, you're going to die.*

Unbridled panic shot jolts of raw energy to her tired arms. A fresh burst of stamina revitalized her and she gave one more last-ditch effort to loosen the metal paneling. She twisted the bar, praying it would come free.

The metal groaned in protest and broke free from the bed. Alice spun around, holding the jagged pole protectively in front of her. March had been steadily closing in, charging with inhuman speed. She was moving so fast, it was impossible for her to stop when Alice brandished her weapon. Forward motion and momentum pushed her straight ahead, directly onto the rusted railing. Physics could only explain how the pole pierced so far up March's body, crushing an anguished screech from her impaled lungs. The ghastly sound reverberated through Alice's eardrums until it was drowned in March's tainted blood flooding through her punctured lungs.

March's bottomless eyes widened in a mixture of shock and pain. Her arms writhed, still clawing and swiping weakly in Alice's direction, fighting to catch her. Finally, a gurgling breath shuddered through her body, spraying bloody spittle as she exhaled. Her remaining strength faded and her arms fell. A soft whine escaped from deep within her throat as she stared ahead, her eyes fixed unblinkingly on Alice. Her gaze held until, suddenly, her head dropped, hanging limply from where she had been skewered. Disgusted, Alice dropped the railing and pulled away, staring at the mutilated mess in front of her.

Ear-splitting feedback ricocheted out of the speakers, immersing Alice in an endless keening. Hatta's voice cut through the system, shrieking into the microphoned loudspeakers, maxing out the wiring. The light flickered on, revealing another darkened window made of double-sided glass. Hatta stood on the other side, seething. His amber eyes were wild with rage, and his meticulous appearance was completely disheveled. Previously styled hair stuck up in tufts around his head, and his silk tie hung crooked over a half-tucked button-down.

The light shining on the glass reflected Hatta's unkempt image, spurring the mad doctor to compose himself. Hastily, he straightened his tie and made a weak attempt at slicking back his hair. His features tightened as he tried to manufacture a calm presence, but the tension in his muscles was palpable, a spring ready to snap.

"It seems you've found a weakness in my creation," he said, voice eerily composed. It didn't match the furious glint of fire blazing in his golden eyes. "Maybe now you can solve my riddle." He scrutinized her through the window. "Why is a raven like a writing desk?"

"You said there was no answer to that question," Alice replied icily. She was getting tired of Hatta's nonsense.

"In actuality, it seems there is," Hatta spoke, an evil smile creeping over his lips. "Both a raven and a writing desk can be destroyed. As can you." He lifted his hands to press a button on the keypad outside the door. A shrill, pulsing screech reverberated through the halls of Borogove. "I think it's time for a tea party, my dear." He smoothed his unruly hair once more and adjusted his lab coat over his shoulders. "Unfortunately, I won't be able to stay. Do give my regards to our guests. I should think they'll be here any minute." He gave a small wave and pressed the keypad again, shrouding the window in darkness.

Alice was once again alone in the remains of the Research Room. Her ears throbbed with the unending cry of Hatta's alarm. Hoping to disable the wretched noise, she took the end of her homemade weapon and speared it into the speakers, as hard as she could. There was a quick popping sound, and the wailing stopped, ending in a low moan as the speaker died. The ghost of the signal whined in her ears until it was overtaken by the snarls and yells of oncoming momerath.

"You've *got* to be kidding me!" Alice groaned. "Can't a girl catch a break?" A loud scrape on the other side of the door warned her she was no longer alone.

"Of course not." She rolled her eyes at the unappreciated irony. "That would make my life too easy." She stepped away from the door, trying to give herself the best vantage point in case her barricade fell.

The momerath arrived, slamming their bodies into the metal door, pounding relentlessly to batter it down. It took several minutes, but soon the door began to weaken. A final crash hit the steel and it pulled away from its paneling with a tired groan. The gap it made between the door and the jamb wasn't wide; the momerath would have to bottleneck in to get to her. It would slow them down at least. She would use it to her advantage.

A rustle behind the door warned that her visitors had almost pushed through the cramped space. Alice raised her pole to bash their skulls in, but paused when she saw a familiar patch of honey blond hair glint in the light.

"What were you saying about breaks?" Nate flashed her a brilliant smile as he stood to greet her.

Alice's knees buckled with relief. "You made it!" She beamed at him, then flushed self-consciously when she saw him staring back at her, a funny look on his face.

Ace squeezed his bulky body through the door with an ugly sneer on his face. He pushed between Nate and Alice on his way in, roughly separating them. Indi slowly trailed in behind him; her pretty bronze skin was ashen and her cheeks streaked with silent tears.

"Where's Johnny?" Alice asked when he didn't fall in after the others. Indi let out a strangled sob and fell to the ground, dropping her head between her knees as she dissolved into messy tears. Nate hurried over to her, and crouched beside her in an attempt to calm her down. To his credit, even Ace looked upset, shifting uncomfortably as he watched her devastation.

"He didn't make it," Nate said gently, his hand light on Indi's shoulder. "We were way outnumbered. I've never seen that many momerath in one place. We almost didn't make it." A gut-wrenching shriek ricocheted down the halls. Nate dropped his head in defeat. Alice knew what he was thinking. They couldn't fight much longer.

"No time to talk." Ace brandished his battle-axe. "Snap her out of it. She's gotta have her head in the game."

Nate's eyes narrowed, but he leaned forward and whispered in Indi's ear. She didn't lift her head from where it was buried in her knees, but she nodded before slowly uncurling herself. She brusquely wiped her tear-stained face with the palms of her hands and drew her weapon. She spared one withering glare at Ace, then faced the door, a professional killer at the ready.

"Nate, I can't stay," Alice interrupted. If she waited to clear out the 'rath, she would lose Hatta. That couldn't happen. She wasn't done with him yet. "I still have to find the antidote."

"What the hell have you been doing this whole time?" Ace roared. He stormed towards her, his oversized muscles bunching as he clenched his fists in outrage. "We're risking our asses so you can find this supposed cure, and you're off playing games!"

Alice stared at Ace in disbelief. A harsh laugh escaped, then burst forth a dam of uncontrollable giggles. Her sore ribs protested, and slowly, she settled, wiping a stray tear from the corner of her eye.

Ace eyed her warily, as if she had lost her mind. Her hysterics subsided, Alice leveled a steely glare at him. "Trust me," she snarled, "it has been anything but fun." She turned to Nate, pointedly ignoring the Marshal behind her. "Please, Nate, I have to go."

The muscles in Nate's jaw tightened. The last attack had clearly taken a large toll on them, but he nodded. "Our orders were to assist you in finding the antidote. That's what we're going to do." His voice was gentle as he addressed her, but in an instant, it filled with authority. "Ace, Indi, get in formation. We have a bit of a vantage point, let's use it. Indi, give Alice your sword."

Alice's body sagged in relief. "Thank you, Nate." The sleek blade would be much easier to wield than the broken bed frame. She thanked them all—even Ace, begrudgingly—then turned to go. Her plan was to sneak out the door to the adjacent room in the back and find Hatta. She remembered the code he had. She would use it to follow him.

"Alice," Nate called before she stepped away. "I don't know how much time we're going to be able to buy you. Hurry."

Alice nodded. Outside the Research Room, raging shouts grew louder as the summoned horde drew nearer. She would hurry. Dinah needed her, and she was *so* over playing in this madhouse.

25

A lice tore through the room, setting off a chain reaction of flickering lights in each compartment she passed. At the door, she punched in Hatta's code, smashing her finger against each button as fast as she could. She ignored the mechanical voice as it granted her access to the research laboratory and burst into the room, blade raised to attack.

The room was quiet. Still. A tall figure stood among the rows of tables, leaning to examine one of the occupied metal cages. Distracted by the noise, he turned to greet her, resting his hand on the metal latch.

"Oh, it's you." Hatta's grin curled in surprised amusement.

"Yeah, well, I guess I'm not like a raven *or* a writing desk," Alice sniped, eyeing him warily. It didn't matter how civilized he was acting, he had tried to kill her. It wasn't something she would soon forget.

Hatta drummed his fingers against his mouth. "Unfortunate, to say the least. I was so hoping I'd found the answer to my riddle."

Alice let out an unattractive snort. "Yeah? Well, sorry about that. Guess your monster missed out. *Darn.*" She appreciated she hadn't lost her penchant for sarcasm. *At least some things are sacred,* she thought as she advanced on the doctor. She gripped the sabre tight in her hand, trying to accustom herself to its light weight. She couldn't blindly attack. She needed to be precise.

Another superior smile flittered across Hatta's expression. "It's not actually you they want, Alice, it's your blood. Really, anyone's blood. The virus, as it has been so *inconsiderately* named, needs the supplementation of fresh blood cells to thrive. Once new blood has been ingested, it bonds with the host and enhances their abilities—their strength, endurance, speed—"

"Their complete lack of emotion or regard for others?" Alice finished in a sickly-sweet voice.

"Oh, Alice," Hatta chuckled. He shook his head good-naturedly at her impertinence. "You have such a unique way of looking at things." He smiled at her fondly.

"That's what Dinah tells me," Alice deadpanned. Her heart thumped in her chest. She was almost close enough to reach him. *Just a few more steps and—*

"And what would Dinah say if I had an antidote for the effects of MR-19?" Hatta asked, hands in his coat pockets, as easily as if he was discussing the weather.

Alice stopped dead in her tracks. *He doesn't have an antidote,* she reasoned. *He couldn't—he wouldn't. He doesn't think this is something that needs to be fixed, remember?* She grimaced. If there was a chance there was an antidote, she needed to take it. She lowered her sword in an attempt to show good faith.

Hatta drew a large syringe from his jacket pocket. A bright green substance sloshed around the glass barrel, and the large needlepoint wickedly reflected the light of the room. "It's no secret I do not see Max Recovery in the same light you do. However, I am a scientist. And as such, I see the validity in having a complete understanding of one's area of study. A microbiologist knows the benefits and dangers of different types of bacterium. A geneticist knows the strengths and weaknesses of various genes. In my field, I must know how to apply and reverse medicinal effects." He paced around Alice, creeping behind her to stand beside another cage. He bumped it, stirring the white rat inside into a fit of crazed squeaks as it thrust itself repeatedly against the door of the cage. Alice watched it warily, shivering as she remembered the mutated Dor-Mouse.

"Alice! Watch out!" a husky voice cried, tearing her gaze from the deranged rodent. Chess stood in the front entryway Dr. Abbott had originally opened for her. A relieved smile sprang to her face when she recognized her friend, but it was chased away by the look of terror on his face. Automatically, she lashed out her arm. It struck Hatta, sending a razor-sharp scalpel spiraling to the floor. It clattered against the ground as it skidded to the book-shelves.

Hatta snarled as he lost grip of his weapon. "It's very rude of him to come and spoil the fun," he seethed, clutching his arm where Alice hit him.

"I thought it was a party," Alice retorted, eyeing the scalpel. It wasn't far. If she moved fast enough, she could get it before Hatta did. Instinctively, she dove, sliding across the floor with her arms outstretched as an indiscriminate yell burst from her lips.

Hatta lunged too, but the scalpel was too far from his reach. By the time his hand brushed against the base of the shelving unit, Alice was on her feet, scalpel in hand.

"Looks like I've got the favors," she taunted.

A brief movement beside Alice grabbed her attention. She startled when she saw Chess standing beside her. *How does he move so fast?*

"Hey, Xena. Still doing your ridiculous battle cries, I see," he teased as he playfully elbowed her in the arm.

A flush burned Alice's cheeks. She fought to keep her face

stern as she stared the doctor down. "While I appreciate the help, this is *really* not the time for jokes," she said dryly, sight set on Hatta. She didn't know what else the doctor had up his sleeves—or in his pockets—and she wasn't about to make the same mistake twice. The doctor's attention, however, had completely abandoned Alice in favor of Chess. He stood rigid, the color drained from his face as if he had seen a ghost.

"Eoghan, what are you doing here?" he asked, his voice barely above a whisper. If the room hadn't been so still, Alice never would have heard him. "You shouldn't be here."

"Trust me," Chess said. His brows knotted together as he glared back at the doctor. "If it was my choice, I wouldn't be." He tipped his head toward Alice. "I'm here for her."

"Why?" Hatta appraised Alice once again, his scientific mind whirling to solve his newest conundrum.

"Because she needed my help and I made a promise. Not that you would know anything about that." Icicles dripped off his words.

"Wait, what?" Alice interrupted. Her thoughts were disjointed, as if she had walked in at the middle of one of Lewis's new reports back in the Sector. She understood fragments of what was going on, but she was missing a piece of vital information that tied everything together. Chess sighed and scratched the back of his head, his frustrated tell.

"I've known Dr. Hatta for a really long time, Alice," he spoke slowly, choosing each word carefully. He choked over the next ones. "He's my father."

"Wait, what?" Alice repeated stupidly. She didn't have any brainpower to spare crafting witty remarks. She was too busy trying to reconcile Chess's revelation with everything else she had learned in the past week.

Alice stared at the two men. Standing in the same room, it was impossible to deny the family resemblance. She couldn't believe she hadn't pieced it together on her own. Both Chess and Hatta—*his father*—had the same tall, lanky build and rugged features. Hatta had the filled-in look of a grown man, but their facial expressions were identical. Everything, from Roman nose to strong jawline, was the same. Even their hair was similar, dusty ash gray, although Hatta's was generously sprinkled with streaks of white. But it was their eyes that confirmed everything— matching almonds colored in a hypnotic shade of amber. Alice looked from boy to man, amazed how identical pairs of eyes could be so different. Chess's were always full of mischief and life, but every time she looked in Hatta's, she only saw cold calculation.

"Only in the loosest sense of the term," Chess hurried to explain. "Really the only thing he's ever done for me was pass on his DNA. Right, Dad?" He glared at the older version of himself, daring him to respond.

Hatta appeared to be waging an internal battle with himself. He hadn't removed his gaze from Chess, and now the rest of his body stood frozen by an invisible force. "You weren't old enough, Eoghan, you couldn't understand," he said. "My work was imperative, but you were important too." His voice trailed off, relinquishing any communication to the pleading in his eyes.

Alice watched the scene unfold in awe, and all her missing puzzle pieces began to fall in place. She snapped them together, clutching to every bit of logic she could.

Chess scoffed, but Alice saw the hurt he hid behind his callous mask. "How can you even say that to me?" he yelled at Hatta. "Your work always came first. I never even stood a chance."

"Don't be childish. I've made sacrifices for you before," the doctor said curtly, his former emotion beginning to fade. "In fact, your friend may appreciate hearing this story as well." A trace of his characteristic smugness tugged at the corners of his lips. The scientist was back.

"I was just telling Alice about my work with Dr. Carroll and his pet project. She didn't seem to believe me, but maybe this will convince her." He took his gaze from Chess for the first time since he had begun speaking to look at Alice. "Eoghan was part of the experiment, too."

Chess froze, and Hatta's smile widened, pleased to be on the offensive once again. "What do you mean?" she asked.

"As I mentioned before, Dr. Carroll made admirable sacrifices for his research to obtain test subjects for his project. Although that particular trial was a failure, we gained valuable insights. Once it concluded, we needed another body. Obviously, it was still very difficult to secure resources. Soon, Dr. Carroll began questioning my dedication. I needed to prove my commitment."

"So you brought in your son," Alice breathed in horror. She peeked at Chess. He looked like he had been slapped in the face. Apparently, this was new information for him too.

A fleeting pang of regret flitted across Hatta's expression. "I did what needed to be done for the progress of science. I brought Eoghan to Borogove and administered a round of the newest Vorpal mixture, VRPL-16, I believe." He turned to Chess. "You wouldn't remember any of this, of course. You were an infant when I brought you in, hardly able to walk."

Alice was convinced Hatta was evil. He just admitted to his own son he had used him as a human guinea pig with no qualms whatsoever. She was going to be sick. Beside her, Chess stood in stunned silence. For once, he had no snarky remarks. She couldn't imagine how he felt. She reached out and squeezed his hand to subtly remind him he wasn't alone. His hand was clammy against her cool skin and he trembled so hard, it made her arm shake.

"After the first round of the serum, you had a terrible allergic reaction. Within minutes of being given the Vorpal, you broke out in hives and your throat sealed shut and almost collapsed. We had to inject you with epinephrine to keep you alive. It was the worst ten minutes of my life." His voice broke with genuine emotion. He coughed and tried to discreetly wipe the corner of his eye. "I decided then, I couldn't continue any longer. I waited until you were completely healed, then shared my sentiments with Dr. Carroll. We parted ways, and I went on to begin the Manxoma project. From there, as they say, the rest was history." Hatta smiled, transformed back into the cold, robotic clinician.

Chess hadn't moved since Hatta began speaking, save the trembling of his arms. Alice continued to squeeze his hand, anchoring him to reality. She felt the slightest pressure against her palm, then Chess released her hand. He stepped slowly towards Hatta, eyes flashing behind his fixed smirk.

"The worst ten minutes of your life," he said. "It must have been terrible for you." His words dripped with venom as he approached his father. "The thing is, *Dad*, you wouldn't have had to live through it at all if you would have just been a decent human being." He laughed, but it had a hard edge, bordering on hysterics.

"And what's funny is, you told me that whole story as your twisted way of explaining how you chose me over your job for once. But you didn't. Not really. I was only *there* because of your job. You only 'saved me' because it would have been more inconvenient if I was dead. Too messy, right? I'm sure it would have been pretty hard to explain to Mom when you came home missing a *whole child*." He ran his hands through his hair in frustration. "Come on, you can't be serious!"

"Eoghan, listen to me," Hatta said firmly. He straightened his coat, bored.

"No, you listen." Chess's voice was husky with emotion. "I don't know what you're doing here, but it's *wrong*. You aren't helping people, or furthering science, or whatever it is you keep telling yourself." His eyes blazed. "You're trying to play God and you're doing a pretty crappy job. You've screwed up your family, your job, hell, you've messed up the *whole freaking world*, and here you are, still trying to 'further science.' Really, you gotta know when to quit." He shook his head sadly, like he already knew the conversation was a lost cause.

"That's up to interpretation, I think," Hatta said, a wry smile creeping across his face. "I was quite successful with you."

"What are you talking about?" Alice cut in, glaring between the two of them. "You don't have *anything* to do with who Chess is."

"Not as a person," Hatta sneered. *"Biologically."* He stared at Chess like he had just made a new discovery. Chess shifted uncomfortably at the attention.

"I can't believe I didn't notice sooner. Although, as you so aptly pointed out, I was rather preoccupied with my work. Had I noticed I could have... oh well. We can make up for lost time," Hatta muttered under his breath. He brought his hand to his chin, covering his mouth as he talked through his thoughts. Suddenly, he pulled back his shoulders and straightened his figure to full height. He smoothed his hand over his hair and readjusted his jacket. When he spoke again, it was with authority.

"Obviously, you had strong genes to begin with, but they have adapted—" Hatta approached Chess to examine him closer. Alice gripped her sabre, but Chess held up his hand, telling her to wait. Hatta circled his son like a vulture, murmuring as he swirled, lost in his own thoughts. "Agility and speed, at the very least. There's no way you should have been able to get into this building undetected, let alone unscathed. And how you got in here with all the momerath outside? I would say impossible, yet here you stand." He grabbed Chess's hand and pulled it to him, flexing it as a physician would during a physical exam. "We'll have to run some tests to find out exactly—"

Chess jerked his hand free from Hatta's grip. "I'm not doing any tests," he growled. "I already know what I am. There is nothing you can or will help me with. I'm not your experiment anymore."

"Eoghan, don't be absurd."

A low snarl rumbled from Chess's throat as he stared at the older version of himself. "My name. Is Chess," he said bitterly.

Hatta rolled his eyes. "Chess, then. Come with me. It's time to go."

"I'm not going with you!" Chess erupted from the tenuous cool he maintained. "You're a failure! As a father, and a scientist. I don't want anything to do with you. Neither of us do." He dropped back to stand with Alice, grabbing her hand in his as he pulled her to the door. "We're leaving."

Conflict warred in Alice as Chess led her through the room. She stopped, pulling against his grip, battling herself. At the same time, Hatta started to laugh. It began small, a soft chuckle until it transformed into all-out hysterics, his head thrown back as he cackled mirthlessly.

Once his outburst settled, Hatta smoothed his tie under his lab coat. "You aren't going anywhere without my permission," he said icily. "And if you won't help me, you are no longer invited to my *party*." He leveled his gaze directly at Alice, the pupils in his eyes dilated almost completely black.

"The time has come, children," he snarled. "Are you ready?"

26

Alice watched apprehensively as Hatta retrieved the syringe he had abandoned in favor of the scalpel earlier. He eyed the contents almost reverently, staring at the thick, neon mixture that clung to the walls of the glass vial. A look of utter adoration covered his face as it sloshed around the syringe. Alice didn't know what it was, but the enormous syringe held a lot of it, and she was willing to bet it was no good.

"You know, Alice, none of this would have happened if you'd never come." He held the syringe to the dim emergency light. "My work wouldn't have been disturbed, I would still have March, my son would not be looking at me with such contempt." He swept a side glance at Chess, quirking his lips in a perverse version of his son's half smile.

Though Hatta spoke calmly, Alice had seen his erratic behavior before. She didn't trust him. *This is probably the most dangerous side of Matt Hatta*, she thought. Electricity crackled through her veins. A fight was coming.

"Be that as it may, you're still here, despite my best efforts," he continued casually. "And that must be remedied. It seems it's time I take matters into my own hands." He looked at them, both trained on the mysterious vial, and another chuckle rumbled from his throat.

"Hypnotic, isn't it?" he asked, studying the serum again. "It is the newest batch of my Max Recovery Serum. I guess you could call it MR-20. I was hoping to test it on March, but sadly, that is no longer an option." He shot a murderous glance at Alice. "But we do what we must for science," he sighed. He rolled up his sleeve, revealing a tan, lean arm. He twisted it to expose the fleshy underside. With his other hand, he deftly pierced the needle through his skin into a visible vein.

The syringe plunged deep into Hatta's arm, the green serum flooding his bloodstream as he pushed the back of the needle in. Once the last of the mixture vanished, Hatta dropped the syringe to the ground, forgotten as he clutched his forearm. His face contorted into a grimace of pain. His arms spasmed so violently his shoulders shuddered. All the color washed from his skin, and its once olive tone now matched the sheet white of his laboratory jacket. He ground his teeth together so intensely, Alice heard them cracking from across the room.

Chess stuttered forward, but Alice squeezed his hand, pulling him back to her.

"Don't," she warned. "It's not safe."

"He's *my* son!" Hatta fumed, his eyes bursting wide open. His irises were still the same glowing amber as Chess's, but the whites were completely bloodshot, as if all the blood vessels inside had erupted simultaneously. He sneered at her, revealing freshly chipped teeth crumbling behind his lips. He smashed his fist down on the table he crouched beside, cratering the metal. "You're the cause of all this!" His body convulsed as he took a trudging step towards Alice, his feet dragging across the floor.

Alice tried to step back, but she was trapped by the bookshelf. She had nowhere to go. A pang of fear ran through her body as her mind worked furiously to figure out what to do.

Hatta continued his tirade. He advanced on Alice, who tugged Chess back next to her and handed him the scalpel so he wasn't defenseless. "You brought him here! You pulled him into this mess, just like your father!" At the mention of Alice's father, Chess looked quizzically at her before standing to face Hatta. She could only shrug helplessly in response before Chess gave her a sly smile, his snark firmly in place as he walked directly towards the convulsing doctor.

"It's not her fault," he said. The overconfident tone in his voice replaced his anger, returning Alice's Chess. "This is all you, Dad."

Enraged, Hatta roared and turned, stumbling over the tables in the middle of the room. He unlatched all the cages he passed, knocking them to the floor and filling the room with disgruntled hisses, squeaks, and screeches.

"Chess, come on!" Alice yelled, tearing after him. Her instincts had kicked in, and she wanted a fight.

She crossed in front of Chess, taking a few more steps before she realized he wasn't moving. When he saw her questioning stare, Chess lowered his gaze and scratched the back of his head. "Alice, I can't—"

He didn't have to finish. She understood. "I know," she said. As much as she hated Mr. Carroll for abandoning her, she probably couldn't have hunted him down either. She gave Chess an encouraging smile. "I'll take care of it. You go get Nate."

"Who's Nate?" Chess asked incredulously, his brows raised in question.

"He's a friend," Alice rushed. She didn't want to lose Hatta again. "He and his team got me into Borogove," she explained, hoping it would appease him.

It didn't.

"His *team*? How do you know him?" Chess demanded.

Alice sighed. Of all the times for him to get overprotective. "He works for the Red Queen—"

"The Queen!" Chess scrubbed his hands through his ashen hair. "You can't be serious. Who've you been running around with, Princess?" His brows mashed against each other as he scowled at her. "I hate to break it to you, but the Queen's bad news, which means your friend probably is, too."

There was a vulnerable edge to his voice Alice had never heard before. If they hadn't been stuck in a room with a mad scientist in a building swarming with momerath, she would have said he was jealous. But considering they might not even live through the next ten minutes, it seemed pointless.

"Chess, seriously, we can't do this right now. You can tell me all about what a big mistake I've made later, but right now, we need Nate!" She spoke forcefully, trying to knock some sense into him.

Chess frowned, silently protesting before he slowly nodded in concession. He reached out to tenderly touch her cheek. "Be careful, kid" was all he said before he was gone in a flash, gliding out of the room like a leaf on the wind.

Once Chess left, Alice was alone. Well, almost. Hatta was with her somewhere, hidden in the dark. She stepped farther into the room, searching for him. The forced silence was eerie, standing her hair on end. Trying to stay hidden, she crept along the tables as quietly as she could. When she reached the end of the row, she crouched to sneak around the other side and bumped the metal paneling with her elbow. A tinny clang resonated through the room, a homing beacon to where she hid.

Alice held her breath, leaning flat against the table. Once the echoes stopped, she crawled forward on hands and knees until a call in the dark made her blood run cold.

"Twinkle twinkle little bat," a sinister voice sang. It sounded like Hatta, but rougher somehow. There was a rasp to his tone she hadn't heard before. The distorted voice let out an evil chuckle before continuing. "How I wonder where you're at!" Hatta swung out around the table with both of his fists clenched together, slamming them into the cold steel. The table crumpled with a huge crash, ringing Alice's ears.

Alice clapped her hands over her mouth, stifling her cry. Hatta was close enough she could see his head peeking over the table in the next row. It was misshapen—a strange, engorged variation of the doctor. His once handsome face was now deformed, with his jutted jaw showcasing jagged, broken teeth. His nose sunk in, cratered, making him appear less than human. His bloodshot eyes darted erratically as he prowled the rows of tables. She shrugged lower to the ground and rolled forward to hide behind the tall counter, forced to use his scuffling steps as her guide.

Monster Hatta ambled along the rows, continuing his bizarre music recital. "Up above the world you fly," he growled before abandoning his song to bellow, "like a tea tray in the sky!"

He flung the table from the middle of the room, sending it crashing against the titanium wall. Its steel frame groaned loudly as it bent under the force of the stronger metal.

Alice flinched as the table crumpled, biting her lip to hold back her scream. The metallic taste of copper tinged her tongue where her teeth cut too far, making her bleed. She hunched to the floor, trying to think. She focused on her surroundings: the cool air on her neck; the sound of Hatta's heavy breathing; the sterile smell of bleach. Hyperaware, she felt something in her back pocket digging into her skin. She removed the offending item and almost cried in relief when she saw the INFERNO spray she nabbed from the minivan her first night in Wanderland. She clutched it in her hand and flinched as another crash sounded against the wall, another mangled table.

"Twinkle twinkle, Alice—" Hatta taunted as he slithered to

the next table and pummeled it into the wall. She peeked around the corner to locate his position. He would be at her row next. She unscrewed the safety on the mace, holding it steady in one hand while she gripped her sword in the other. She closed her eyes, shutting out all other distractions to focus on Hatta's movements. Her heart pounded incredibly fast, filling her body with adrenaline. Hatta scuffled to her table, muscles bunched as he prepared to destroy it. Hatta's nails traveled through the steel, betraying his position. Using the advantage, she sprung to her feet, crossing her sword and blasting a stream of INFERNO in his face.

He roared in agony, tearing at his eyes to wipe away the pepper spray. Mutated claws bit into his flesh, ripping huge gashes across his cheeks and nose. Alice kept on, directing the stream straight at his eyes. When the last bit petered out, she tossed the useless can aside. It clattered against the tile, and Hatta blindly struck at the noise.

Alice narrowly jumped out of reach before his bulging arm swung through the air where she stood. Incensed at missing his mark, Hatta let out another wild howl, more animal than human. He fumbled against the remaining rows of tables, one hand clasped over his burning eyes while the other thrashed in search of her.

Seizing her opportunity, Alice lunged. She drew her sword, ready to attack, when Hatta pulled his hand away from his injured face revealing eyes that were completely healed. The strength of the INFERNO should have blinded him for at least thirty minutes, but it had been less than five and he was already blinking away final tears. His pupils dilated, surrounded by amber irises. A sickly gray ring separated them from the whites, making them appear even more dead.

She hesitated, providing Hatta enough time to fend her strike. The counter protected his neck, but his arm took the brunt of Alice's hit. The sabre sliced through his quickly graying skin like butter, splitting it from wrist to elbow. Hatta roared and swung with his free hand, smashing his fist into her gut and flinging her against the wall like a rag doll.

A huge grunt whooshed from Alice's lungs as they collapsed under the pressure of her ribs and the wall. Her head spun, and when she touched her hand to the base of her skull, her fingers came back drenched in fresh blood.

A roar across the room drew her attention to two Hattas barreling towards her. She wondered where the second one came from before they seamlessly merged into a single rampaging unit. She struggled to lift herself off the floor, but clumsily stumbled back. Hatta hit her again, slapping her with the force of a wrecking ball.

She felt the cool of the tile on her cheek before she realized she was laid out across the floor. Her head throbbed, and she swore she could feel the earth's rotation from where she lay. She forced her neck to lift her sluggish head to find Hatta. A sick grin spread across his deformed jaw as he sized up her broken body. She dropped her head, unable to support it any longer. All she could see was Hatta's malformed legs scuffling towards her. Dangling in his hand, the edge of another long surgical tool glinted wickedly in the light. Her vision didn't reach high enough to see the whole instrument, but she could tell by the serrated blade at the end she didn't want it anywhere near her.

Get up, Alice! her brain shrieked at her listless body, willing her leaden limbs to move. Her muscles screamed in protest, rebelling against the abuse they had taken. Spasms shot through her nerves, turning her arms and legs to jelly. Everything hurt. She couldn't possibly move; her body wouldn't let her.

Again, she tried to push herself up, but her arms slipped under her weight and dropped her to the tile. A small whimper slipped from her throat. He wasn't far now. Three, maybe four steps away. Alice couldn't see the blade he was holding anymore.

A pang of fear shot through her, igniting the remaining adrenaline she had in her body. The tiny spark lit, searing through her blood and giving her one final burst of energy. *You have to move.* "Now!" The word ripped from her throat and ricocheted through the room as Alice twisted out of Hatta's path. She kicked her foot as she rolled, swiping at the monster's ankles, sending him tumbling on top of her.

Alice cried out as one of her ribs snapped, cracking like a walnut. She tried to push him off, but he was too heavy. The best she could do was punch at him, each swing burning hot coals in her chest. She gritted her teeth and swung, landing a solid right hook in the middle of his oversized jaw, whiplashing his neck. Hatta growled at her and lifted up on his arms to leverage himself, pressing down on her already broken ribs. His eyes gleamed as he seethed at her.

"Your hair wants cutting, Alice." He brandished the enormous scalpel. A gravelly laugh escaped his chest as he smashed it down, straight at her heart. Alice cringed, her mind envisioning the day at the beach with her mother and Dinah as she waited for the black to take her.

ALICE'S EVIDENCE

27

With a haunted cry, another body crashed into Hatta, shoving him off of Alice's chest. They toppled to the floor in a tangle of limbs, ending in a feeble whimper followed by another furious roar from Hatta. Alice turned to her savior and was shocked to see Dr. Abbott.

Crumpled beneath the monster, Abbott was even more frail than she remembered. His hair still stuck up at odd angles, and his hands shook, but as she looked more closely, she noticed his piercing blue eyes were clear. Alert. Abbott coughed and peered at the mutated version of Hatta, shaking his head sadly at his former friend. His breath came in shallow gasps as he stirred and pulled a tiny pocket watch from his slacks.

"The time has come," he said weakly, unclasping the golden watch cover to show a hollowed-out case filled with snow white powder.

Hatta's neck swiveled from Abbott to Alice then back to Abbott where his serrated scalpel jutted out from the doctor's chest. He released an unnatural, grating shriek and dove to rip out Abbott's throat. Before he could administer his kill strike, the smaller doctor took a deep breath and blew the powder into his face.

A cloud of white dusted Hatta, seemingly harmless until he began bellowing in pain. Alice watched in horror as the parts of his skin that the powder touched began to bubble and peel, covering his body in instant third-degree burns. Hatta tore at his flesh to wipe away the powder, but the damage had been done. His erratic clawing only worsened the effects by cutting horrific gashes into his decaying skin.

While Hatta writhed in pain, Dr. Abbott stirred, trying to push himself off the tile. The movement caught Hatta's attention, and he backhanded the white-haired doctor before turning once more to Alice. His fury, mixed with the cocktail of chemicals he'd ingested, made him gruesomely different from the handsome man he had been before. He lurched forward, prepared to attack, but Alice was ready. Abbott's diversion had given her enough time for her dizziness to subside. She was unsteady on her feet but she planted them firmly against the floor and raised her blade in challenge. She hurt, but Abbott's hit severely weakened the mad doctor. She could take him.

She leveled her gaze at the disintegrating monster. Skin was sloughing off his bones into puddles of slime around his feet. Alice's stomach lurched. The smell of rot was almost overpowering. She had to force herself not to retch. She tightened her grip and stepped forward.

Hatta released one last furious cry and flung himself across the room at her. Alice responded in turn and shot towards him, sabre at the ready. She barreled into him, plowing through his chest with the sabre. He let out a surprised gasp and looked down at the hilt of the blade, the only visible piece of the weapon. He whipped his gaze to Alice. He hissed and made a sudden jerking motion, trying to bite a chunk from her neck. Alice bobbed her head back and wrenched her arms up. The sabre tore through the former doctor and burst from the top of his head, splitting the upper part of his body in half.

Hatta's vacant stare fixed on her as his body fell. Blood and brain matter pooled around his head, scrambled from where the blade ran its course. Alice closed her eyes, but the vision was imprinted in her mind.

A weak moan from behind pulled Alice's attention from the grisly scene back to the man who had saved her. She rushed to Abbott's side where she found him wheezing on the floor, clutching the scalpel in his chest. The tool had plunged deep, far enough to puncture his lungs. If his ragged gasps were any indication, she was sure each breath was excruciating.

Alice spoke gently to soothe him while assessing his wounds. She had gone on enough rounds with Dinah to be able to mend basic injuries, but this was severe. She pressed her hand to his chest to staunch the bleeding. She left the knife alone. She knew if she pulled it out without properly sealing the wound, Abbott would die.

"Dr. Abbott, why are you here?" she asked mournfully. Frustrated, she pushed her bangs from her face. She wasn't equipped to handle this.

A gurgling cough ripped through Abbott's chest. He winced, brow scrunched in pain as the serrated blade burrowed farther into his flesh. "I wasn't late this time," he said weakly, a small smile on his lips.

He handed Alice his pocket watch, and she took it warily. It spun at the end of its chain, its golden casing glinting innocently in the light.

"Take this. It's a new development I've been working on to combat the momerath." He wheezed. "I had to fix my mistake..." His words were drowned out by another bloody cough squelching from his chest.

Alice pushed harder on Dr. Abbott's chest. She had to stop

the bleeding. She ripped off a large piece of fabric from his lab coat to soak up the blood. Her hands weren't enough to hold it in his body, which was evident by her stained fingers and clothes. She needed someone to help her.

"Chess!" she called desperately, "Nate! *Anybody*! Dr. Abbott needs help!"

A trembling hand brushed against her own and brought her attention back to the dying man in front of her. Even in his current state, Abbott was the most lucid Alice had ever seen, his sky blue eyes bright as they bored into hers. "Alice, you need to listen."

How could she listen when his voice was so weak? She could hardly hear him! She fought to remain calm. She nodded, not trusting her voice.

"You can save your sister," Abbott said through wheezing breaths. "Only you."

"I don't understand," she whimpered, pressing stubbornly against the blood-soaked rag.

"*You* can save your sister." He looked meaningfully at her. He reached into his pocket and pulled out a crumpled, folded piece of paper and a plastic pouch containing an empty syringe.

"The answer is in your blood, Alice. Take it to her." Abbott's hands shook so badly, Alice was surprised she took the items without dropping them.

She stared at the paper and needle dumbly, willing them to give her an answer. Dr. Abbott wasn't going to last much longer, let alone be able to explain himself. *Think, Alice!*

Behind her, a throat cleared awkwardly. She turned and saw Chess, staring around the room with wide eyes.

"Chess..." She breathed a sigh of relief. Her heart lurched when his gaze flickered over to the mess of Hatta's body, but Abbott wouldn't last much longer. "Hurry, come help me!" She stuffed the paper Dr. Abbott gave her into her back pocket as she looked for the others. "Where's Nate?"

"Right here," his strong voice called from the dim. Nate rushed towards her, glancing warily at the needle on the floor beside her. "What do you need?" He hurried to take Alice's place so she could work freely.

Dr. Abbott coughed again. All the color had vanished from his face, leaving his cheeks as white as his hair. It made the blue in his eyes even more intense as they pierced hers. She cradled his head to make him as comfortable as possible. Her traitorous nose tickle warned of tears as she gazed at the feeble man. He didn't deserve to die this way.

Abbott raised a trembling hand to her cheek, a small smile on his face. "Wasn't late... this... time..." He panted between pained breaths. Alice didn't realize she was crying until he wiped the tears from the corner of her eye. Chess stood behind her, hand on her shoulder as she watched the doctor.

"No," she said tenderly as tears fell freely down her cheeks. "You weren't."

Abbott sighed his last breath. His eyes closed, but his smile remained, finally free from his imagined guilt. Alice stared stone-faced at the man who had given up everything to save her, until her vision blurred with tears.

"It's alright." Chess wrapped his arm around her. She turned and buried her face in his shoulder. She was sorry Dr. Abbott had died. Sorry she had pulled him into it— *No,* she told herself, *he was in the middle of it to begin with. You can only control what you do. And you need to take care of Dinah.* Thinking of her mission calmed her. She took a deep breath, noting the scent of cinnamon coming from Chess's jacket.

When she calmed, Chess crushed her against his chest. Suddenly, he stepped back, bewildered. "Ow!" He held his arm where Alice punched him, his eyes wide with confusion.

"Weren't you just hugging me, Doll-face?" he asked. "Can't we go back to that?" His lazy smile replaced his shock as he tried to wrap his arms around Alice to draw her towards him, but she smacked them away.

"You left me again, you idiot!" she scolded. "After all those momerath showed up, I thought you were dead!" Her eyes narrowed and she punched him once more for good measure.

"Left you?" Chess asked, pretending to be wounded. "I would never leave you, Cream Puff. You just didn't see me." He winked and danced out of Alice's reach before she could smack him again.

Another throat cleared behind her, and Alice turned to Nate, her cheeks blazing red. "Nate!" she said a little too quickly, wondering why she felt a twinge of guilt as he watched her. His jaw was stiff as he glared at Chess. Standing between the two, Alice noticed how different they were from each other. Chess was tall and dark and filled with electric energy, while Nate was gold and strength and duty-bound. Both were looking protectively at her, tension radiating off them in waves.

Alice chattered nervously. "You're all right! But...where's everyone else?" she asked, feeling like Wanderland's biggest jerk for not noticing he was alone sooner.

"Ace went to go radio for backup. We fought off the momerath, but there were a lot more of them. Indi got hurt pretty bad, and we need a pick up. Good news is, the building's clear." He forced a smile to his face. It didn't quite reach his cheeks, leaving a haunted expression. "Did you find the antidote?"

"I think so," Alice said. "And if the building is clear, I need to go." She felt bad running out on him again so soon, but she didn't know how much time Dinah had left.

"I'm coming with you," Chess said. He leaned to grab the syringe she left on the floor and inconspicuously pocketed it before walking to her side.

"See you later, pretty boy." He gave Nate a mock salute and a wink. Nate grimaced before turning to Alice, sorrow in his eyes. She lifted her hand in a small wave and turned to go, but was stopped short.

"No one's going anywhere," a low voice rumbled as Ace's hulking figure hustled towards them. Behind him, Alice saw about ten more soldiers, each with small blinking green lights on the side of their necks. Jokers. He leered at Alice. His smug smile made her skin crawl.

"We have strict orders to take you back to the Queen," he said. "She would like to speak with you. Immediately."

28

"What? No!" Alice stomped towards Ace. She realized how ridiculous she probably looked, her tiny blond frame standing menacingly before the towering hulk of a soldier. It didn't matter. She wasn't going to deal with Ace's nonsense. "The Queen and I have a deal. I get to go back home to Dinah first."

Ace didn't even give her the courtesy of eye contact. "Deal's changed," he barked.

Frustrated, she appealed to Nate. "What *is* this? You were there! You know what she said!" Her nose pricked. After she had survived the madness of Borogove, this couldn't be what was keeping her away from Dinah.

Nate shot a dubious look at Ace, bristling at his declaration. "That wasn't the deal, Ace. The Queen told Alice she could report back after she saw to her sister."

Ace's sneer deepened. "The Queen said you'd say that." He let out a derisive snort as one of the Jokers handed him a red envelope. He passed it to Nate. "Told me to give you this."

Nate snatched the letter in disbelief. But as he read it, he ground his teeth in anger. He shot one last stormy glare at Ace, who chuckled.

"I'm sorry, Alice." Nate wouldn't meet her gaze. "We have orders to return you to Tulgey Wood. Please come with us, and it will be quick."

"No!" Alice yelled. "I need to see my sister!" She searched the room, pleading for sympathy, but the Jokers behind Ace all held the same vacant stare as they awaited orders. Nate seemed upset, but stood impassive, following his Queen's directive. He wasn't going to help. She turned to Chess. His features set in stone as the guards surrounded them, his amber eyes blazing. He gave her the smallest shake of his head, as if he knew it was a lost cause. Outrage burned through Alice. She had been lied to.

What kind of person would I be? the Queen had said. Now she knew exactly what kind of person.

"Fine," Alice seethed. "Take me to her, but I *won't* be staying long." Nate only nodded.

Ace chuckled as he led Alice and Chess through the empty halls of Borogove flanked by the other Jokers. With only the sound of the soldier's heavy boots clomping down the still, metal corridors, the building suddenly felt very sad. There had been so much death here. Alice shuddered.

When they reached the vans, Ace shoved Alice into the first one between a pair of bulking guards, intentionally separating her from Chess, who was sent to the vehicle behind her. "So you don't try anything stupid," Ace growled as she sullenly watched them escort her comrade away.

Trapped in the van, Alice sat surrounded by the Queen's lackeys on all sides. The monstrous Jokers sat stoically, their mechanical necklaces enforcing good behavior with their presence. In front of her, Ace lounged in the driver's seat, lazily picking his teeth with an old playing card as he drove the van over the bumpy desert road to Tulgey. Nate sat on his right, shoulders tense as he stared out the passenger side window, sullen. At one point, he turned to give Alice a sympathetic glance, but she ignored him. His eyes lingered on her for a few moments before he swiveled to resume his silent observation of the desert's twisted landscape.

When they reached camp, Alice and Chess were marched directly to the Queen's quarters, separated and swarmed by a dozen Jokers. Ace and Nate walked side by side in front of the procession, forcing the residents of Tulgey to make way for the group.

"Alice, so nice to see you again!" the Queen breezed as they were escorted through the doors to her quarters. Her oily voice was fully loaded with charm, but it only made Alice sick. "I hear you wreaked quite the havoc on Borogove," she said, clapping her hands together delightedly.

Alice wasn't sure why Her Royal Redness was suddenly acting so friendly, but she wasn't interested in entertaining her playacting. "I want to see my sister," she responded flatly.

The Queen's smiled faltered, puckering into the slightest frown before reclaiming its upturned quirk. "And you will, my dear, you will. We just need to have a quick chat."

"What do you want?" Alice asked petulantly. The Queen might be able to use her Jokers to force Alice to be there, but she couldn't make her like it.

"Don't be juvenile," the Queen snapped. "It's so very dreary." Irritation laced her pretty features. "I merely need a report of what transpired at Borogove, then you can be on your way. Ace says it was *very* exciting." She stared at Alice hungrily.

"We went in, we got attacked. We found Dr. Hatta, we got attacked. Found Hatta *again*, got attacked again. Killed lots of momerath, managed to escape. It was all very exciting," Alice answered, deadpan. Chess snorted into his jacket, forcing her to bite her lip to keep a straight face.

"Yes, sounds like it." The Queen's lips pursed. She leaned back in her chair as she considered. "Nathan. Tell me, what did you see?"

Nate stepped forward, sparing one last remorseful glance at Alice, who stood defiantly in front of the Queen, refusing to acknowledge him. He sighed and cleared his throat before recapping what happened in Borogove. Some parts were muddled where he had separated from Alice, but ever the dutiful soldier, he recalled the details succinctly, ending when they met in the Research Laboratory after Alice had fought Hatta the last time.

"By the time I arrived, Hatta was gone and Dr. Abbott was critically wounded." He brought forward the doctor's broken wristwatch. He must have taken it from the doctor when Alice was talking to Chess. "He didn't make it, Your Majesty."

The Queen accepted the watch from Nate, and Alice was surprised to find genuine sorrow in her expression. She clasped it in her hand for a moment before she let out a small sniffle and directed her attention back to Alice. "Is that everything?" she asked.

"That's it," Alice said, tight-lipped.

The Queen stood, stretching her legs as she walked to Alice. She peered at her as if trying to telekinetically pull unspoken words from them. When it failed, she slowly returned to her chair.

"I wish you would have been more forthcoming with me, Alice." Faux disappointment laced her features as she *tsked* insincerely. "As it is, now, you must stay with me. *Indefinitely.*"

"*What?*" Alice erupted at the same time Nate and Chess yelled their own objections.

The Queen's eyes widened, a delighted smile springing to her lips at the sudden excitement. "If you had been honest, I could have let you go. But here you came, escorted by my guards, withholding vital mission intelligence, accompanied by this..." She gestured at Chess, her mouth turned down in a cold sneer. "...traitor."

Alice whirled around to Chess. He made no effort to deny the accusation and stood, glaring daggers at the Queen. His amber eyes blazed as he leveled a look of pure hatred at the woman. For her part, the Queen just laughed.

"Oh, don't look at me like that, Chess darling. You had to know I would find you and Bug one day." She casually checked her nails. "Where is my old surveillance specialist these days? I'm sure he can't have gone too far into the "scary" world of Wanderland." The Queen dropped her hand and turned to watch Chess wolfishly.

"He's doing fine," Chess seethed. "Better than your old Guard, I'd say." He surveyed her collection of Jokers. "Don't see many old faces, but lots of new ones. Been busy, Majesty?"

The Queen grimaced and clenched her jaw, a habit she apparently shared with her nephew. "Good help is hard to come by, it seems. It's a shame Bug turned you so against me." She pouted. "You were such an excellent reconnaissance soldier. But we all make our choices." The Queen gave Chess another girlish look, and Alice's stomach twisted with an unfamiliar emotion.

"I wonder, what made you come back?" The Queen advanced on Chess like a spider closing in on a fly entangled in its web. Chess stiffened, not moving as she studied him. He flashed the smallest glance to Alice, betraying his thoughts.

"Oh my." The Queen giggled in a way Alice supposed was intended to be flirtatious, but came out sounding more like a spoiled child. "Well. Isn't *that* interesting." She walked back to Alice, circling her like a hungry vulture.

"You see, Alice? I just can't let you go. It would make things far too complicated for me, and I don't like complications."

"But, Your Majesty—" Nate stepped forward then paused,

surprised at his brashness. It caught the Queen off guard as well. She turned to her nephew wonderingly. "Yes, Nathan?"

"What about her sister?" he asked. He looked at Alice with concern. Alice smiled at him, relief flooding her body as she instantly forgot she was furious with him. The Queen's brow raised again as she considered her nephew's request.

"What about her?" the Queen bristled. "She's probably already turned. I'm doing you a favor." She sniffed, dismissing the matter.

Alice, however, was far from dismissing it.

"You bitch!" She surged forward, stopped only by a pair of guards grabbing her arms to restrain her. She had the satisfaction of seeing Chess had followed her lead and also tried to rush the dishonest dictator. "You promised I could help her!"

The Queen crossed her arms, watching indifferently as Alice struggled against her guards. "That was when I thought you could be useful to me," she clipped.

Outrage seared through Alice's body, shooting burning adrenaline through her veins. She was going to knock the condescending smirk off the Queen's face if it was the last thing she did. She lunged again, this time taking the astonished Jokers with her. The element of surprise enabled her to quickly shake her escorts off her arms, setting her free to attack. The Queen's emerald eyes widened as she backed away, hidden behind two more Jokers who leapt to protect their lady. Alice clawed and scratched, trying to get through to her as more soldiers struggled to subdue her.

"Ace! Nate! Bring me a ContraBand," the Queen shouted to conceal her panic. She stood to the side of her chair, her body crackling with nervous energy as she surveyed the scuffle in front of her. Ace hurried forward with one of the sinister collars in his hands at her request. "Put it on her. She may still be useful after all—if I can control her."

"Your Majesty, are you sure this is a good idea?" Nate looked confused, as if he still couldn't believe he was questioning his commanding officer. He eyed the explosive ContraBand before turning to Alice, faltering as her rampage against the Queen negated any argument he could make in her favor. "She just needs time—" he finished lamely.

"Shut up, Nathan!" the Queen demanded. Bits of spittle flew from her mouth as she raged. "Once she's been tamed, you can keep her as your pet if you want her so badly. But I will *not* have her in my court without an insurance policy!"

Her remark turned Nate a brilliant shade of red before, shamefaced, he stormed from the Queen's chambers.

"Let him go!" the Queen commanded when Ace moved to chase Nate. "I'll handle him later."

Alice continued to fight against the guards in an attempt to reach the Queen. Utilizing the distraction, Chess had even managed to shake loose one of his Jokers and struggled to best the other. They might have stood a chance if a shrill whistle hadn't sounded through the camp, summoning more Jokers to subdue her.

Alice scanned the chambers hopelessly as another wave of Jokers surrounded them. A familiar shock of sleek black hair entered her peripheral, and her heart sank as she recognized Indi. She didn't want to fight her.

The pretty Joker ran in, still in her combat gear from Borogove, her eyes tinged red. She took in the scene in front of her, and rushed to defend the Queen. She fell into the protective circle around her, forming a secondary guard in case Alice managed to break free. Alice's strength was fading fast, but she continued to struggle to reach her mark.

The Queen must have realized she was tiring and ventured an emboldened step from behind her protective shield. "That was fun," she purred, her smug grin securely back in place now that the threat had been neutralized. "Ace, bring me the Contra-Band. I want to do this one myself," she said, accepting the metal collar from her lackey.

"Wait!" Indi's voice rang out across the crowded room. She held a control similar to the one Ace had in Borogove. She waved it in the air threateningly, her eyes burning holes into Ace.

"How did you—" the Queen began, then stopped as she patted down her coat and realized she had been pickpocketed. The soldiers by Indi quickly distanced themselves so as not to be found guilty by association. Her emerald eyes flashed as they narrowed at Indi and the unexpected problem she presented.

"Return my control at once!" she demanded, but her voice faltered, obviously shaken by Indi's act of defiance.

"Let them go," Indi said evenly, tightening her grip on the control.

The Queen glanced from Indi to Alice, buried under a mound of soldiers. She waged a silent battle, then bitterly gave the command. "Release them."

The Jokers backed away, freeing Alice and Chess. They eyed the Queen skeptically, her rage palpable as it reddened her cheeks, emanating from her in waves. Alice looked mournfully at Indi. She knew what was going to happen once the Queen got hold of her. Indi only winked and smiled.

"Do better for your sister—better than I did for Johnny and Mikey," she said. A single tear ran down her cheek as she waved goodbye.

Alice and Chess hurried to the door, but didn't quite reach it before Ace took his own control from his pocket and pressed down on the button, initiating the countdown sequence. Behind her, Alice heard the Queen yell something unintelligibly before Ace's voice retorted in ire.

They didn't wait to see what happened. She yelled at Chess

to hurry as they fled the room, followed by the Queen's repeated shouts of *"Off with their heads!"*

They slammed the door behind them as the explosion sounded from the building. Spurred by the chaos, they tore through the campsite like madmen, putting as much distance between themselves and the Jokers as they could. Alice was going off of memory to get them back to the lot where the vans were kept. She made a mental note to congratulate herself later when they managed to get there after taking only one wrong turn. They slid into the lot, loose rocks skittering along the desert landscaping as they rushed to the first van they reached. Locked.

"Check the other ones," Chess said, hurrying to the next vehicle. "You take that side, I'll get these."

Every door was locked. Apparently, the Queen didn't trust her followers as much as she let on. "What are we going to do?" Alice asked, panic in her chest. It would take at least four hours to get to Dinah if they went on foot. And that was only accounting for the walking—not the soldiers in pursuit or the momerath they might run into. She pulled the handle again, praying it would magically unlock. She practically flew backwards when, to her surprise, there was a small click and it unlatched, flinging the door wide open.

Alice caught herself ungracefully and looked around, bewildered. Across the lot, Nate hurried towards her, a small set of keys jangling in his hand.

"Here, take these." He handed them quickly to her. "I just filled the tank so it should run awhile. This is Ace's car," he said meaningfully. Alice took the keys, shocked, then wrapped her arms around Nate's neck, hugging him tight.

"Thank you," she whispered, pulling away.

"Just be careful," he said, then turned to Chess. He had come to Alice's side when the door flew open and stared at Nate with a mixture of resentment and gratitude. "Take care of her," Nate said, acknowledging his glare.

Chess nodded and pushed Alice into the passenger seat. "I'm driving," he said. Alice didn't argue. She was more than happy to let Chess take care of the mechanical beast. She gave a small wave to Nate as they tore out of the parking space, careening through the desert away from Tulgey Wood, neither of them daring to look back.

Alice and Chess rode in nervous silence until they were back on the interstate. Alice anxiously checked the rearview mirror several times expecting to see a chain of Tulgey vans in pursuit, kicking up clouds of dust behind them, but none showed. It made her uneasy, but she decided not to dwell on it and considered it a sign the universe was finally giving her a break.

A much needed break, she thought. Her mind flitted through all the things that had happened over the past few days. *Wonderland. Borogove. The Queen. Hatta. Chess.*

She peeked over at Chess, watching him drum his fingers on the steering wheel in time to a bad '80s album he found and had dubbed "Escape Music." He acted like nothing was wrong, but Alice noticed he hadn't looked at her since they had made it out of Tulgey.

"I'm sorry about your father," she said, her voice very small. She twisted her hands in her lap. She imagined that was what her insides were doing.

Chess let out a strangled laugh. "It's not your fault," he

sighed. "I lost my father a long time ago." He tried to smile at her, but it didn't quite reach his eyes. Without their familiar spark, they looked incredibly empty.

Alice tried to say something, but her words had all disappeared. Her chest was tight. It was hard to breathe.

"Alice, that thing was not my father," Chess said, his voice like stone. "I don't blame you." He looked like he was going to say more, but stopped and focused his attention back on the road. They drove in awkward silence until Alice couldn't bear it any longer.

"Why did you follow me to Borogove?"

"Because I told you I would," he said. He glanced at her, a quick smile turning up the corners of his lips.

"But you were gone. I hadn't seen you since right after we left Bug's house," Alice said, hoping her voice didn't sound as accusing as she thought.

Chess scratched the back of his head while he tried to figure out what to say. "Alice..." He paused, then sighed. "How can I explain this?"

He was quiet another minute as he considered. Alice could practically see the wheels turning in his head. She waited patiently, not wanting to interrupt his train of thought. He opened and shut his mouth a few times before finally deciding on his words.

"While we were in Borogove, do you remember what Hatta said to me?"

Alice nodded. She remembered quite a few things Hatta said, the main one being he was Chess's father. To be honest, she still hadn't quite wrapped her head around that one. "He called you Eoghan." She smiled slyly.

"Besides that," Chess said, exasperated at the mention of his real name.

She smirked. "Oh! So you think it's annoying when someone

calls you the wrong thing, huh?" Chess looked at her with a pained expression. "So, are you gonna stop with the terrible nicknames?" she asked pointedly.

"Heck no, Techno!" Chess scoffed as if that was the craziest thing he ever heard. "Now focus, or I'm going to start calling you Squirrel Girl."

Alice gave a withering look to show him exactly how she felt about that idea. He grinned and continued. "What did Hatta say to me?"

Alice scanned her memory through the jumbled mess that was the Borogove experience. She thought about Chess showing up in the room, drawing Hatta's attention from her, the mad doctor's admission that he was his son, then...

"He said he ran an experiment on you."

"And—" Chess prompted.

"And then he wanted you to go with him so he could run more tests on you," she said.

"To which I responded—" he coaxed, trying to lead her to some hidden revelation.

Alice paused. What did it matter how he responded? "He said he wanted to do more tests on you! Wasn't that bad enough?" she asked incredulously.

"Think, Squirrelly. What did I say?"

Alice rolled her eyes, but paused to think about what Chess had said. She tried to visualize the scene to see if it would jog her memory.

"You said..." She fought to remember, her eyes shut tight. "You said you already—"

"—know what I am," Chess finished with her, emphasizing each word. Alice scoffed, frustrated he was entertaining such silliness.

" 'Know what you are.' What does that even mean?" She scoffed. Alice liked logic and order. Chess was speaking gibberish like his father. Soon, he'd be asking her how chipmunks were better than dinner plates or something equally ridiculous. She rolled her eyes. "What are you then?"

"I'm different," he answered seriously, ignoring her disbelieving laugh. She had to fight not to say she was aware exactly how different he was in the head, but Chess pressed on.

"But it doesn't show all the time. Only if I get nervous or scared. Then it's like something tells me I need to get away, and everything about me helps it happen faster. I can move quicker, breathe easier, and run longer. I can also jump really high so if anything is in my way, I can get around it." He spoke quickly, a mixture of excitement and nerves. He kept glancing at her to gauge her reaction.

So, run track, Alice thought. But she didn't want to sound judgmental, so she said instead, "Okay, so you're a... Runner. Do you always have to run?"

"Not always," he said. "But sometimes, it's like no matter what I do, or how bad I want to stay, the message my brain tells me overrides everything and the only thing I can do is run. That's why I disappeared on you the first time, outside of Borogove." He looked at her apologetically. "My brain sent the message for me to run, and it shorted out everything else except for how my autonomic system wanted my body to respond. I wanted to stay," he added softly.

"Autonomic system?" Alice asked, amused by his fancy wording.

"Dad's a doctor, remember?" He winked at her.

"Alright, Mr. Genius, help me figure this out. Dr. Abbott said only I could help Dinah. That it was my blood she needed. What does that mean?"

Chess's eyes widened and he let out a startled sound as if her statement reminded him of something. He reached into his pocket and pulled out the syringe Dr. Abbott had given her earlier. "I don't know, but you'll probably need this. Didn't he give you something else too?"

"Yeah," Alice said, reaching into her back pocket. "Some paper."

Nothing was there. Her other pocket was empty too. She checked again with her other hand. Still nothing. "I can't find it, it's not in my pocket!" she said, a queasy feeling budding in the pit of her stomach.

"What was on it?" Chess asked.

"I don't know," she snapped. "I didn't exactly get a chance to sit down and read it. I've been kind of busy."

"Calm down." Chess ignored her temper. "You'll find it," he reassured her. "And if not, it was only a piece of paper. No one will even notice it, let alone read it." He changed the subject to divert her attention.

"Your blood...why would it need to be your blood?"

"I don't know." Alice was still distracted by the missing paper, but as she mulled over reasons her blood could be important, the puzzle pulled her attention from the lost page.

Chess supplied the first guess. "Because you guys are related?"

"Not biologically," Alice countered. "We were both adopted." She stared out the window as she thought. They were making good time, quickly leaving Wanderland behind them. They would be at the Sector soon. She would have to have an answer by then. Alice growled and pressed the heels of her hands against her eyes, fighting a headache. She was tired of overanalyzing everything. It was time to act.

"I don't know, but if Dr. Abbott thinks it will work, it's worth a shot," she said and fearlessly stuck the needle into her vein to take the sample she would need.

"EW!" Chess cried out, jerking away from her as he watched

in disgust. He looked at her like she was an alien. "Where did you learn how to do that?"

"Dinah showed me. It didn't happen often, but there were a couple of times she had to use a syringe in the Sector." The bottle filled and she nimbly removed the needle from her skin. She clamped her thumb over the pin prick to staunch the bleeding.

"Gross." Chess shivered. Alice smirked. Needles had never bothered her. Talking to strangers? *That* was terrifying. A little blood? Meh.

Chess squirmed uncomfortably from the driver's seat as she studied the syringe. Such a small thing to be so important. In her peripheral, she noticed the roads began to look familiar. They were getting closer to the Sector. *Hang on, Dinah. Just a little longer. I'm almost home.*

Thinking of her sister set Alice's nerves on edge. What if she didn't get there in time? She had worked so hard to find the cure. But what she had wasn't exactly a sure bet. What if she got there in time only to find out her blood was no good? The possibility made her sick. She needed to find something else to think about.

She glanced at Chess to divert her anxiety. He started as a stranger who threw her into an empty van, like some bad episode of *Criminal Minds*, but then had stuck with her even when it endangered him. If she was in his position, would she have done the same?

"Why did you stay?" She twisted in her seat to face him. "If you knew the Red Queen was involved in Borogove, why did you stick with me?"

He smirked, his gaze fixed on the road. "That's easy, Alice," he said. His amber eyes melted into hers. "It's the first rule of chess: always protect your queen."

Alice's cheeks warmed under the intensity of his gaze. "You used my name."

Chess winked at her, all seriousness gone. "Yeah, well, you

know. Gotta keep things interesting." He pulled off the freeway exit to Tolleson and followed Alice's directions to the Sector. She had him park right outside the opening she and Dinah had made in the fence and showed him how to squeeze through and avoid the land traps. A minute later, they were both in and dashing madly to Alice's house at full speed.

30

The first thing Alice saw when she burst through her front
door was Lewis staring at her in shock.

"Alice!" The words poured from his mouth as he hurried
towards her. "Where have you been? It's been *three days*. I
thought you were dead! And Dinah's gotten worse."

Dinah's gotten worse.

"Go home, Lewis. I'll explain later," she yelled, feeling only
slightly guilty. She pushed past him, dashing upstairs as he called
after her to wait. Chess stopped him, running interference. She
wasn't even a quarter of the way upstairs when a wheezing cough
wrenched through the house. She couldn't believe how bad it
sounded. It didn't seem possible. She practically launched herself
off the top of the stairs into Dinah's door. Throwing it open, she
ran to the side of Dinah's bed, praying she wasn't too late.

The dark room smelled of rot, like something had spoiled.
And it was *hot*. The heat hit Alice like a wave of lava as she
walked towards her feverish sister. Dinah lay on the bed, curled
in a ball with beads of sweat covering her skin. Her bed reeked, as
if she had been sitting in the same dirty clothes for months. Her

beautiful chocolate skin had paled to a dingy ash gray. She looked like a distorted black-and-white movie figurine in a full color world—the reverse *Wizard of Oz*. Her only color was on her hands, where the navy blue tinge at the base of her nails spread, mingling with her pallid gray complexion like some rotting corpse. *Shut up, Alice.*

Another gurgling cough erupted through the room, and Dinah's whole body contracted. Alice rushed to her side. "Shh, Dinah, it's okay. I'm here," she said softly.

"Alice?" Dinah turned to the sound of Alice's voice, her eyes shifting feverishly to find her. Their color had dimmed, the rich mahogany now dulled to mud.

"I'm here," Alice repeated, more to herself than Dinah, steeling her resolve as she uncapped the needle and plunged it deep into her sister's thigh. Dinah swatted at it weakly to chase away the pain.

Alice stared at her sister, trying to will her better. The final contents of the syringe emptied into her bloodstream and Dinah's eyes widened, then snapped shut.

Please work, please work, please work. Alice's monologue kept her company as she waited for Dinah to wake.

Dinah shifted, unfolding her arms and legs from the fetal position she had been tucked in. Her eyelids fluttered, and a massive, hacking cough broke free from her chest as her eyes flew open.

But they weren't her eyes anymore.

A stranger watched Alice from Dinah's body. No. A mutation, like a bad clone. Alice tried to look away, but could only stare in horror as the washed-out skin on Dinah's arms and face mottled, transforming from sickly to decaying in front of her eyes.

"No..." Alice backed away from the bed, her mind a haze. This couldn't be happening. "*No!*" she yelled. Dinah startled and jumped from the bed, crouching low to the floor and growling menacingly.

"Dinah," Alice whispered, her whole body trembled. "It's me." Tears pricked the corners of Alice's eyes.

Dinah craned her neck until her head was practically turned upside down. An evil smile crawled across her lips as she deliberately raised her hand to the top of her cheek. She let out a hiss and dug her nails into her flesh and dragged them to the base of her chin, carving four jagged gashes into her face. She stared at Alice, black blood flowing from the wounds as a raspy chuckle rumbled from her chest.

"Dinah, it's *me*," Alice plead again, desperately holding onto hope that Dr. Abbott hadn't been wrong, that her sister would come back. *You have to know it's me.*

Dinah froze. Her chest rose and fell softly as she angled her head to the other side.

"Don't be gone," Alice breathed. A single tear ran down her cheek. Dinah's empty gaze trained on her face. She raised her bloodied hand and flexed her fingers, watching the blood drip to the floor.

Alarms rang in Alice's ears, screaming danger. Suddenly, Dinah attacked. Alice leapt back, barely escaping her extended reach. Dinah screeched in frustration when her claws scratched nothing but air and lunged again, swinging wildly.

Alice dodged left to avoid the attack, but she refused to retaliate. Dinah prowled after her, sending her things flying onto the floor and against the walls. Still, Alice wouldn't take offense.

Frustrated with the cat-and-mouse game, Dinah crept onto her disheveled bed, giving her a height advantage. Alice tried to back away, but she was already cornered against the far wall. There was nowhere to go. Dinah let out a weird chattering sound, then launched herself at Alice like a torpedo. She pinned her against the wall, smashing her head, and reopening her congealed wound.

Alice panicked. "Dinah, it's me!" she yelled desperately. "I know you know me!" Her body screamed to fight, warning if she didn't, she was going to die. She screamed as Dinah leaned in and sniffed her wound, her own oozing blood still pouring from her cheek. Her sister watched from dead eyes, and it finally sunk in.

This isn't Dinah. Dinah's gone.

Ugly tears streamed down Alice's face as she felt her strength surge. Visions of Borogove flashed through her mind, followed by patchy memories with Dinah and Mom. Behind it all, Chess's voice played through her head. *"The message my brain tells me overrides everything... I get stronger, faster..."*

It was too much for Alice to take. She screamed, a raw, blood-curdling sound that ricocheted from her throat around the small room, drowning out everything else as she put all her strength into pushing Dinah off her. Dinah flew against the wall, cracking it underneath her weight. Her eyes glazed over as she sagged to the ground, disoriented. Her body spasmed, jerking her limbs like an electric shock coursed through her. She stiffened and slumped over until her eyes flung open, capturing Alice in their dark gaze.

"Alice?"

A jolt ran through Alice's body as she recognized her sister's eyes. "Dinah?" she asked, taking a careful step towards her. Though her sister still wore a momerath mask, the eyes were hers.

"Don't come near me!" Dinah yelled, her cry ending in a hiss. "I don't want to hurt you." She extended her arm in front of her to hold Alice back, revealing grayed hands that ended in claws.

Dinah's transformation unnerved Alice, but she wouldn't be deterred. "You wouldn't hurt me," she said, stepping towards her. "You're my sister." Her nose pricked and tears formed in the corners of her eyes, but she held Dinah's gaze.

"I said stay back!" Dinah roared, her voice deep and

distorted. "You don't know what I could do!" She smothered her hands against her face, waging a battle within.

Alice took another tentative step. Just a few more, and she would reach Dinah. Dinah swiveled her head towards the motion. Her eyes narrowed and she let out a menacing snarl.

Alice hesitated at her sister's hungry gaze. Her body stiffened, but she released her sabre, dropping it to the floor. It hit the carpet with a soft thud, leaving her completely defenseless.

Dinah roared and whipped her arm out, smashing the window beside her. Alice flinched when the glass shattered and sprayed across the room. In one smooth motion, Dinah hopped to the window sill. She cast a final wistful look at Alice, her gorgeous brown eyes filled with sorrow.

"Dinah, wait," Alice begged as she reached for her sister's hand. But it was too late. Dinah was gone.

31

Alice stood in stunned silence. She dropped to her knees, clutching the window sill. The quiet broke when Chess barged in with Lewis trailing behind him. Alice heard their sharp intake of breath at the state of the room, but kept her eyes trained out the window, down the path Dinah had taken out from the Sector.

Chess slowly approached Alice and knelt beside her. "What happened?" he asked softly, watching her with concern. Alice could only imagine what was going through his mind as he observed the tiny destroyed room. She decided she didn't care.

"I've had such a curious dream," she murmured. Her hand fell heavily from the sill as she remembered her sister's crazed glare and terrified voice.

"Alice, where's Dinah?" Lewis asked, his voice laced with panic.

"She's gone," Alice said. Tears streamed freely down her face while her hands knotted in her lap. Chess shifted uncomfortably beside her, then tenderly rested his hand against her shoulder.

Alice's vision blurred as his touch summoned a new wave of tears.

Lewis turned a sick shade of green. "What do you mean she's gone?" He looked around the room, stopping at the window covered in blood.

"I don't know," Alice whispered. "She attacked me..." She trailed off as her mind was bombarded with memories. Her cheeks were cold where the night air hit her tears. "I injected her. She changed." *Sort of.* Alice struggled to formulate the rest of her thought. "I think it worked. I think she's cured."

Chess forced a small smile to his face that didn't quite reach his eyes. "That was a curious dream," he said, then tenderly brushed her bangs from her eyes.

Alice's head spun as she tried to make sense of it all. She was going to burst into a million pieces. Only Chess's touch anchored her to the present. She took an unsteady breath and reached to touch the shattered window. She pulled her hand back, then extended it to Chess, showing him the black blood pooling on her fingers.

"But it was real," she breathed.

Chess gently pressed her wrist to lower her hand. He searched her face, as if afraid to believe the possibility. "There's a cure?"

She nodded. "There's a cure." Alice didn't understand what happened, but she knew Dinah wasn't a momerath. She may not be one hundred percent human, but she wasn't a monster. Her brain buzzed as an idea began to form. She didn't know why Dinah ran, but she was going to bring her back. No matter what.

The million thoughts assaulting her mind settled as Alice stood with a new air of determination. She looked at Chess, the boy who helped her survive the madness of Wanderland.

"Why is a raven like a writing desk?" She spoke quietly, but her eyes sparkled with intensity. A wave of hope thrilled through her as she recalled Hatta's riddle.

"What?" Confusion laced Chess's features, but he rose to stand beside her. His amber eyes bored into hers, fueling her resolve.

"I don't know," Alice admitted, smiling at the impossibility, "but I intend to find out."

EPILOGUE

Adelighted grin danced across the Red Queen's face as she peered at the paperwork in front of her. She had worked closely enough with Waite that she was able to recognize his messy script. She could even identify the more common documents he worked with. This was a medical document of some sort, perhaps a blood panel. It would take some time to read in detail, but as she scanned the page, the Queen saw something that told her it would be worth the effort.

"Alice Carroll."

A loud knock on her chamber doors startled her from her reverie. She pulled her attention from her prize to seethe at the Battle Marshal pushing through her chamber doors.

"What is it, Ace?" she snarled. She had explicitly told him she didn't want to be disturbed for any reason. Clearly, he needed clarification on what *any reason* meant. He had never been the brightest of her men. His brawn was good if you needed a strong arm in a pinch, but otherwise, he tended to be useless.

He was devoted to her though, which was more than she could say for her sentimental nephew. She growled. Thinking of

Nathan reminded her why she had locked herself in her chambers to begin with. She sighed. Her day had started so well. Her sting operation into Borogove had been more successful than she had planned. After years of waiting, Waite finally allowed her men access into the mysterious building. He didn't even suffer one of those irritating episodes that so often interfered with her business. Once inside, all her suspicions had been confirmed: Dr. Hatta was still working on modifying the Momerath Virus. That was excellent news. After her men swept the building, detaining Alice along with the added bonus of that blasted defector, Chess, they cleared out Hatta's offices and collected all of his data. Now it was her data. She could have even used Chess as one of her guinea pigs to see how some of the serums worked. It would have been fun.

Everything was exactly where she wanted it, until that stupid girl—one of her own guards!—had turned on her. At least it was one thing she was able to do something about. Annie, or Andi, or Indi—whatever her name was—could never choose to disobey her again.

She tapped her fingers on the top of the desk, irritated. She didn't know what it was about the annoying little blonde that seemed to endear her to so many people, her nephew included. But there was definitely something different about her. Perhaps the panel would reveal the key to her "Alice-ness." She hoped so. It put her off immensely. The Queen's eyes narrowed as she focused on her Battle Marshal. His intrusion had better be worth her time.

"Your Majesty, we've found something you might be interested in." He leaned over, his muscles bulging as he whispered, "Something we've never seen before."

He had piqued her curiosity, but she mustn't look too eager. She threw a withering stare at him, filling her emerald eyes with as much disdain as she could muster. "And whatever may that be?" she drawled.

Ace pressed open the door and let out a low whistle. Ten members of her Guard walked in, led by none other than her own darling nephew. Her eyes narrowed. She still hadn't decided whether she had forgiven him or not. But her rage was cut short when she noticed each man carried a piece of chain, all attached to a figure walking in the middle of their group.

The Queen pulled her hand to her face to cover her surprise when the Guard marched a momerath into the middle of her room.

"What is the meaning of this, Ace?" she snapped, trying to determine if a coup was being staged. "Where did you get this thing?" She sneered. This was all that girl's fault. She reached for her pocket to grab her ContraControl when Nate's voice cut across the room.

"Actually, Your Majesty," he stepped to the side to give the Queen a clearer view of the creature. "She found us."

"She," the Queen scoffed. "You know as well as I, Nathan, these creatures don't—" She stopped abruptly as her mind registered the monster before her. From a distance, it resembled any other momerath she had seen: the pallid, decaying flesh, gnarled hands, and disjointed posture. But looking closer, she noticed some subtle but significant differences. Unlike the other monsters who paced restlessly when cornered, this one stood calmly before her, almost as if she—*it*—understood what was going on. There was no manic look on its face or crazed hunger in its eyes—its eyes. That was where the true difference was, the Queen realized. Every other 'rath she'd ever seen had the same dead-gray orbs. The creature in front of her stared back from behind warm, dark cinnamon eyes, waiting for a response.

The Queen stood and marched to where the momerath stood, sure to maintain a safe distance. It may have seemed civilized, but that didn't change protocol. As a matter of fact, she would have to have a word with her Marshals later about bringing one of the monsters into her camp. Later.

"*She* found us," the Queen purred, still marveling at the thing in front of her. "However did that come to pass?" Though she addressed the question to her Guard, she looked to the creature for a response.

"I only recently turned... Your Majesty." It hesitated, as if searching for the words. The Queen stepped back, amazed that it had managed to string the words together. Ace was right. This *was* something she had never seen before. "I lived in a small Sector when I fell ill. I didn't want to harm any of my friends, so I ran away." The monster's voice was low and gravelly, and its words came out in a mixture of speech and hisses. It was fascinating.

"And you decided you'd rather take a shot at my camp?" The Queen's brows raised. "I'm not in the habit of harboring monsters."

The momerath stared back unapologetically. "When I saw your guards and your facilities, I thought maybe you could help me, or that you might know of someone who could."

"Well, aren't we a bright little monster," the Queen mused. The momerath's eyes narrowed and a low growl escaped its lips before it dropped its gaze.

"Forgive me, Majesty. I'm still learning to control myself."

The Queen flashed a brilliant smile. *A monster with control. Now, wouldn't that be a splendid addition to my collection.* "I understand, my dear. I can only imagine what it must be like for someone in your...condition." The momerath stirred under the Queen's shrewd gaze. "But you are correct. I *can* help you—for a cost."

"I don't have anything to offer you, Majesty."

"I should think an agreement for you to work under my employ should be sufficient," the Queen said casually.

"Really? That's all?"

The Queen's eyes gleamed. "That's it. Of course, I will also have to run a few tests to make sure you don't pose any threats to my citizens. There will also be the matter of my insurance policy..."

"I understand," it nodded. "I don't want to hurt anyone either. If it helps, I also have some training in medicine. I'm not a doctor or anything, but I can perform basic tasks."

"Thank you for sharing, my dear. I will keep that in mind when I finalize your assignment," she said. She waved her hand at Ace. "Fetch me a ContraBand, Ace. It seems Tulgey has a new resident."

An unsettling smile crept across the Battle Marshal's face, and he hurried to oblige. Within a matter of moments, he was back in the room with a flashing metal collar in hand. The momerath eyed it nervously, but stood its ground as Ace approached it and clicked it into place around its neck. The 'rath gingerly raised a clawed hand to the device, and rubbed where the metal met its skin.

"Excellent." The Queen beamed, her eyes filled with a predatory gaze. The momerath looked back at her, and for the first time, a look of concern covered her face. "Simply wonderful. I am so glad you stopped by, my dear. I think we have a lovely partnership ahead of us. What should we call you?" she asked as she returned to her desk.

"Dinah," the creature growled, looking incredibly sad. "My name is Dinah."

ALTERNATE CHAPTER

The door to the Queen's room burst open with a bang. It startled the Queen, who jerked back and blotted red ink across the letter she was writing. She glanced up at the messenger, annoyed. He was one of her younger servants, brought into camp along with an older brother a couple of months ago. He was slight, but that was only because he wasn't grown. He would make an excellent addition to her Guard in a few years' time—if he lived that long.

The boy eagerly hurried across the room, but paused uncertainly when he caught her narrowed gaze. He swallowed, and rubbed his hand along the underside of his ContraBand, hazel eyes wide as he watched her.

"Well, what is it?" She crumpled the paper in front of her, thankful that she had only just started the message.

The boy looked from the balled page back to his Queen. "Th-the Raiders are back, Your Majesty," he said timidly. "And they have a girl with them."

The Queen's brow quirked. "I daresay you've seen a girl before, Jack. I can't imagine this being such important news."

Jack blushed furiously. It tinged his caramel skin the faintest pink, but he held his ground. "But, Your Majesty, they found her in the middle of a momerath nest fighting them all by herself! And..." He paused to swallow nervously. "The girl had no reaction to the Unveiling Serum."

"At all?" Both eyebrows disappeared behind her curls. Jack shook his head, lips drawn in a hard line. Of course he was telling the truth; he wouldn't dare otherwise. She looked at the Contra-Band wrapped around his neck. It looked like it was getting a little snug. It was probably uncomfortable. She would have to give him a new one. Eventually.

"Where's Nathan?" Her nephew would have more information than the errand boy.

Jack bounced on his heels like an exuberant puppy. "They're headed this way now, Your Majesty. Nate and the girl, Alice. He's very protective of her—Ace isn't pleased. They'll be here in just a moment."

"Wonderful." She cleared the correspondence off her desk. She would attend to that later.

"If that's all, Jack, you are dismissed. Tell Nathan to hurry."

Jack bowed low. "Yes, Your Majesty." He scurried off, his wavy black hair bobbing along as he ran.

"And Jack," the Queen called. The boy stopped immediately. She smiled, pleased by his obedience. "Send the Doctor in. I need to speak with him."

"Yes, Your Majesty." His head bounced, and he was out the door, running to fetch Dr. Abbott. The door hadn't even shut all the way before the Raiding party filed in, led proudly by her Battle Marshal. Ace's face twisted in a smug grin as he stomped across the room. Killing always put him in a good mood. It was the bond that connected her to him.

"We brought you a present, Your Majesty," he boomed before he knelt in front of her.

She tipped her head, indicating for him to take his position beside her. "So I've heard," she purred, fixing him with a flirty grin.

"Had a hard time convincing Junior to administer the serum," he said, then let out a low growl. "Seemed more concerned about the girl's safety than the camp's. It needs to be addressed."

The Queen's eyes flashed. "I will let you know who needs to be addressed, Ace. Not the other way around." She didn't look at her Battle Marshal but she heard Ace shuffle awkwardly beside her. Appeased, she settled into her chair and watched the remainder of the party troop in, with Nathan bringing up the rear.

The Queen felt a familiar pang as she watched her nephew. He looked so much like his father at his age, sometimes she almost forgot he was gone. She chased away her sentiments and straightened in her seat. Now was not the time for softness. There never was anymore. She looked from Nathan to the girl trailing behind him. She was not nearly as sure of herself. Her eyes darted around the room nervously, lingering especially on the ContraBand collars the Guard wore.

"You wanted to see the refugee, Your Majesty?" He knelt before her, dipping his head so low that his golden hair brushed against the floor. The girl stood behind him, looking up at the Queen warily. She was annoyingly pretty, a waif of a thing with flowing silver hair and striking blue eyes. She looked like she could be snapped in half with a flick of Ace's wrist.

The Queen pressed her finger to her temple as she returned the girl's fixed stare. When the girl remained standing, she cleared her throat and directed a pointed look at Nathan. "No accounting for manners, I see."

The waif-girl's eyes widened. She bumbled into a mess of a curtsey before squeaking out an uncertain "How do you do?"

The Queen pressed her lips together and made a mental note

to speak to Nathan about informing her guests of proper etiquette before they audienced with her. "So you're the girl my men found taking on a nest of runners on her own." She touched her lips as she studied the unimpressive girl in front of her. Though it pained her to admit, she was curious how this girl could possibly fit the stories she was hearing. "Either you're very good, or very stupid. Maybe both." The girl shuffled awkwardly, but her eyes blazed. The corners of the Queen's lips quirked in a smile. Maybe there *was* more to her than just a pretty face. "Either way, you may be useful." She motioned for Nathan to stand. "Is it true nothing happened when she drank the elixir?"

Nathan clasped his hands behind his back and addressed her like a proper soldier. He had been trained well. "Yes ma'am."

"Interesting," the Queen said. She stood and walked a lazy circle around the girl. She raked her eyes over her as she tried to find *anything* extraordinary about her. She certainly didn't look exceptional. "There's never been anyone who hasn't had *any* response to my Unveiling Serum," she mused, thinking of all the different reactions she had seen. There had been many, some milder than others, but all unpleasant. *All.*

The girl's eyes dipped, but her voice was stone. "So I've heard." She raised her head and looked directly at the Queen, her blue eyes filled with cool heat.

The Queen's temper flared at the unspoken challenge, but she flashed a brilliant smile back at her visitor.

"I'd love the opportunity to examine *your* reaction," she said. "Or rather, your lack of one." Her smile stretched from confident to menacing. If she was lucky, the girl's body would have twice the response to the serum. It would make up for her impertinence.

Once again, the girl's eyes flitted to Nathan before she looked back at the Queen. The Queen's eyes narrowed. She didn't understand why Nathan kept coddling her, but it was starting to irritate her immensely. She turned her attention to her nephew, whose eyes still lingered on her guest. "Excellent." She clapped loudly and was pleased when the harsh noise pulled his attention off the girl. "Nathan, bring me two vials of Serum for our guest." She wondered how fond of her Nathan would be after she broke out in hives. Or maybe she would retch violently. Her lips quirked as she imagined some of the nastier reactions she'd witnessed. This pretty little thing wouldn't be pretty much longer.

Nathan's brow furrowed, but he obeyed. He walked to the armoire where she kept all of her "treats." The Queen didn't have to watch him to know he would comply. Nathan was one of her best soldiers, rivaled only by Ace. She trusted him implicitly. He was family, after all.

No, she was much more interested in her visitor. While Nathan retrieved the serum, the Queen kept her gaze fixated on the girl. She had grown more confident in the time she had been in the quarters, and was now openly studying her surroundings. She gazed around the room, not shying away from the Queen's gaze. The Queen tipped her head, but held her stare as she waited for Nathan to return. She heard the shuffle of steps behind her and stretched out her hand to receive the vials.

The glass was cool against her skin as she clutched her fingers around the bottles. She was satisfied to see the girl staring at the bottles with a mixture of curiosity and apprehension. "Would you like to see what happens?" she asked. When the girl didn't respond, she signaled for the guard nearest to her. A tremor ran through his body, but he complied, shuffling towards her, his eyes also trained on the tiny vial.

"Majesty," Nathan stepped toward her, his voice filled with concern.

She waved him silent. "Not now, Nathan." She didn't have time for his bleeding heart. Sometimes her nephew just didn't understand the grit required to be a leader. "Some things can't just be explained."

The Queen turned back to the guard. He stood in front of her, panic plastered across his face. "But, Your Majesty," he blubbered, "I'm not sick—"

"Of course you are, Lyons. That's why you're in a Contra-Band." She snapped her lips together. Begging irritated her. She was amazed how people believed whining would somehow bring them mercy. She swirled the vial in her hands, much more entertained by the mixture inside than the man before her. Although *man* was a generous classification. He was infected. A momerath. And his whining made him seem more childish than anything. She fought back a grimace as she addressed his sniveling frame. "Your service has been greatly appreciated, and now I need you to do one last thing for me."

Lyons took another step forward, his hands clasped in front of his body, pleading. "I can be of better use to you!" The Queen rolled her eyes. She would not entertain his ridiculousness any longer.

"This is what I need you to do," she clipped. She dipped her free hand into her pocket and pulled out her ContraControl. She held it up to locate the button wired to Lyons's ContraBand. The guard fell back a step when he saw the device, his eyes wide with fright.

The Queen briskly stepped forward and extended her hand, pressing one of the vials into Lyon's sweaty palms. She clasped her hands around his clammy skin to make sure his sniveling didn't drop her precious bottle. When she was certain his grip would hold, she stepped back, putting a safe distance between herself and her guard.

"Lyons, show Alice what happens when a Carrier takes the Unveiling Serum," she ordered. Her eyes flicked to the girl, who watched with a mixture of concern and curiosity evident on her delicate features.

Lyons directed one last pitiful gaze in her direction. When he saw her hardened stare, he made a last-ditch effort to search the room for someone who would help him. There was no one. Each pair of eyes Lyons met averted their gaze or stared straight ahead. None of them were willing to risk her wrath. She had seen to that long ago.

When Lyons' last ditch effort failed, the Queen sighed. This was turning into a production, and she was getting bored. Her thumb itched to press Lyons' ContraControl switch, but then she would have to sacrifice another guard to showcase her Serum. While the Queen had no qualms making the occasional sacrifice, she didn't have unlimited resources.

The threat of the control proved enough, however. Lyons' gaze fixed on the device, and the Queen could almost see the cogs working in his small mind. Resistance was futile. She was glad he'd finally realized it.

He raised the vial to his lips. The coward shook so badly, the Queen was certain he was going to drop the glass, but somehow, he managed to keep it firm in his grasp. He squeezed his eyes shut as he downed the contents with a dramatic gulp, and dropped the vial.

Before the bottle hit the ground, Lyons let out a loud groan and doubled over, clutching his stomach. He looked like he was trying to crawl in on himself, like one of those bugs that clamps shut when it feels threatened. Suddenly, he stiffened and his arms shot out, flailing wildly in the air. She had seen enough serum transformations to know he didn't have much time. She gripped the control, comforted by the bite of its plastic against her grip. The Queen turned to the girl, who watched the scene in front of her in horror. Her lips formed a perfect O and her fists clenched tight against her legs. She was learning her lesson well.

Lyons let out a final roar, drawing the Queen's focus. The guard was gone, replaced by a momerath in Guard's clothes and collar. He stared at her, his filmy eyes forming slits as he snarled. His muscles bunched and she knew what was coming. He didn't even get to finish his lunge before she whipped the control up and smashed the button down into the plastic. The ContraBand responded, initiating the detonation sequence. High-pitched beeps shrilled through the room before a muffled explosion, followed by the squelch of bloody splatters hitting the ground.

So messy.

The Queen's nose turned at the gore. Even with her rose-bushes, the smell was incredibly strong. "Take care of the mess," she ordered, startling two guards to action. They hurried to obey, lest they share Lyons' fate. Satisfied by her demonstration, she fixed her gaze on her guest. To her delight, the girl was aghast. She certainly wasn't going to like her next trick.

"It's an interesting little potion," the Queen crooned, examining her remaining bottle. "My head scientist brought it to me when he joined my camp. We don't generally use it at home base." She looked at Lyons' remains and let out a dainty sniff. "Too... *messy*. Although it has been particularly helpful for my men in the field." She indicated to Nathan. He shifted uncomfortably as the girl's soft eyes flitted over to his face. The Queen's lips pursed. "But I guess there is an exception to every rule." She passed the vial to the girl.

Nathan's sharp intake of breath drew a small smile to the corner of the Queen's lips. But the girl before her returned her gaze with a steely glare of her own.

Interesting.

The girl stood still a brief moment before she snapped the bottle to her lips and drained the contents. Without taking her eyes off the Queen, she extended her hand and dropped the glass back into her outstretched hand, the barest trace of a smile dancing on her lips.

Impertinent.

Now it was the Queen's turn. Her breath caught as she watched in anticipation, waiting for the girl's reaction. There had to be *something*. Time stretched as the girl stood, completely unbothered. The Queen held a moment more, prepared for a response that never came.

Different.

She could be useful.

"Fascinating," the Queen murmured. She circled the girl once more before she returned to her seat, certain she was missing something. The girl appeared ordinary as she had before. The Queen didn't trust it. Best to keep a close eye on this one. "I have a proposition for you..." She trailed off, realizing she had forgotten the girl's name. A-something.

"Alice," the girl supplied tartly.

That was it. "Yes. Alice." The Queen paused. She'd never heard of an Alice. Obviously, she wasn't from around Wanderland. That would make it difficult to gather intel, but not impossible.

"I have a proposition for you, *Alice*, if you would be so inclined." She smoothed her hair as she waited for the girl's response.

Alice's answer came back too quickly. "That depends." The Queen's eyes narrowed. Her generosity wasn't often denied. Or ever denied, for that matter. Not that the Queen was any stranger to persuasion.

She leaned casually against the back of her chair, carefully arranging her face into a forced smile.

"Clearly, you have experience as a fighter, and I can always use skilled soldiers." She gestured toward the soldiers standing attentively around the room. "Especially female soldiers. Tulgey has an exceptional combat force, but it is tragically lacking in female representation. And I wouldn't be truthful if I didn't admit I find you most entertaining." She pressed a finger to her lip as she considered the best way to hook the girl. "But more than that, there are benefits we can offer. Most obviously, a high security facility where you are free to pursue your own interests —so long as they further the interests of Tulgey. You would be welcome to stay and make it your home if you agreed to work for me." She spread her arms to show the expanse of her generosity.

Alice's gaze trained on the Queen. There was indecision in her eyes. After an annoyingly long pause, she finally answered, "I'm flattered, but unfortunately, I can't."

The Queen's smile faltered as her brows laced together in confusion, but it was a brief flash before she fixed it firmly in place. She let out a haughty chuckle. "You enjoy roaming the wilderness on your own?" Her eyes gleamed as she stared across the room at Alice. "Want to keep it a one-woman act?"

If the girl was intimidated, she didn't show it. "Not exactly," she snipped.

Impertinent beast.

The Queen frowned, her glare morphing quickly into a glower. "I'm working for myself right now," she amended, balking under the Queen's furious scrutiny.

"Really." The Queen smiled at her discomfort. Much better. That was the attitude the Queen expected from her visitors. "Do tell."

Alice's eyes flitted to where Nathan stood at attention. The Queen fought to suppress an eye roll. How very like her nephew to make another conquest. If the girl before her wasn't so irritating, she might have been happy for him. But for now, Nathan's training paid off. He didn't pay the blonde any notice. She gulped and turned her attention back to the Queen. "My sister's sick," she said, barely concealing the whine in her voice. "I need to find a cure."

Impossible.

"There is no cure," The Queen said brusquely. "You'd be better off putting her out of her misery." There was no reason to entertain such nonsense.

To her surprise, Alice didn't stand down. Instead, she stepped forward. "What do you know about 'better off'?" Fury blazed behind her blue eyes as she leveled a matching glare at the Queen. "From what you just showed me with that Joker, you don't seem to care too much about anyone."

The Queen ground her teeth together to keep her jaw from dropping. Suddenly, she thrust her head back, forcing out a malicious laugh. When she settled, she leaned back in her chair and locked her eyes on Alice. "You are a fighter, I'll give you that." She held the girl's gaze with narrowed eyes. "I haven't been spoken to like that in a very long time."

She waited for the girl to respond to her unspoken challenge, but Alice stood stoically across the room, sandwiched between two of her guards. For all intents and purposes, she should be terrified, yet she held firm. That could be problematic. If she decided to stay, she would have to be broken. Later.

The corners of the Queen's lip quirked in a tight smile. "You see, my dear," she said, calmly, "there are actually two different tests to find if someone is a Carrier." She directed a pointed look at Lyons' remains. "The first you have already seen and experienced—several times, I may add. This particular test is the nastier of the two, either resulting in the subject getting disgustingly ill or transforming into a momerath, with you being the sole exception." The Queen paused to let her words sink in. Alice kept her face carefully neutral, but the Queen didn't miss the way her fists clenched and unclenched at her sides.

"The other test is exclusively for my base, also developed by my head doctor," the Queen continued, eager to boast. "He has a certain... *brilliance* when it comes to the Plague. He discovered the Carrier gene is unique to one specific blood type, as the antigens in that particular strand do not register the virus as a threat. If someone has that specific antigen, they have the potential to be a Carrier. However, the only way to test this without triggering an immediate reaction is through a complex series of blood work."

She glanced down at her desk. Nestled inside were hundreds of screenings from Tulgey Resident "applicants." She wouldn't be surprised if she had one of the most comprehensive Plague research databases in the country. Not that it was particularly difficult at this point. The CDC had long since fallen. After all, it was hard to be an expert when you couldn't even control your own hunger pangs. She fought back another gleeful laugh. "When my men are out in the field, they don't have the time or resources for this test, so the Unveiling Serum is sufficient to identify potential threats. Generally, if someone is invited to my camp, they are required to complete the blood screen before they are allowed in. There is also a generic screening process they must pass to see if they are worth my physicians' time and supplies. If they are valuable, then I run the blood work. If they are clean, they can stay in Tulgey and come and go as they please."

Alice raised an eyebrow. "If they don't pass?" The disbelief laced through her voice made the Queen's lip curl in irritation.

"If they *don't* pass," she responded, forcing honey into her voice, "they are still welcome to stay, but they must agree to my terms." She caressed the collar of the guard beside her with her index finger. She was pleased to feel her involuntary shiver of fear.

"How does that work?" Alice asked, a mixture of curiosity and judgement evident in her voice.

"It's simple, really. The collar has a detonator installed,

controlled by a device only I have access to." The Queen jiggled her ContraControl to showcase its sleek design. "In the event one of my Carriers turns," *or gets a little too irritating,* she thought, "I have a way of *expediting* their removal from my camp." She smiled, recalling one of her more infuriating patrons and the way his head squelched. He forgot that Queens don't share. She turned to Alice. Her face was pinched in distaste.

She's a martyr. The Queen's eyes fluttered. The self-righteous were *so* exhausting. "Don't look at me like that," she sighed. "It's not as bad as it sounds. The Carriers under my employ have a much higher quality of life than any other Carriers in Wanderland. Better even than non-Carriers in outside sectors, I'd wager." Looking at Alice's scrawny figure, she was certain wherever she was from had nothing on Tulgey. "They can continue to live normally until they turn, and in the unfortunate event it happens, I have a safety net in place to protect my other citizens. And honestly, at that point, if they could, they'd thank me. It's sad, but necessary."

Alice didn't look convinced, but the Queen was saved from having to waste any more time on her antics when Waite entered her chambers. "Doctor. So nice to see you." As always, he looked like a nervous wreck, his clothes and hair twisted in disarray, but he was calm, which was promising. If he wasn't so brilliant, the Queen would have tired of his episodes long ago.

Waite pushed to the front, and without sparing her guest a passing glance, bowed low. "Majesty."

The Queen smiled, pleased that *someone* remembered the proper etiquette for addressing royalty. "We have a guest who needs your assistance." She indicated to Alice. "See to her wounds, then return to your research."

Waite seemed to notice the girl for the first time. He gave a curt nod, then turned and began prodding at her in true physician form. He asked her several questions, but the Queen's focus was no longer on Alice. It was on her nephew. He had moved closer to the girl once Waite began his inspection and was anxiously watching over the doctor's shoulder while he tended to her. There was a clear look of concern on his face as his eyes jumped from her to the doctor, and back again. His preoccupation with the girl was unsettling. She wondered whether this was something that would need to be formally addressed. She rather hoped not.

"We're all done here," The finality in Waite's voice drew the Queen from her musing. "The wound isn't that deep. A couple of butterfly bandages should hold it together nicely." He stood to go, but surprisingly, Nathan stopped him.

"Band-Aids? Doctor, she needs stitches! Can't you see how much blood she lost? There's a huge gash in her head!" Nathan waved his arm towards the girl's head. The Queen followed his movement. Granted, her hair was a mess in clumps of blood, but Waite was correct: her forehead was clear. Perhaps she should have Nathan examined while the doctor was here.

Waite's lips pursed. "While I admire your concern, Marshal, I can assure you, the wound on her head is minor." He sounded incredibly put out. "Head traumas generally do have more blood loss, so it makes sense you would think the injury more severe. But I can assure you, a simple bandaging will be sufficient."

"But I saw it!" Nathan's outburst surprised the entire room.

"Nathan, that's quite enough." The Queen's eyes narrowed. She was more than aware he and the doctor rarely saw eye to eye, but his tantrum was beginning to irk her. Her nephew was overstepping boundaries. It wasn't like him.

Waite seemed to share her sentiments. He gave her a tired glance. "Is there anything else I can help with, Majesty?"

The Queen smiled. There *was* something she wanted to address. "As a matter of fact, Waite, there is." She made her voice smooth as silk. Her request was certain to agitate the doctor and she needed to keep him calm as long as possible. "My guest is here looking for something for her sister." She glanced at Alice with a feeling of smug superiority. She knew very well what Waite's response would be. It was the same answer she'd been given the past three years. "A cure for the Plague."

Waite paled. It was an appropriate response, considering he had *yet* to deliver an antidote. The doctor may have been unstable, but he was no fool. He knew she was tiring of waiting. "A cure, Majesty?"

"Yes, a cure." Her lips twisted in a disappointed pout. "But I informed her it was just not possible, as there *is* no cure. Isn't that right?"

"Y-yes, Majesty." The doctor's hands started to tremble. He was spiraling. "Unfortunately, we have been unable to manufacture an antidote. We're still trying."

"Oh, calm down, Doctor." The Queen's voice was harsh, but she gently touched the doctor's shoulder to anchor his nerves. "You still have time," she soothed.

Waite took in a steadying breath, then turned to the girl. "There is no cure for the Plague."

Alice's face contorted, finally stealing the pretty from her features. Suddenly she was no longer a dainty slip of a thing, but a little fighter. The Queen watched with interest, finally privy to the secrets she hid behind her surface. This girl, she could imagine holding her own against a pack of momerath.

Intriguing.

The Queen was content studying the girl, but suddenly, her outburst escalated. "There's not enough *time!*" she shouted angrily at the doctor. Waite stiffened at her words, but she continued yelling, too wrapped up in her own problems to notice the effect her words had on him. "I've already been away from home for almost two days, getting sent on wild goose chases and hunted and forced to drink these god-awful concoctions, and it's all been just a huge waste of time!"

There it was again. The T-word. One look at Waite, and the Queen knew that she was about to lose him. She hurried towards Abbott in an attempt to keep him in the present. "Calm down, Doctor," she began, but it was pointless. The impossible girl had triggered him. His mind had fractured.

"Late. I'm late!" Waite swatted at her extended hand, forcing her Guard to jump to action. They surged toward the doctor to subdue him.

"Don't touch him!" she yelled. Physical contact would only further his paranoia at this point. Her command did not come quick enough. One of the burly guards tapped Abbott on the shoulder, setting him into a full-on panic.

"I'm late!" Abbott beat back the guard's hand. "So very, very late!" He pushed the soldier back and sprinted through the hall, followed by echoes of his screams. "I'm late! I'm late! I'm late!"

The door slammed shut, closing out Waite's frantic screams and leaving the room encased in a silent tomb. The Guards all shifted uncomfortably, waiting for her command. The Queen's temper blazed. She did not have time to deal with a riled physician. "Wonderful," she snapped. She massaged her temple where the beginning of a migraine was starting to form. "He's absolutely useless when he gets like this."

The irritating girl stepped forward. "I'm sorry, I didn't mean to." Her words were meant to be an apology, but the whiny tone behind them pierced the Queen's head, inflaming her headache. "I didn't think—"

"Clearly." The Queen seethed. She didn't know what she had done to earn this vexation, but she was quickly tiring of this Alice and all the trouble she seemed to cause. She vaguely wondered if she was worth it. She continued rubbing her forehead. She needed to stay calm. She was certain the girl could be useful. How, she didn't know.

But she was determined to find out.

"Nathan, take our guest to her quarters for the evening," she commanded. She needed some time to figure out what to do with her new ward. "Ace, monitor the doctor and make sure he doesn't hurt himself. Perhaps if he snaps out of it, he can still get something worthwhile done tonight." She waved her hands to dismiss her audience. Within a few moments, her chambers were cleared and she was gloriously alone.

"Alice," she murmured to herself, thinking of the things she had just witnessed. "Whatever am I going to do with you?" A sly giggle escaped her lips. The possibilities were endless.

ACKNOWLEDGMENTS

First and foremost I would like to God for giving me the passion and the opportunity to bring stories to life. There is nothing I would have without his blessings, and for that I am truly thankful.

Next, I want to thank my husband, Steven, without whom this book would not be possible. Thank you for spending countless hours supporting, encouraging, and sharing ideas with me. We may have a mess, but it's ours, and it's beautiful. I love you.

I would also like to thank my children, Brody, Zoie, and Liam. You fill my heart with such joy and make me a better person. Thank you for being patient with my countless hours behind the computer screen and for pulling me back into the reality when I needed it. I love you all so much.

For my parents, thank you for instilling a love for literature and words in my life from a young age and for always encouraging me to follow my dreams. For my mother- and father-in-law, thank you for so graciously inviting me into your family and treating me as if I always belonged there. Not everyone is lucky enough to have an amazing set of parental units. I have two.

For the rest of my family, thank you for being the best support group a girl could ever ask for. Aunt Sarah, I love you more than chocolate chip cookies. Uncle Steve, thank you for fostering my wit and snark. Shawna (and Mark), thank you for always being there for Steven, the kids, and I whenever we need you. Zach, Daniel, Paul, Beth, Logan, and Makenna, thank you for teaching me how strong the bond between siblings can be.

For my friends, specifically those who encouraged me to follow this crazy writing thing. You have helped me more than you can ever know. Indi, thank you for patiently listening to me blather on about all things Alice on our daily work commute and for volunteering your namesake to one of my favorite characters. Nicole, Amiri, Miss Terri and Amanda, thank you for always lending your writer's ears to talk through my ideas. Brittany and Jesse, thank you for reading Alice when she wasn't at her prettiest, and for telling me she was worth the effort. Without you, she may have been shelved forever.

For all my friends who supported my writing through my Publishizer campaign, please know that your contributions to jumpstarting Alice is the only reason I'm where I am today. Your belief in me and support of my work means more to me than I can ever express, and for that I am truly grateful.

Of course, I want to thank Dionne and Trisha. Dionne, thank you for taking your time and energy and investing them in my dreams. Trisha, thank you for being the most kind-hearted but strict editor I could ever imagine. You whittled my prose with patience and grace and I am absolutely in awe of you.

And for Jon and Sherry, thank you so much for believing in my work and accepting Alice into the Bleeding Ink family. You are bringing new worlds to life every day, and I am so thankful that you have included mine.

I would also like to thank Mr. Lewis Carroll for creating the wondrous world of Wonderland and sharing it with us all those years ago. Without your whimsy, Wanderland would never have come to be. I am eternally in your debt.

And last but definitely not least, I would like to thank my readers. You are the reason for the countless hours, coffee binges, and excessive keyboard abuse. Wanderland may be a piece of my heart, but it was written for you.

Thank you.